Penguin Books
Spring Fever

P. G. Wodehouse was born in Guildford in 1881 and educated at Dulwich College. After working for the Hong Kong and Shanghai Bank for two years, he left to earn his living as a journalist and storywriter, writing the 'By the Way' column in the old *Globe*. He also contributed a series of school stories to a magazine for boys, the *Captain*, in one of which Psmith made his first appearance. Going to America before the First World War, he sold a serial to the *Saturday Evening Post* and for the next twenty-five years almost all his books appeared first in this magazine. He was part author and writer of the lyrics of eighteen musical comedies including *Kissing Time*; he married in 1914 and in 1955 took American citizenship. He wrote over ninety books and his work has won world-wide acclaim, being translated into many languages. *The Times* hailed him as 'a comic genius recognized in his lifetime as a classic and an old master of farce'.

P. G. Wodehouse said 'I believe there are two ways of writing novels. One is mine, making a sort of musical comedy without music and ignoring real life altogether; the other is going right deep down into life and not caring a damn . . .' He was created a Knight of the British Empire in the New Year's Honours List in 1975. In a BBC interview he said that he had no ambitions left, now that he had been knighted and there was a waxwork of him in Madame Tussauds. He died on St Valentine's Day in 1975 at the age of ninety-three.

P. G. Wodehouse

Spring Fever

Penguin Books

PENGUIN BOOKS

Published by the Penguin Group
Penguin Books Ltd, 27 Wrights Lane, London W8 5TZ, England
Viking Penguin, a division of Penguin Books USA Inc.
375 Hudson Street, New York, New York 10014, USA
Penguin Books Australia Ltd, Ringwood, Victoria, Australia
Penguin Books Canada Ltd, 2801 John Street, Markham, Ontario, Canada L3R 1B4
Penguin Books (NZ) Ltd, 182–190 Wairau Road, Auckland 10, New Zealand

Penguin Books Ltd, Registered Offices: Harmondsworth, Middlesex, England

First published by Herbert Jenkins 1948
Published in Penguin Books, 1969
10 9 8

Printed in England by Clays Ltd, St Ives plc
Set in Intertype Times

Book One

Chapter 1

Spring had come to New York, the eight-fifteen train from Great Neck had come to the Pennsylvania terminus, and G. Ellery Cobbold, that stout economic royalist, had come to his downtown office, all set to prise another wad of currency out of the common people.

It was a lovely morning, breathing of bock beer and the birth of a new baseball season, and the sap was running strongly in Mr Cobbold's veins. He looked like a cartoon of Capital in a labour paper, but he felt fine. It would not have taken much to make him break into a buck-and-wing dance, and if he had had roses in his possession it is more than probable that he would have strewn them from his hat.

Borne aloft in the elevator, he counted his blessings one by one and found them totting up to a highly satisfactory total. The boil on the back of his neck had yielded to treatment. His golf handicap was down to twenty-four. His son Stanwood was in London, safely removed from the wiles of Miss Eileen Stoker of Beverly Hills, Cal. He was on the point of concluding remunerative deals with the Messrs Simms and Weinstein of Detroit and the Consolidated Nail File and Eyebrow Tweezer Corporation of Scranton, Pa. And a fortunate glance at Debrett's Peerage that morning had reminded him that tomorrow was Lord Shortlands's birthday.

He floated lightly into the office and found Miss Sharples, his efficient secretary, there, right on the job as always, and a mass of torn envelopes in the wastepaper basket told him that she had attended to his correspondence and was all ready to give him the headline news. But though that correspondence almost certainly included vital communications from both Simms and Weinstein and the Nail File and Eyebrow Tweezer boys, it was the matter of Lord Shortland's natal day that claimed his immediate attention.

'Morning, Miss Sharples,' he said, and you could see that what he really meant was 'Good morning, good morning, Miss Sharples, what a beautiful morning it is, is it not? With a Hey and a Ho and a Hey nonny no, Miss Sharples.' 'Take a memo.'

'Yes, Mr Cobbold.'

'Western Union.'

'Western Union,' echoed Miss Sharples, inscribing on her tablets something that resembled an impressionistic sketch of a pneumonia germ.

'Tell them to put in a personal call at ... Say, what time do you reckon an English peer would be waking up in the morning?'

He had come to the woman who knew.

'Eleven, Mr Cobbold.'

'*Eleven?*'

'That's the time young Lord Peebles wakes up in the novel I'm reading. He props his eyes open with his fingers and presses the bell, and Meadowes, his man, brings him a bromo seltzer and an anchovy on hot toast.'

Mr Cobbold uttered a revolted 'Pshaw!'

'This fellow isn't one of those dissolute Society playboys. He lives in the country, and he's fifty-two. At least, he will be tomorrow. Seems to me seven would be more like it. Have Western Union put in a personal call at seven, English time, tomorrow, to the Earl of Shortlands, Beevor Castle, Kent, and sing "Happy birthday" to him.'

'"Happy birthday",' murmured Miss Sharples, pencilling in two squiggles and a streptococcus.

'Tell them to pick out a fellow with a nice tenor voice.'

'Yes, Mr Cobbold.'

'Or maybe they tear it off in a bunch, like a barbershop quartette?'

'I don't think so, Mr Cobbold. Just one vocalist, I believe.'

'Ah? Well, see that they do it, anyway. It's important. I wouldn't like Lord Shortlands to think I'd forgotten his birthday. He's the head of my family.'

'You don't say!'

8

'Sure. Cobbold's the family name. There's a son, Lord Beevor, who's out in Kenya, but all the others are Cobbolds. Three daughters. The eldest married a fellow named Topping I was in college with. I'll tell you how I first came to hear of them. I was in the club one day, and I happened to pick up one of those English illustrated weeklies, and there was a photograph of a darned pretty girl with the caption under it "Lady Teresa Cobbold, youngest daughter of the Earl of Shortlands". "Hello," I said to myself. "Cobbold? Well, what do you know about that?" and I had the College of Arms in London get busy and look into the thing.'

'And it turned out that you were a relation?'

'That's right. Just what kind I couldn't exactly tell you. Sort of cousin is the way I figure it out. I've written Lord Shortlands a letter or two about it and sent him a few cables, but he hasn't got around to answering yet. Busy, maybe. Still, there it is. Seems that in 1700 or thereabouts one of the younger sons sailed for America –'

Mr Cobbold broke off the gossip from the old home and gave a rather formal cough. He perceived that the spirit of Spring had lured him on to jeopardize office discipline by chewing the fat with one who, however efficient and however capital a listener, was after all an underling.

'Well, that's that,' he said. 'And now,' becoming his business self after this frivolous interlude, 'what's new?'

Miss Sharples would have been glad to hear more of the younger son who had sailed for America and all the rest of the Hands-Across-the-Sea stuff, for hers was a romantic nature, but she, too, recognized that this was not the time and place. She consulted her notes.

'Simms and Weinstein will meet your terms, Mr Cobbold,' she said, translating the one that looked like part of Grover Whalen's moustache.

'They better.'

'But the Nail File and Eyebrow Tweezer people don't seem any too well pleased.'

'They don't, don't they?'

'They say they are at a loss to comprehend.'

'Is that so? I'll fix 'em. Anything else?'

9

'No letters of importance, Mr Cobbold. There is a cable from Mr Stanwood.'

'Asking for money?'

'Yes, Mr Cobbold.'

'He would be. Seems to me he spends more in London than he did over here.'

A frown came into Ellery Cobbold's bulbous face. He was a man of enviable financial standing for, despite the notorious hardness of the times, he always managed to get his, but this did not make it any the more agreeable to him to be tapped by his son. A great many prosperous fathers have this adhesive attitude towards their wealth when the issue show a disposition to declare themselves in on the gross.

A song of his youth flitted through Mr Cobbold's mind:

> My son Joshu-ay
> Went to Philadelphi-ay;
> Writes home sayin' he's doin' mighty well:
> But seems kind of funny
> That he's always short of money,
> And Ma says the boy's up to some kind of hell.

Then he brightened. Whatever kind of hell Stanwood might be up to, his father's heart had this consolation, that he was not up to it in the society of Miss Eileen Stoker.

With restored equanimity he dismissed him from his thoughts and settled down to dictate a letter to the Consolidated Nail File and Eyebrow Tweezer Corporation of Scranton, Pa., which would make them realize that life is stern and earnest and that Nail File and Eyebrow Tweezer Corporations are not put into this world for pleasure alone.

The morning wore on, filled with its little tasks and duties. Lunch-time came. The afternoon followed. In due season everything needed to keep Mr Cobbold's affairs in applepie order for another day had been done, and he took the six-ten train back to his Great Neck home. At eight he dined, and by nine he was in his favourite armchair, a cigar between his lips and a highball at his side, preparing to read the evening paper which the intrusion of a garrulous neighbour had prevented him perusing on the train.

But even when settled in his chair he did not begin to read immediately. Dreamily watching the smoke curl up from his perfecto, he found his thoughts turning to his son Stanwood and the adroitness with which he had flung the necessary spanner into that young man's incipient romance with Miss Eileen Stoker of Hollywood.

The discovery that his offspring was contemplating marrying into celluloid circles had come as an unpleasant shock to Mr Cobbold, filling him with alarm and, until he rallied and took action, despondency. During the first anxious days he had twice refused a second helping of Spaghetti Caruso at lunch, and his golf handicap, always a sensitive plant, had gone up into the thirties.

He mistrusted Stanwood's ability to choose wisely in this vital matter of selecting a life partner, for though he loved his child he did not think highly of his intelligence. Stanwood, a doughty performer on the football field during his college career, was a mass of muscle and bone, and it was Mr Cobbold's opinion that the bone extended to his head. And he had a good deal of support for this view. Even those who had applauded the young man when he made the All American in his last season had never claimed for him that he was bright. Excellent at blocking a punt or giving a playmate the quick sleeve across the windpipe, but not bright. It seemed to Mr Cobbold that he must be saved from himself.

If the bride-to-be had been the Lady Teresa Cobbold whose photograph he had seen in the English illustrated weekly, that would have been a vastly different matter. A union between his son and the daughter of the head of the family he would have welcomed with fervour. But a film star, no. He knew all about film stars. Scarcely had they settled down in the love nest before they were bringing actions for divorce on the ground of ingrowing incompatibility or whatever it might be and stinging the bridegroom for slathers of alimony. And the thought that at the conclusion of the romance under advisement it would be he, the groom's father, who would be called upon to foot the bills had acted on him as a powerful spur, causing him to think on his feet and do it now.

He had shipped Stanwood off to England on the next boat in

the custody of an admirable fellow named Augustus Robb, whom he had engaged, principally on the strength of the horn-rimmed spectacles he wore, at an agency which supplied gentlemen's personal gentlemen, with instructions to remain in England till further notice. It is one of the great advantages of being a tycoon that your life trains you to take decisions at the drop of the hat. Where lesser men scratch their heads and twiddle their fingers, the tycoon acts.

To Mr Cobbold, as he sat there drawing at his cigar, it was a very soothing reflection that three thousand miles of land and another three thousand miles of water separated his son and Miss Stoker, and for some moments he savoured it like some rare and refreshing fruit. Then with a contented sigh he opened his paper.

It was to the financial section that he turned first; then to the funnies, in which he surprisingly retained a boyish interest. After that he allowed his eye to wander at random through the remainder of the sheet. And it was while it was doing so, flitting idly from spot to spot like a hovering butterfly, that it found itself arrested by a photograph on one of the inner pages of a personable young woman with large eyes, curving lips and apparently lemon-coloured hair.

He had been on the verge of sleep at the moment, for he generally sank into a light doze at about this time in the evening, but there was something about those wistful eyes gazing into his, with their suggestion of having at last found a strong man on whom they could rely, which imparted sufficient wakefulness to lead him to glance at the name under the photograph. And having done so he sat up with a jerk.

MISS EILEEN STOKER

A snort broke from Mr Cobbold's lips. He frowned, as if he had found a snake on his lap.

So this was Eileen by golly Stoker, was it? No devotee of the silver screen, he had never seen her before, and now that he was seeing her he did not like her looks. A siren, he thought. Designing, he felt. Not to be trusted as far as you could throw an elephant, he considered, and just the sort who would spring with joy to the task of nicking a good man's bank-roll. He eyed the lady askance, as he eyed all things askance that seemed potential threats to his current account.

The phrase 'universally beloved' is, of course, a loose one. It cannot ever really include everybody. In this instance it did not include Mr Cobbold. All over the United States, and in other countries, too, for Art knows no frontiers, there were clubs in existence whose aim it was to boost for Eileen Stoker, to do homage to Eileen Stoker and to get the public thinking the Eileen Stoker way, but the possibility of Ellery Cobbold joining one of them was remote. A society for dipping Eileen Stoker in tar and sprinkling feathers on her he would have supported with pleasure.

There were a few lines in smaller print below this absurd statement that Miss Stoker was universally beloved, and Mr Cobbold's eye, having nothing better to do at the moment, gave them a casual glance. And scarcely had it done so when its proprietor leaped in his chair with a wordless cry like that of a sleeping cat on whose tail some careless number eleven shoe has descended.

Once at the country club, coming out of the showers in the nude and sitting down on the nearest bench to dry himself, Mr Cobbold's attention had been drawn to the fact that a fellow member had left a lighted cigar there, and until tonight he had always regarded this as the high spot of his emotional life. He was now inclined to relegate it to second place.

For this was what he had read:

MISS EILEEN STOKER
Universally Beloved Hollywood Star
Has arrived in England to take up her contract for
two pictures with the Beaumont Co. of London

The words seemed to print themselves in letters of fire on his soul. So devastating was their effect that for quite an appreciable time he sat paralysed, blowing little air bubbles and incapable of movement. Then, once more his alert, executive self, he rose and bounded to the telephone.

'Gimme Western Union!'

It occurred to him as a passing thought that he seemed to be putting a lot of business in the way of Western Union these days.

'Western Union?'

He was suffering much the same mental anguish as that experienced by Generals who have allowed themselves to become outflanked. But how, he asked himself, could he have anticipated this? How could he have foreseen this mobility on the part of the foe? He had always supposed that Hollywood stars were a permanency in Hollywood, like swimming-pools and the relations by marriage of a studio chief.

'Western Union?' said Mr Cobbold, still finding a difficulty in controlling his voice. 'I want to send a couple of cables.'

Chapter 2

On the following morning, at about the time when the Lord Peebles of whose habits Miss Sharples had spoken was accustomed to begin his day, a young man lay sleeping in the bedroom of a service flat at Bloxham House, Park Lane, London. A silk hat, dress trousers, a pair of evening shoes, two coloured balloons and a squeaker were distributed about the floor beside the bed. From time to time the young man moaned softly, as if in pain. He was dreaming that he was being bitten in half by a shark, which is always trying.

We really do not know why we keep saying 'young man' in this guarded way. There is no need for secrecy and concealment. It was Stanwood Cobbold, and he was sleeping at this advanced hour because he had got home at four in the morning from the party which he had given to welcome Miss Eileen Stoker to England.

Except for the bulge under the bedclothes which covered his enormous frame, very little of Stanwood Cobbold was visible, and that little scarcely worth a second look, for Nature, doubtless with the best motives, had given him, together with a heart of gold, a face like that of an amiable hippopotamus. And everybody knows that unless you are particularly fond of hippopotami, a single cursory glance at them is enough. Many blasé explorers do not even take that.

Augustus Robb came softly in, bearing a tray. Augustus Robb always came into rooms softly. Before getting saved at a revival meeting and taking up valeting as a career, he had been a burglar in a fair way of practice, and coming into rooms softly had grown to be a habit.

Once in, his movements became less stealthy. He deposited the tray on the table with a bang and a rattle and raised the blind noisily.

'Hoy!' he cried, in a voice like someone calling the cattle home across the Sands of Dee. He had rather a bad bedside manner.

Stanwood parted company with his shark and returned to the world of living things. Having done so, he clasped his forehead with both hands and said: 'Oh, God!' He had the illusion that everything, including his personal attendant, had turned yellow.

'Brekfuss,' roared Augustus Robb, still apparently under the impression that he was addressing a deaf friend a quarter of a mile away. 'Eat it while it's hot, cocky. I've done you a poached egg.'

There are certain words which at certain times seem to go straight to the foundations of the soul. 'Egg' is one of these, especially when preceded by the participle 'poached'. A strong shudder passed through Stanwood's sensitive person.

'Take it away,' he said in a low, tense voice. 'And quit making such a darned noise. I've got a headache.'

Augustus Robb adjusted the horn-rimmed spectacles which had made so powerful an appeal to Mr Cobbold senior, and gazed down at the fishy-eyed ruin before him with something of the air of a shepherd about to chide an unruly lamb. He was a large, spreading man with a bald forehead, small eyes, extensive ears and a pasty face. He sucked a front tooth censoriously, his unpleasant habit when in reproachful mood.

'Got a headache, have you? Well, don't forget you asked for it, chum. I heard you come in this morning. Stumbling all over the place you was and knocking down the furniture. "Ah," I says to myself. "You wait," I says. "The day of retribution is at hand," I says, "when there will be wailing and gnashing of

15

teeth." And so there is, cocky, so there is. Well, now you're awake, better eat your brekfuss and get up and go out and 'ave a good brisk walk around the Park.'

The suggestion seemed to strike Stanwood Cobbold like a blow. He drew the bedclothes higher, partly to exclude the light, but principally so that he might avoid seeing his personal attendant. Even when at his most robust he found the sight of the latter disagreeable, for there seemed to him something all wrong about a valet in horn-rimmed spectacles, and at a time like this it was insupportable.

'It's a lovely day, the sun's shining a treat and the little dicky birds are singing fit to bust,' said his personal attendant, by way of added inducement. 'Upsy-daisy, and I'll have your clob- ber all ready for you by the time you're out of your tub.'

The effort was almost too much for his frail strength, but Stanwood managed to open an eye.

'Get me a highball.'

'I won't get you no such thing.'

'You're fired!'

'No, I'm not. Don't talk so silly. Fired, indeed! No, cocky, you can't have no highball, but I'll tell you what you can have. I stepped out to the chemist's just now and asked him to recom- mend something suitable for your condition, and he give me this.'

Stanwood, examining the bottle, brightened a little, as if he had met an old friend.

'This is good stuff,' he said, shaking up its dark contents. 'I've tried it before, and it's always saved my life.'

Removing the cork, he took a hearty draft, and after a brief interval during which his eyeballs revolved in their sockets and his whole aspect became that of one struck by a thunderbolt, seemed to obtain a certain relief. His drawn features relaxed, and he was able to remove the hand which he had placed on the top of his head to prevent it coming off.

'Wow!' he said in a self-congratulatory manner.

Augustus Robb was still amused at the idea of his employer dispensing with his services.

'Fired?' he said, chuckling at the quaint conceit. 'How can you fire me, when I was specially engaged by your Pop to look

16

after you and be your good angel? "Robb," he says to me. I can see him now, standing in his office with his weskit unbuttoned and that appealing look in his eyes. "Robb, my faithful feller," he says, "I put my son in your charge. Take the young barstard over to England, cocky, and keep an eye on him and try to make him like what you are," he says. Meaning by that a bloke of religious principles and a strict teetotaller.'

'And a burglar?' said Stanwood, with a flicker of spirit.

'Ex-burglar,' corrected Augustus Robb coldly. It was a point on which he was touchy. 'Seen the light this many a year past, hallelujah, and put all that behind me. And listen,' he went on, stirred by a grievance. 'Why did you go and tell Mr Cardinal I'd been a burglar once?'

'I didn't.'

'Yes, you did, and you know it. How else could he have found out? I wish I'd never mentioned it now. That's the trouble with you, chum. You're a babbler. You can't keep from spilling the beans. "So you used to be a burglar, used you?" says Mr Cardinal, day before yesterday it was, when you'd asked me to step over to his apartment and borrow his new *Esquire*. "And your name's Robb." "What about it?" I says. "Ha, ha," he says, laughing a sort of silvery laugh. "Very suitable name for a burglar," he says. "You're the fifty-seventh feller that's told me that," I says. "Then you have known fifty-seven brilliantly witty people," he says. "I congratulate you." And he takes a couple of little what-nots off the mantlepiece and locks 'em in a cupboard, as it were ostentatiously. Wounding, that was. I wish you'd be more careful.'

'Mike won't tell anyone.'

'That's not the point. It's the principle of the thing. A feller that's been saved don't want his sinful past jumping out at him all the time like a ruddy jack-in-the-box. Was he at that do of yours last night?'

'Yes, Mike was along,' said Stanwood.

He spoke with a trace of flatness in his voice, for the question had awakened unpleasant memories. It might have been his imagination, but it had seemed to him that, during the course of the festivities alluded to, his friend Mike Cardinal had paid rather too marked attentions to Miss Stoker, and that the latter had not been insensible to his approaches. Of course, the whole thing might have been just a manifestation of the party spirit, but Mike was such an exceptionally good-looking bird that a lover, especially a lover who had no illusions about his own appearance, was inclined to be uneasy.

'And was strictly moderate in his potations, I've no doubt,' proceeded Augustus Robb. 'Always is. I've seen Mr Cardinal dine here with you and be perfectly satisfied with his simple half-bot. And him with his spirit on the rack, as you might say, and so with every excuse for getting stinko. Fine feller. You ought to take example by him.'

Stanwood found himself mystified.

'How do you mean?'

'How do I mean what?'

'Why is Mike's spirit on the rack?'

'Because he's suffering the torments of frustrated love because he can't get the little bit of fluff to say Yus. That's why his ruddy spirit's on the rack.'

'What little bit of fluff?'

'This Lady Teresa Cobbold.'

Stanwood was intrigued. Terry Cobbold was an old friend of his.

'You don't say!'

'Yus, I do.'

'This is the first I've heard of this.'

'The story's only just broke.'

'Mike never said a word to me.'

'Why would he? Fellers don't go around singing of their love like tenors in a comic opera. Specially if the girl's giving 'em the raspberry and they can't seem to make no 'eadway.'

'Well, he told you.'

'No, he didn't any such thing. So 'appened that when I was in his apartment day before yesterday there was an envelope lying on his desk addressed to Lady Teresa Cobbold, Beevor Castle, Kent, and beside it a 'alf-finished letter, beginning "Terry, my wingless angel." I chanced to glance at it, and it told the 'ole story.'

'You've got a hell of a nerve, reading people's letters.'

'Language. There's a habit you want to break yourself of.

Let your Yea be Yea and your Nay be Nay, as the Good Book says. I've a tract in my room that bears on that. I'll fetch it along. Yus, pleading with her to be his, this letter was. Very well-expressed, I thought, as far as he'd got, and so I told him.'

A sudden spasm of pain contorted Stanwood's homely features, and the comment he had been about to make died on his lips. The telephone at his side had rung with a shattering abruptness.

'Gimme,' said Augustus Robb. 'I'll answer it. 'Ullo? Yus? Oh, 'ullo Mr Cardinal, we was just talking about you. Yus, cocky, I'll tell him. It's Mr Cardinal. Says not to forget you're giving him lunch at Barribault's Hotel today.'

'Lunch?' Stanwood quivered. 'Tell him it's off. Tell him I'm dead.'

'I won't do no such thing. You can't evade your social obligations. Yus, that's all right, chum. One-fifteen pip emma in the small bar. Right. Goo'bye. What I'd advise,' said Augustus Robb, replacing the receiver, 'is a nice Turkish bath. That'll bring the roses back to your cheeks, and Gawd knows they need 'em. You look more like a blinkin' corpse than anything 'uman. Well, I can't stand here all day chinning with you, cocky. Got my work to do. 'Ullo, the front door bell. Wonder who that is.'

'If it's anyone for me, don't let them in.'

'Unless it's the undertaker, eh? Haw, haw, haw,' laughed Augustus Robb, and exited trilling.

Left alone, Stanwood gave himself up to his thoughts, and very pleasant thoughts they were too, though interrupted at intervals by the activities of some unseen person who appeared to be driving white-hot rivets into his skull. The news about Mike Cardinal and Terry Cobbold had taken a great weight off his mind and, his being a mind not constructed to bear heavy weights, the relief was enormous.

For obviously, he reasoned, if Mike Cardinal was that way about young Terry, he could scarcely be making surreptitious passes at Eileen Stoker.

Or could he?

Surely not?

No, definitely not, Stanwood decided. What he had witnessed at last night's supper party must have been merely the routine civilities of a conscientious guest making himself agreeable to his host's future bride. Odd, of course, that Mike had said nothing to him about Terry. But then, if things were not going too well, no doubt, as Augustus Robb had pointed out, he wouldn't.

Too bad, felt Stanwood, that the course of true love was not batting .400. Inexplicable, moreover. To him, Mike Cardinal seemed to have everything; looks, personality and, seeing that he was a partner in one of Hollywood's most prosperous firms of motion picture agents, money, of course, to burn. Difficult to see why Terry should be giving him the runaround.

He grieved for Mike Cardinal. Mike was his best friend, and he wished him well. He had, besides, during the month or two which she had spent in London as a member of the chorus of a popular musical comedy, conceived a solid affection for Terry. They had lunched together a good deal, and he had told her about his love for Eileen Stoker, and she had told him about her life at home and the motives which had led her to run away from that home and try to earn her living.

A peach of a girl, was Stanwood's view, pretty and cheerful and abounding in pep. Just, in short, the sort for Mike. Nothing would have given Stanwood more pleasure than to have seen the young couple fading out on the clinch.

Still, that was the way things went, he supposed, and he turned his thoughts to the more agreeable subject of Eileen Stoker and the big times they were going to have together, now that she had hit London. So soothing was the effect of these meditations that he fell asleep.

His slumber was not long-lived. 'Hoy!' roared a voice almost before he had closed his eyes, and he saw that Augustus Robb was with him once more.

'Now what?' he said wearily.

Augustus Robb was brandishing a document.

'Cable from your Pop,' he announced. 'I'll read it and give you the gist.'

He removed his spectacles, fished in his pocket, produced a case, opened it, took out another pair of spectacles, placed these on his nose, put the first pair in the case and the case in his pocket and cleared his throat with a sound like the backfiring of a motor truck, causing Stanwood, who had sat up, to sag down again as if he had been hit over the head with a blunt instrument.

'Here's the substance, chum. He says –'

'Is it money?'

'Yus, he's cabled a thousand dollars to your account, if you must know, but you think too much of money, cocky. Money is but dross, and the sooner you get that clearly into your nut, the 'appier you'll be. But that's only the start. There's a lot more. He says . . . 'Ullo, what's this?'

'What?'

'Well, well, well!'

'What is it?'

'Well, well, well, *well*! Quite a coincidence, I'd call that. Your Pop,' said Augustus Robb, becoming less cryptic, 'says you're to proceed immediately to Beevor Castle –'

It was foreign to Stanwood's policy to keep sitting up, for the process accentuated the unpleasant illusion that somebody was driving white-hot rivets into his skull, but in his emotion he did so now.

'What's that?'

'You 'eard. You're to proceed immediately to Beevor Castle and stay there till he blows the All Clear. You can guess what's happened, of course. He's been apprised that this Stoker jane of yours has come to London, and he's took steps. But you see what I meant about it being a coincidence. Beevor Castle's where this little number of Mr Cardinal's lives that we was talking about.'

Stanwood was still endeavouring to grasp the appalling news.

'Leave London and go to some darned castle?'

'I shall enjoy a breath of country air. Do you good, too. It's what you need, cocky. Fresh air, milk and new-laid eggs.'

Stanwood struggled for utterance.

'I'm not going anywhere near any darned castle.'

'That's what *you* say. Cloth-headed remark to make, if you ask me. You've got to do what your Pop tells you, or he'll cut off supplies, and then where'll you be? It's like in the Good Book, where the feller said "Go" and they goeth and "Come" and they cometh. Or, putting it another way, when Father says "Turn," we all turn. It's an am-parce.'

Even to Stanwood, clouded though his mind was at the moment, the truth of this was evident. With a hollow groan he buried his face in the pillow.

'Oh, gosh!'

Fruitless now those dreams of sitting beside Eileen Stoker with her little hand in his, and pouring into her little ear all the good stuff he had been storing up for so many weeks. Good-bye to all that. She would be in London, pursuing her art, and he would be at this blasted castle. As so often occurred in the pictures in which she appeared, two young hearts in Springtime had been torn asunder.

'Beevor Castle,' said Augustus Robb, seeming to roll the words round his tongue like some priceless wine. No more fervent worshipper of the aristocracy than he existed among London's millions. He read all the Society columns, and the only episode of his burglarious past to which in his present saved condition he could look back with real pleasure was the occasion when he had got in through a scullery window belonging to a Countess in her own right and been bitten in the seat of his trousers by what virtually amounted to a titled wire-haired terrier. 'Come to think of it, I've seen Beevor Castle. Cycled there once when I was a lad. Took sandwiches. Nice place. Romantic. One of those stately homes of England they talk about. Who'd have thought I'd of ever got inside of it? It just shows, don't it? What I mean is, you never know. And now, cocky, you'd better hop out of that bed and go and have your Turkish bath. I'll be putting out your things. The blue suit with a heliotrope shirt and similarly coloured socks will be about the ticket, I think,' said Augustus Robb, who had an eye for the rare and the beautiful.

Nothing, in his opinion, could actually convert his employer into an oil painting, but the blue suit and the heliotrope shirt might help to some small extent.

Chapter 3

Some four and a quarter hours after a silver-voiced Western Union songster, even more of a human nightingale than usual owing to sucking throat pastilles, had chanted into the receiver of his telephone that beautiful lyric which begins:

> Happy birthday to you,
> Happy birthday to you,

and goes on (in case the reader has forgotten):

> Happy birthday to you,
> Happy birthday to you.

Claude Percival John Delamere Cobbold, the fifth Earl of Shortlands, was standing at the window of his study on the ground floor of Beevor Castle in the county of Kent, rattling in his trousers pocket the two shillings and eightpence which was all that remained of his month's pocket money, and feeling how different everything would be if only it were two hundred pounds.

The sun which had evoked the enthusiasm of Augustus Robb in London at eleven o'clock was shining with equal, or even superior, radiance on Beevor Castle at eleven-fifteen. It glittered on the moat. It also glittered on the battlements and played about the ivied walls, from the disused wing which had been built in 1259 to the modernized section where the family lived and had their being. But when a couple of rays of adventurous disposition started to muscle into the study, they backed out hastily at the sight of this stout, smoothfaced man who looked like a discontented butler, finding his aspect forbidding and discouraging.

For the morning of May the twelfth, the fifty-second anniversary of his birth, had caught Lord Shortlands in poor shape. A dark despondency had him in its grip, and he could see no future for the human race. He glowered at the moat, thinking, as he had so often thought before, what a beastly moat it was.

As a matter of fact, except for smelling a little of mud and dead eels, it was, as moats go, rather a good moat. But you would have been wasting your time if you had tried to sell that idea to Lord Shortlands. A sullen dislike for the home of his ancestors and everything connected with it had been part of his spiritual make-up for some years now, and today, as has been indicated, he was in the acute stage of that malady which, for want of a better name, scientists call the heeby-jeebies.

It generally takes a man who likes to sleep till nine much more than four and a quarter hours to recover from the shock of having 'Happy birthday' sung to him over the transatlantic telephone at seven, and in addition to this shattering experience there had been other slings and arrows of outrageous Fortune whistling about the fifth Earl's ears this morning.

His dog Whiskers was sick of a fever. His favourite hat, the one with the broken rim and the grease stains, had disappeared, stolen, he strongly suspected, by his daughter Clare, who was collecting odds and ends for the vicar's jumble sale. Breakfast, in the absence of Mrs Punter, the cook, away visiting relatives in Walham Green, had been prepared by the kitchen maid, an indifferent performer who had used the scorched earth policy on the bacon again. Cosmo Blair, the playwright, who had been staying at the castle for the past week, much against his lordship's wishes, was extending his visit indefinitely, in spite of the fact that there had been a clean-cut gentleman's agreement that he would leave this afternoon.

And, shrewdest buffet of all, his daughter Adela, a woman who, being the wife of Desborough Topping, one of those Americans at the mention of whose name Bradstreet raises his hat with a deferential flourish, could have fed such sums to the birds, had refused to lend him two hundred pounds.

Wanted to know why he wanted two hundred pounds, of all silly questions. As if he could possibly tell her that he wanted it in order to buy a public house and marry Mrs Punter, the cook.

What the average rate or norm of misfortune for Earls on their birthdays might be Lord Shortlands did not know, but he would have been greatly surprised to discover that he had not been given an unusually liberal helping: and he was about to sink for the third time in a sea of self-pity when he became aware of a presence and, turning, saw that his daughter Clare had entered the room.

Self-pity gave way to righteous wrath. There are men from whom old hats can be snitched with impunity, and men from whom they cannot. Lord Shortlands was a charter member of the second and sturdier class. His prominent eyes glowed dangerously, and he spoke in a voice the tones of which King Lear, had he been present, would have memorized for personal use.

'Clare,' he boomed, 'did you take that hat of mine?'

She paid no attention to the question. She was a girl who had an annoying habit of paying no attention to questions, being brisk and masterful and concentrated on her own affairs; the sort of girl, so familiar a feature of the English countryside, who goes about in brogue shoes and tweeds and meddles vigorously in the lives of the villagers, sprucing up their manners and morals till you wonder that something in the nature of a popular uprising does not take place. The thought sometimes crossed Lord Shortlands's mind that, if he had been a villager, compelled to cope with Lady Clare Cobbold and her sister Lady Adela Topping, he would have turned his face to the wall and given up the struggle.

'Whose is this, father?' she asked, and he saw that she was extending towards him a battered volume of some kind. It might have been, as indeed it was, an album for the reception of postage stamps.

It is interesting to reflect that this stamp album, which was to play so considerable a part in Lord Shortlands's affairs, made upon him at its first introduction but a slight impression. It was to be instrumental, before the week was out, in leading him to break Commandments and court nervous prostration, but now he merely looked at it in distaste, like a butler inspecting a bottle of wine of an inferior vintage. Coming events do not always cast their shadow before them.

'Don't point that beastly thing at me,' he said. 'It's all over dust. What is it?'

'A stamp album.'

'Well, it's caked with grime. Put it on the table. Where did you get it?'

'I found it in a cupboard,' said Clare, deviating from her practice of not answering questions. 'Whose is it, do you know?

Because if it doesn't belong to anyone, I want it for my jumble sale.'

This would have been an excellent cue for the restating of the hat *motif*, but Lord Shortlands had now begun to be interested in this album. Like most people, he had once collected stamps, and strange nostalgic emotions were stirring within him. He approached the table and gave the book a tentative prod with the tip of his fingers, like a puppy pawing at a tortoise.

'Why, this is mine.'

'Why should it be yours?'

'I used to collect stamps.'

'I should imagine it's Tony's.'

'Why should it be Tony's any more than mine?'

'I've told Desborough, and he's coming here to look through it. He knows all about stamps.'

This was true. A confirmed philatelist from his early years, Desborough Topping was as much looked up to by Stanley Gibbons as by Bradstreet. Stamps and the reading of detective stories were his two great passions.

'There may be something valuable in it. If there is,' said Clare, who, while she believed in supporting jumble sales in aid of indigent villagers, did not believe in overdoing it, 'we can take it out.'

She moved towards the door, and Lord Shortlands remembered that the vital issue was still unsettled.

'Just a minute. How about that hat? Somebody has taken my hat. I left it last night hanging on a peg in the coat-room. I go there this morning, and no hat. Hats don't run away. Hats don't leap lightly off pegs and take to the great open spaces. Have you seen my hat?'

'Have you seen Terry?' asked Clare. Unquestionably she was a difficult girl to talk to about hats.

The eccentricity of her conversational methods bewildered Lord Shortlands, who had never been nimble-minded.

'Terry?'

'Have you seen her?'

'No.'

'Well, if you do, tell her that Cosmo Blair wants to read her his second act.'

The name seemed to grate upon Lord Shortlands's sensibilities.

'Cosmo Blair!'

'Why do you say "Cosmo Blair" like that?'

'Like what?'

'Like you did.'

'I didn't.'

'Yes, you did.'

'Well, why shouldn't I?' demanded Lord Shortlands, driven out into the open. 'He's a pot-bellied perisher.'

Clare quivered from head to foot.

'Don't call him a pot-bellied perisher!'

'Well, what else can you call him?' asked Lord Shortlands, like Roget trying to collect material for his Thesaurus. 'I've studied him closely, and I say he's a pot-bellied perisher.'

'He's a very brilliant man,' said Clare, and swept from the room, banging the door behind her.

'His last play ran nine months in London,' she added, re-opening and re-banging the door.

'And a year in New York,' she said, opening the door again and closing it with perhaps the loudest bang of the series.

Lord Shortlands was not a patient man. He resented the spectacle of a daughter behaving like a cuckoo in a cuckoo clock. When the door opened once more a moment later, he was all ready with a blistering reproof, and was on the point of delivering it when he perceived that this was not his child playing a return date, but a godlike figure, with short side-whiskers, that carried a glass of malted milk on a salver. One of Lord Shortlands's numerous grievances against his daughter Adela was the fact that she made him drink a glass of malted milk every morning, and this was Spink, the butler, bringing it.

Nature is a haphazard caster, and no better example of her sloppy methods could have been afforded than the outer husks of the fifth Earl of Shortlands and Spink, his butler. Called upon to provide an Earl and a butler, she had produced an Earl who looked like a butler and a butler who looked like an Earl. Mervyn Spink was tall and aristocratic and elegant, Lord Shortlands square and stout and plebeian. No judge in a beauty contest would have hesitated between them for an instant, and no one was more keenly aware of this than Lord Shortlands. He would willingly have given half his fortune – amounting at the moment, as we have seen, to two shillings and eightpence – to have possessed a tithe of this malted milk carrier's lissomeness and grace. For something even remotely resembling his profile he would probably have gone still higher.

The butler advanced into the room with the air of an ambassador about to deliver important despatches to a reigning monarch, and Lord Shortlands turned to the window to avoid looking at him. He did not like Mervyn Spink.

It is to be doubted if he would have liked him even in the most favourable circumstances; say, just after the other had saved him from drowning or death by fire, for some people are made incompatible by nature, like film stars and their husbands. And the circumstances were very far from favourable. Lord Shortlands wanted to marry Mrs Alice Punter, the cook, and so did Spink. And it is not agreeable for the last of a proud line to have his butler as a rival in love.

Not that you have to be the last of a proud line to chafe at such a state of affairs. No householder would like it. In a race for which the hand of a cook is the prize a butler starts with the enormous advantage of being constantly at her side. While the *seigneur* has to snatch what surreptitious interviews he can, quivering all the while at the thought that his daughter Adela may pop in at any moment and catch him, the butler can hobnob with her by the hour, freely exerting the full force of his fascination.

And you simply could not afford to be handicapped like that in a struggle against such an adversary as Mervyn Spink, facially a feast for the eye and in addition a travelled sophisticate who had seen men and cities. Spink had been for a time in service in the United States, and so was able to bring to his wooing a breath of the great world outside. He also had a nephew on the stage. And while it was true that this nephew had so far played only minor character parts, and those only intermittently, a nephew on the stage is always a nephew on the stage.

Add the fact that he could imitate Spencer Tracy and do

tricks with bits of string, and it was only too easy to picture the impact of such a personality on a woman of Mrs Punter's cloistered outlook. Lord Shortlands, who was doing it now, shuddered and gave vent to a little sighing sound like the last gurgle of an expiring soda-water syphon.

Had happier conditions prevailed, there might have taken place at this juncture a word or two of that genial conversation which does so much to smooth relations between employer and employed. Such snatches as 'Nice day, Spink,' 'Yes, indeed, m'lord,' or 'Your malted milk, m'lord,' 'Eh? Oh? Ah. Right. Thanks!' suggest themselves. But now the silence was strained and unbroken. Spink put the salver on the table without comment, and Lord Shortlands continued to present a chilly back. The shadow of Alice Punter lay between these men.

Spink withdrew, gracefully and sinuously, with a touch of the smugness of the ambassador who is pluming himself on having delivered the important despatches without dropping them, and Lord Shortlands pursued the train of thought which the man's entry had started. He was musing dejectedly on Mervyn Spink's profile, and trying to make himself believe that it was not really so perfectly chiselled as he knew in his heart it was, when the telephone rang.

He approached it warily, as any man would have done whose most recent unhooking of the receiver had resulted in the impact on his ear drum of a Western Union tenor's 'Happy birthday.' The burned child fears the fire.

'Hullo?' he said.

'Hello,' replied a pleasant male voice. 'Can I speak to Lady Teresa?'

'Terry? I haven't seen her this morning.'

'Who is that speaking?'

'Lord Shortlands.'

'Oh, how do you do, Lord Shortlands? You've probably forgotten me. Mike Cardinal.'

Lord Shortlands was obliged to confess that the name did not seem familiar.

'I was afraid it wouldn't. Well, would you mind telling Terry I called up. Good-bye.'

'Good-bye,' said Lord Shortlands, and returned to meditations. He was sinking steadily again into the Slough of Despond in which he had spent most of the morning, when the door opened again, this time to admit the Lady Teresa of whom the pleasant voice had spoken.

'Ha!' said Lord Shortlands, brightening.

To say that he beamed at the girl would be too much. A man who has lost his favourite hat, and is contending in the lists of love against a butler who might have stepped out of a collar advertisement in a magazine, does not readily beam. But his gloom perceptibly lightened. A moment before, you would have taken him for a corpse that had been some days in the water. Now, he might have passed for such a corpse at a fairly early stage of its immersion. After his trying morning the sight of Terry had come to him like that of a sail on the horizon to a shipwrecked mariner.

Even at the nadir of his depression Lord Shortlands, contemplating the inky clouds that loomed about him as far as the eye could reach, had always recognized that there was among them a speck of silver lining; the fact that his youngest daughter, who some time previously had run off to London to seek a venturous freedom in the chorus of a musical comedy, had now run back again and was once more at his side to comfort and advise.

His oldest daughter Adela might be hard to bear, his second daughter Clare difficult to endure. A man might well come near to cracking under the strain of Mervyn Spink and Cosmo Blair. But Terry, God bless her, was all right.

Chapter 4

Lady Teresa Cobbold was considerably better worth looking at than the Lady Clare, her sister. The latter took after her father in appearance, which was an unfortunate thing for any girl to do, for it has already been stressed that the fifth Earl of Shortlands, though a worthy soul and no thicker in the head than the average member of the House of Peers, presented to the eye the façade of an Eric Blore rather than that of a Robert Taylor.

Terry had had the good sense to resemble her late mother, who had been in her day one of the prettiest débutantes in London. Slim, blue-eyed, fair-haired and bearing Youth like a banner, she was the sort of girl at the sight of whom strong men quiver and straighten their ties.

'Good morning, Shorty,' she said. 'Many happy returns, darling.'

'Thank you, my dear.'

'Here's my little gift. Only a pipe, I'm afraid.'

'It's a jolly good pipe,' said Lord Shortlands stoutly. 'Just what I wanted. There was a fellow on the phone for you just now.'

'Name of Cardinal.'

'Yes. Seemed to know me, but I couldn't place him.'

'You wouldn't. It's years since you saw him. Well, never mind young Mike Cardinal,' said Terry, perching herself on the end of the battered sofa. 'How have you come out on the takings? Did the others do their bit?'

Lord Shortlands's face clouded. He had had a lean birthday.

'Adela gave me a couple of ties. Desborough gave me a book called Murder at some dashed place or other. Clare –"

'No cash?'

'Not a penny.'

'What a shame. I was hoping we could have slunk up to London and had lunch somewhere. How much have you?'

'Two and eightpence. How much have you?'

'Three bob.'

'You see. That's how it goes.'

'That's how it goes, Shorty.'

'Yes, that's how it goes,' said Lord Shortlands, and fell into a moody silence.

These times in which we live are not good times for Earls. Theirs was a great racket while it lasted, but the boom days are over. A scattered few may still have a pittance, but the majority, after they have paid their income tax and their land tax and all their other taxes, and invested in one or two of the get-rich-quick schemes thrown together for their benefit by bright-eyed gentlemen in the City, are generally pretty close to the bread line. Lord Shortlands, with two and eightpence in his pocket, was more happily situated than most.

But even he cannot be considered affluent. There had been a time, for he had seen better days, when he had thought nothing of walking into his club and ordering a bottle of the best. We find him now reduced to malted milk and dependent for the necessities of life on the bounty of his daughter Adela, that level-headed girl who had had the intelligence to marry into Bradstreet.

Dependence in itself was not a state of being which would have grafted on the fifth Earl. He had always preferred not to have to pay for things. But it was another matter to be dependent on a daughter who checked his expenditure so closely; who so consistently refused to loosen up – as it might be when a fellow wanted two hundred pounds in order to marry the cook; and, above all, who was so devoted to the ancestral home that she insisted on staying in it all the year round.

Why anyone with the money to live elsewhere should elect to live at Beevor Castle, which was stuffy in summer and cold in winter, was one of the mysteries which Lord Shortlands knew that he would never solve.

'Do you realize, Terry,' he said, his thoughts during the lull in the conversation having turned to this perennial grievance, 'that the last time I was away from this place for even a couple of hours was when those Americans took it last summer? And then Adela made me go with her to Harrogate, of all loathsome holes. Some nonsense about Desborough's lumbago. I offered to rough it at my club, but she said she couldn't trust me alone in London.'

'I suppose you aren't the sort of man who can be trusted alone in London.'

'I suppose not,' said Lord Shortlands, with modest pride.

'You used to paint it red in the old days, didn't you?'

'Reddish,' admitted Lord Shortlands. 'And since then I've not been out of the damned place. I'm just a bird in a gilded cage.'

'Would you call it a gilded cage?'

'Well, a bird in a bally mausoleum.'

'Poor old Shorty. You don't like Ye Olde much, do you?'

'And this infernal feeling of dependence. "Adela, could I have a shilling?" "What do you want a shilling for?" "For tobacco." "I thought you had tobacco." "I've smoked it." "Oh? Well, here you are. But you smoke a great deal too much." It offends one's manly pride. I can't tell you how much I admired your spirited behaviour, Terry, in breaking away as you did. It thrilled me to the core. A bold bid for freedom. I wish I had the nerve to do it, too.'

'Perhaps the mistake we made was in not going away together and working as a team. We might have got bookings in vaudeville as a cross-talk act."

'What on earth made you come back?'

'Hunger, my angel. The show I was in collapsed, and I couldn't get another job. Have you ever tried not eating, Shorty?'

'Do you mean you didn't get enough to eat?'

'If it hadn't been for one faithful friend, who was a perfect lamb, I should have starved. He used to take me out to lunch and tell me about the girl he was in love with. His father had sent him to England to get him out of her way. He was an American, and, oddly enough, his name was the same as mine.'

'What, Cobbold?'

'Well, you didn't think I meant Teresa?'

Lord Shortlands was interested. Since seven that morning the name Cobbold had been graven on his heart.

'I wonder if he was any relation of that lunatic of mine. There's a borderline case in New York named Ellery Cobbold who keeps writing me letters and sending me cables. And this morning he incited some blasted friend of his to ring me up on the telephone and howl into my ear a lot of dashed rot about "Happy birthday". At seven! Seven sharp. The stable clock was just striking when the beastly outrage occurred.'

'I should imagine Stanwood is his son. He told me his father lived in New York, or somewhere just outside. Well, he kept me alive, though growing thinner every day, but I found I couldn't take it, Shorty, so I came back.'

'Why couldn't you get another job? I should have thought a girl as pretty as you could have walked into something.'

'I couldn't even crawl. And I couldn't afford to wait.'

'No cash?'

'No cash.'

Lord Shortlands nodded.

'Yes, that's it. The problem of cash. One comes up against it at every turn. Look at me. If I had two hundred pounds, I could strike off the shackles. Mrs Punter still sticks rigidly to her terms.'

'I know. She told me.'

'She will only marry a man who can set her up in a pub in London. Wants to chuck service and settle down. Enjoy the evening of her life, and all that. One can understand it, of course. Women must have the little home with their own sticks of furniture about them. But it makes it dashed awkward. I don't see how I can raise the money, and there's Spink piling it up hand over fist. I saw that chap Blair slip him a quid the other day. It nearly made me sick. And who knows what those Rossiters may not have tipped him last summer? Spink must be getting very near the goal by now.'

'But he bets.'

'Yes, and suppose one of these days he strikes a long-priced winner.'

'According to Mrs Punter, he loses all the time, and it prejudices her against him. She wants a steady husband.'

'Did she tell you that?'

'Yes, that comes straight from the horse's mouth. I went to her just before she left for her holiday, and pleaded your cause. It seems that she once had a sad experience in her life. She didn't tell me what it was, but I gathered that some man had let her down pretty badly, and now she's looking for someone she can rely on.'

'The sturdy oak, not the sapling.'

'Exactly. I plugged your reliable qualities, and she quite agreed. "Your Pa hasn't got Mr Spink's fascination and polish," she said. "He isn't so much the gentleman as Mr Spink. But he's steady."'

'Ha!'

'So carry on and fear nothing, is my advice. Don't give a thought to Spink's fascination and polish. It's the soul that counts, and that's where you have the bulge on him. I think you're Our Five Horse Special and Captain Coe's Final Selection. You'll romp home, darling.'

Lord Shortlands, though not insensible to this pep talk, was unable to bring himself to rejoice wholeheartedly. The sort of life he had been living for the last few years makes a man a realist.

'Not if I can't get that two hundred.'

'Yes, we shall have to look into that.'

The telephone rang, and Lord Shortlands went to it more confidently this time, like one who feels that the danger is past.

'It's for you.'

'Mike Cardinal?'

'Yes. He says did you get his letter?'

'Yes, I did. Tell him I won't.'

'Won't?'

'Won't.'

'Won't what?'

'Just won't. He'll understand.'

'Yes,' said Lord Shortlands into the instrument, mystified but dutifully obeying instructions, 'she says she did, but she won't. Eh? I'll ask her. He wants to know if you're still doing your hair the same way.'

'Yes.'

'She says yes. Eh? Yes, I'll tell her. Good-bye. He says very sensible of you, because it makes you look like a Botticelli angel. What won't you do?' asked Lord Shortlands, who still found the phrase perplexing.

Terry laughed.

'Marry him.'

'Does he want to marry you?'

'He keeps saying so.'

Lord Shortlands looked as like a conscientious father with his child's welfare at heart as it was possible for him to do.

'You ought to marry.'

'I suppose so.'

'Think what it would mean. Liberty. Freedom. You would never have to see that moat again.'

'Adela wants me to marry Cosmo Blair,'

'Don't do it.'

'I won't.'

'That's the spirit. I mean to say, dash it, it's all very well wanting to get away from the moat, but you can pay too high a price.'

'I feel like that, too. Besides, he's going to marry Clare.'

'Good God! Does he know it?'

'Not yet. But he will.'

Lord Shortlands reflected.

'By George, I believe you're right. She bit my head off just now because I called him a pot-bellied perisher. Even at the time it struck me as significant. Well, I'm glad there's no danger as far as you're concerned.'

'None whatever. I can't stand that superior manner of his. He talks to me as if I were a child.'

'He talks to me as if I were a bally fathead,' said Lord Shortlands, who, being one, was sensitive about it. 'Well, tell me about this fellow Cardinal. When did you meet him?'

'Do you remember Tony bringing a school friend of his here for the summer holidays about eight years ago?'

'How can I possibly remember all Tony's repulsive friends?'

'This one wasn't repulsive. Dazzlingly good-looking. I met him again when I was lunching with Stanwood Cobbold one day. They knew each other in America.'

'He's American, is he?'

'Yes. He was at school with Tony, but he comes from California. He came up and asked me if I remembered him.'

'And did you?'

'Vividly. So he sat down and joined us, and after lunch Stanwood went off to write to his girl and Mike immediately proposed to me over the coffee cups.'

'Quick work.'

'So I pointed out to him. He then said he had loved me from the first moment we met, but had been too shy to speak.'

'He doesn't sound shy.'

'I suppose he's got over it.'

'What is he?'

'A Greek god, Shorty. No less.'

'I mean, what does he do?'

'He's a motion picture agent in Hollywood. Motion picture

agents are the people who fix up the stars with engagements at the studios. They get ten per cent of the salaries.'

Lord Shortland's eyes widened. He had read all about motion picture stars' salaries.

'Good heavens. He must make a fortune.'

'Well, he's only a junior partner, but I suppose he does pretty well.'

Lord Shortlands gulped emotionally.

'I'd have grabbed him.'

'Well, I didn't.'

'Don't you like him?'

'Yes, I do. Very much. But I'm not going to marry him.'

'Why not?'

'There's a reason.'

'What reason?'

'Oh, just a reason. But don't let's talk about me any more. Let's talk about you – you and your two hundred pounds.'

Lord Shortlands would have preferred to continue the probe into his daughter's reasons for being unwilling to marry a rich and good-looking young man, whom she admitted to liking, but it was plain that she considered the subject closed. And he was always ready to talk about his two hundred pounds.

'That still remains the insuperable obstacle. I don't see how I can raise it.'

'Have you tried Desborough?'

'I keep starting to pave the way, but he always vanishes like a homing rabbit. The impression he gives me is that he sees it coming.'

'Well, he'll be here at any moment to look at that stamp album Clare found. And he can't vanish like a rabbit this time, because he's got lumbago again.'

'That's true.'

'Tackle him firmly. Don't pave the way. Use shock tactics. Oh, hullo, Desborough.'

A small, slight, pince-nezed man in the middle forties, who looked like the second vice-president of something, had entered. He came in slowly, for he was supporting himself with a walking stick, but his manner was eager. When there were stamps about, Desborough Topping always resembled a second vice-president on the verge of discovering some leakage in the monthly accounts.

'Hello, Terry. Say, where's this ... Ah,' he said, sighting the album and becoming lost to all external things.

The eyes of Lord Shortlands and his daughter met in a significant glance. 'Do it now,' said Terry's. 'Quite. Certainly. Oh, rather,' said Lord Shortlands's. He advanced to the table and laid a gentle hand on his son-in-law's shoulder.

'Some interesting stamps here, eh?' he said, affectionately. 'Desborough, old chap, can you lend me two hundred pounds?'

The invalid started, as any man might on finding so substantial a touch coming out of a blue sky.

'Two hundred pounds?'

'It would be a great convenience.'

'Why don't you ask Adela?'

'I did. But she wouldn't.'

Desborough Topping was looking like a stag at bay.

'Well, you know me. I'd give you the shirt off my back.'

Lord Shortlands disclaimed any desire for the shirt off his son-in-law's back. What he wanted, he stressed once more, was not haberdashery but two hundred pounds.

'Well, look. Here's the trouble. Adela and I have a joint account.'

It was the end. A man cannot go on struggling against Fate beyond a certain point. Lord Shortlands turned and walked to the window, where he gave the moat a look compared with which all previous looks had been loving and appreciative.

'This whole matter of joint accounts for married couples,' he was beginning, speaking warmly, for the subject was one on which he held strong views, when his observations were interrupted. The door had opened again, and his eldest daughter was coming in.

Lady Adela Topping, some fifteen years younger than her husband, was tall and handsome and built rather on the lines of Catherine of Russia, whom she resembled also in force of character and that imperiousness of outlook which makes a woman disinclined to stand any nonsense. And that she had recently been confronted with nonsense of some nature was plainly shown in her demeanour now. She was visibly annoyed; so visibly that if Desborough Topping had not become immersed in the stamp album once more and so missed the tilt of her chin and the flash of her eye, he would have curled up in a ball and rolled under the sofa.

'Do you know a man named Cobbold, father?' she said. She consulted the buff sheet of paper in her hand. ' "Ellery Cobbold" he signs himself.'

Like a bull which, suddenly annoyed by a picador, turns from the matador who had previously engrossed its attention, Lord Shortlands shelved the thought of joint accounts for the time being and puffed belligerently.

'Ellery Cobbold? That fellow in New York? I should say I do. He sours my life.'

'But how do you come to be connected with him?'

'He's connected with me. Or says he is. Claims he's a sort of cousin.'

'Well, I cannot see that that entitles him to expect us to put his son Stanwood up for an indeterminate visit.'

'Does he?'

'That's what he says in his cable. I never heard such impertinence.'

'Bally crust,' agreed Lord Shortlands, indignant but not surprised. After what had occurred that morning when the stable clock was striking seven, he could scarcely be astonished at any excesses on Mr Cobbold's part.

Only Terry seemed pleased.

'Is Stanwood Cobbold coming here?' she said. 'Splendid.'

'Do you know him?'

'We're like ham and eggs.'

'Like what?'

'I mean that's how well we get along together. Stanwood's an angel. He saved my life in London.'

Down at the table something stirred. It was Desborough Topping coming to the surface.

'Ellery Cobbold?' he said, the name having just penetrated to his stamp-drugged consciousness. 'I was in college with Ellery Cobbold. Fat fellow.'

'Indeed?'

'Very rich now, I believe.'

Lady Adela started.

'Rich?'

'Worth millions, I guess,' said Desborough, and dived back into the album.

A change had come over Lady Adela's iron front. Her eyes seemed softer. They had lost their stern anti-Cobbold glare.

'Oh, *is* he? And you say he's some connexion of ours, father? And his son is a friend of yours, Terry? Then of course we must ask him here,' said Lady Adela heartily. 'Desborough, go and send him a telegram – here's the address – saying that we shall be delighted to put him up. Sign it "Shortlands". The cable was addressed to you, father.'

'Was that why you opened it?' asked Lord Shortlands, who had begun to feel ruffled again about that joint account.

'Say that father will be coming in this afternoon in the car –'

A sigh escaped Lord Shortlands. Permission to go to London, and only two-and-eightpence to spend when he got there. This, he supposed, was the sort of thing Cosmo Blair had been alluding to at dinner last night, when he had spoken of tragic irony.

'– and will bring him back with him. Have you got that clear? Then run along. Oh, and you had better cable Mr Cobbold saying how delighted we are. Pistachio, New York. New York is one word.'

'Yes, dear. I'll take this album with me. It's quite interesting. I've already found a stamp that's worth several pounds.'

'Then Clare must certainly not give the thing to her jumble sale until you have thoroughly examined it,' said Lady Adela with decision. She shared her sister's views about not overdoing it when you are aiding indigent villagers.

It seemed to Lord Shortlands that the time had come to get his property rights firmly established. The mention of stamps worth several pounds had stirred him profoundly, and all this loose talk about jumble sales, he felt, must be checked without delay.

'Just a minute, just a minute,' he said. 'Clare isn't going to have that album. Ridiculous. Absurd.'

'What do you mean?'

'Perfect rot. Never heard of such a thing.'

40

'But what has it to do with you?'

'It's my album.'

'Nonsense.'

'It is, I tell you. I used to collect stamps.'

'Years ago.'

'Well, the thing's probably been in that cupboard for years. Look at the dust on it. What more likely than that I should have put my album in a cupboard and forgotten all about it?'

'Well, I haven't time to discuss it now. Run along, Desborough.'

'Yes, dear.'

As the door closed, Lady Adela had another idea.

'It might be a good thing, father, if you were to start at once. Then you could give Mr Cobbold lunch.'

'What!'

Lady Adela repeated her remark, and Lord Shortlands closed his eyes for a moment, as if he were praying.

'An excellent idea,' he said in a hushed voice. 'At the Ritz.'

'You're off the beat, Shorty,' said Terry. 'Barribault's is Stanwood's stamping ground.'

'Then make it Barribault's,' said Lord Shortlands agreeably.

'And you can take Terry with you.'

Terry blinked.

'Did you hear what I heard, Shorty?'

'"Take Terry with you" was the way I got it.'

'That's what it sounded like to me, too. Do you really mean this, Adela?'

'Make yourself look nice.'

'A vision,' said Terry, and started off to do so.

She left Lord Shortlands uplifted but bewildered. He was at a loss to account for this sudden spasm of open-handedness in a daughter generally prudent to a fault. He found himself reminded of the Christmas Day activities of the late Scrooge.

'This may be a most fortunate thing that has happened, father,' said Lady Adela. 'Terry is a very attractive girl, and apparently she and this Mr Cobbold are good friends already. And he saved her life, she says. Odd she should not have mentioned that before. I wonder how it happened. It seems to me that, being here together, they might quite easily –'

'Good Lord!' said Lord Shortlands, enlightened. He was also a little shocked. 'Don't you women ever think of anything but trying to fix up weddings?'

'Well, it's quite time that Terry got married. It would steady her.'

'Terry doesn't need steadying.'

'How can you talk like that, father, after the way she ran off and –'

'Oh, all right, all right. And now,' said Lord Shortlands, for he felt that too much time was being wasted on these trivialities, 'in the matter of expenses. I shall need quite a bit of working capital.'

'Nonsense. Two pounds will be ample.'

It is not often that anyone sees an Earl in the act of not believing his ears. Lady Adela was privileged to do so now. Lord Shortlands's prominent eyes, so well adapted for staring incredulously, seemed in danger of leaping from their sockets.

'Two pounds?' he cried. 'Great heavens! How about cocktails? How about cigars? How about wines, liqueurs and spirits?'

'I'm not going to have you stuffing yourself with wines and liqueurs. You know how weak your head is.'

'My head is not weak. It's as strong as an ox. And it is not a question of stuffing myself, as you call it, with wines and liqueurs. I shall have to do this boy well, shan't I? You don't want him thinking he's accepting the hospitality of Gaspard the miser, do you? It's a little hard,' said Lord Shortlands, quivering with the self-pity which came so easily to him. 'You bundle me off to London at a moment's notice, upsetting my day and causing me all sorts of inconvenience, to entertain a young man of whom I know nothing except that his father is off his bally onion, and you expect me to keep the expenses down to an absurd sum like two pounds.'

'Oh, very well.'

'It's going to be a nice thing for me at the end of lunch, when the coffee is served and this young fellow gazes at me with a wistful look in his eyes, to have to say "No liqueurs, Cobbold. It won't run to them. Chew a tooth-pick." I should blush to my very bones.'

'Oh, very well, very well. Here is five pounds.'

'Couldn't you make it ten?'

'No, I could not make it ten,' said Lady Adela, with the testiness of a conjurer asked to do too difficult a trick.

'Well, all right. Though it's running it fine. I foresee a painful moment at the table, when this chap is swilling down his wine and I am compelled to say "Not quite so rapidly, young Cobbold. Eke it out, my boy, eke it out. There isn't going to be a second bottle." How about seven pounds ten? Splitting the difference, if you see what I mean. Well, I merely asked,' said Lord Shortlands, addressing the closing door.

For some moments after the founder of the feast had left him he stood gazing – in a kindlier spirit now – at the moat. In spite of the misgivings which he had expressed, he was not really ill-pleased. For a proper slap-up binge, of course, on the lines of Belshazzar's Feast, five pounds is an inadequate capital, but you can unquestionably do something with it. Many a poor Earl, he knew, would have screamed with joy at the sight of a fiver. It was only that he did wish that some angel could have descended from on high and increased his holdings to ten, in his opinion the minimum sum for true self-expression.

So softly did the door open that it was not until he heard his emotional breathing that he became aware of his son-in-law's presence. Desborough Topping had stolen into the room furtively, like a nervous member of the Black Hand attending his first general meting.

'Psst!' he said.

He glanced over his shoulder. The door was well and truly closed. Nevertheless, he continued to speak in a hushed, conspiratorial whisper.

'Say, look, about that two hundred. I can't manage two hundred, but –'

Something crisp and crackling slid into Lord Shortlands's hand. Staring, he saw his son-in-law receding towards the door. His pince-nezed eyes were shining with an appealing light, and Lord Shortlands had no difficulty in reading their message. It was that fine old family slogan 'Not a word to the wife!' The next moment his benefactor had gone.

Terry, returning some minutes later, was stunned by a father's tale of manna in the wilderness.

'Ten quid, Terry! Desborough's come across with ten quid! I cannot speak in too high terms of the fellow's courage – no, dash it, heroism. Men have got the V.C. for less. Fifteen quid in my kick that makes. Fifteen solid jimmy-o'-goblins. Not counting my two-and-eightpence.'

'Golly, Shorty, what a birthday you've had.'

'Nothing to the birthday I'm going to have. Today, my child, a luncheon will be served in Barribault's Hotel which will ring through the ages. It will go down in story and song.'

'That will be nice for Stanwood.'

'Stanwood?' Lord Shortlands snorted. 'Stanwood isn't going to get a smell of it. Just you and I, my dear. A pretty thing, wasting my hard-earned money on a fellow whose father eggs his confederates on to getting people out of bed at seven in the morning and bellowing "Happy birthday" at them,' said Lord Shortlands severely.

In the drawing-room Lady Adela had rung the bell.

'Oh, Spink,' she said, as the butler slid gracefully over the threshold.

'M'lady?'

'A Mr Cobbold, who is over here from America, will be coming to stay this afternoon. Will you put him in the Blue Room.'

'Very good, m'lady.' A touch of human interest showed itself in Mervyn Spink's frigid eye. 'Pardon me, m'lady, but would that be Mr Ellery Cobbold of Great Neck, Long Island?'

'His son. You know Mr Cobbold?'

'I was for some time in his employment, m'lady, during my sojourn in the United States of America.'

'Then you have met Mr Stanwood Cobbold?'

'Oh, yes, m'lady. A very agreeable young gentleman.'

'Ah,' said Lady Adela.

She had invited this guest of hers to the castle in the spirit of the man who bites into a luncheon counter sausage, hoping for the best but not quite knowing what he is going to get, and this statement from an authoritative source relieved her.

Chapter 5

It is pleasant to be able to record that Stanwood Cobbold's Turkish bath did him a world of good, proving itself well worth the price of admission. They took him and stripped him and stewed him till he bubbled at every seam, and rubbed him and kneaded him and put him under a cold shower and dumped him into a cold plunge, and sent him out into the world a pinker and stronger young man. It was with almost the old oomph and elasticity that shortly after one o'clock he strode into Barribault's Hotel and made purposefully for the smaller of its two bars. This was not because he had anything against the large bar – he yielded to none in his appreciation of its catering and service – but it was in the small bar, it will be remembered, that he had arranged to meet Mike Cardinal.

His friend was not yet at the tryst, the only occupant of the room, except for the white-jacketed ministering angel behind the counter, being a stout, smooth-faced man in the early fifties of butlerine aspect. He was seated at one of the tables, sipping what Stanwood's experienced eye told him was a McGuffy's Special, a happy invention on the part of the ministering angel, whose name – not that it matters, for except for this one appearance he does not come into the story – was Aloyius St X. McGuffy. He had the air of a man in whose edifice of revelry this McGuffy's Special was not the foundation stone but one of the bricks somewhat higher up. Unless Stanwood's eye deceived him, and it seldom did in these matters, this comfortable stranger had made an early start.

And such was indeed the case. A lunch of really majestic proportions, a lunch that is to ring down the ages, a lunch, in short, of the kind to which Lord Shortlands had been looking forward ever since his daughter Adela with that wave of her magic wand had transformed the world for him, demands a certain ritual of preparation. The fifth Earl's first move, on arriving in the centre of things and giving Terry three pounds and sending her off to buy a hat, after arranging to meet her in the lobby of Barribault's Hotel at one-thirty, had been to proceed to his club and knock back a bottle of his favourite champagne, following this with a stiff whisky and soda. Then, and only then, was he ready for Aloysius McGuffy and his Specials.

Stanwood took a seat at an adjoining table, and after he in his turn had called on the talented Aloysius to start pouring, a restful silence reigned in the bar. From time to time Stanwood shot a sidelong glance at Lord Shortlands, and from time to time Lord Shortlands shot a sidelong glance at Stanwood. Neither spoke, not even to comment on the beauty of the weather, which was still considerable, yet each found in the other's personality much that was attractive.

There is probably something about men crossed in love which tends to draw them together, some subtle aura or emanation which tells them that they have found a kindred soul. At any rate, every time Lord Shortlands looked at Stanwood, he felt that, while Stanwood unquestionably resembled a hippopotamus in appearance, it would be a genuine pleasure to fraternize with him. And every time Stanwood looked at Lord Shortlands, it was to say to himself: 'Granted that this bimbo looks like a butler out on the loose, nevertheless something whispers to me that we could be friends.' But for a while they remained mute and aloof. It was only when London's first wasp thrust itself into the picture that the barriers fell.

One is inclined to describe this wasp as the Wasp of Fate. Only by supposing it an instrument of destiny can one account for its presence that morning in the small bar of Barribault's Hotel. Even in the country its arrival on the twelfth of May would have been unusual, the official wasping season not beginning till well on in July, and how it came to be in the heart of London's steel and brick at such a time is a problem from which speculation recoils.

Still there it was, and for a space it volplaned and looped the loop about Lord Shortlands's nose, occasioning him no little concern. It then settled down for a brief breather on the back of Stanwood's coat, and Lord Shortlands, feeling that this was an opportunity which might not occur again, remembered his swashing blow, like Gregory in *Romeo and Juliet,* and downed it in its tracks with a large, flat hand.

46

A buffet between the shoulder blades does something to a man who is drinking a cocktail at the moment. Stanwood choked and turned purple. Recovering his breath, he said (with some justice): 'Hey!' and Lord Shortlands hastened to explain. He said:

'Wasp.'

'Wasp?'

'Wasp,' repeated Lord Shortlands, and with a pointing finger directed the other's attention to the remains. 'Wasp,' he added, driving the thing home.

Stanwood viewed the body, and all doubt concerning the purity of his preserver's motives left him.

'Wasp,' he said, fully concurring.

'Wasp,' said Lord Shortlands, summing the thing up rather neatly. 'Messing about on your back. I squashed it.'

'Darned good of you.'

'Not at all.'

'Courageous, too.'

'No, no. Perhaps a certain presence of mind. Nothing more. Offer you a cocktail?'

'Or me you?'

'No, me you.'

'Well, you me this time,' said Stanwood, yielding the point with a pleasant grace. 'But next time me you.'

The ice was broken.

When two men get together who are not only crossed in love but are both reasonably full of McGuffy's Specials, it is inevitable that before long confidences will be exchanged. The bruised heart demands utterance. Gradually, as he sat there drawing closer and closer spiritually to this new friend, there came upon Stanwood an irresistible urge to tell his troubles to Lord Shortlands.

The orthodox thing, of course, would have been to tell them to Aloysius McGuffy, who may be said to have been there more or less for the purpose, but this would have involved getting up and walking to the bar and putting his foot on the rail and leaning forward and pawing at Aloysius McGuffy's shoulder. Far simpler to dish it out to this sympathetic stranger.

47

Very soon, accordingly, he was explaining his whole unhappy position to Lord Shortlands in minute detail. He told him of his great love for Eileen Stoker, of his father's short way with sons who loved Eileen Stoker, of his ecstasy on learning of Eileen Stoker's impending arrival in London, of his welcome to her when she did arrive and finally of the crushing blow which had befallen him, knocking his new-found happiness base over apex; this wholly unforeseen cable from his father, ordering him to leave the metropolis immediately and go to some ghastly castle, the name of which had escaped him for the moment.

Throughout the long and at times rambling exposition Lord Shortlands had listened with the owlish intentness of a man who has already started lunching, uttering now a kindly 'Ah?' and anon a commiserating 'Good gad!' At this mention of going to castles a grave look came into his face. He had grown fond of this young man, and did not like to see him heading for misery and disaster.

'Keep away from castles,' he advised.

'But I can't, darn it.'

'Castles,' said Lord Shortlands, speaking the word with a bitter intonation. 'I could tell you something about castles. They have moats.'

'Yay, but –'

'Nasty smelly moats. Stinking away there since the Middle Ages. Be guided by me, my dear boy, and steer jolly clear of all castles.'

Stanwood was beginning to wonder if it would not have been wiser to stick to the sound old conservative policy of telling his troubles to the barman. This stranger, though sympathetic, seemed slow in the uptake.

'But don't you understand? I've got to go to this castle.'

'Why?'

'My father says so.'

Lord Shortlands considered this. Until now, though Stanwood had been at some pains to elaborate it, the point had escaped him. It was not long before a happy solution presented itself.

'Kick him in the eye.'

'How can I? He's in America.'

'Your father is?'

'Yay.'

'I could tell you something about fathers in America, too,' said Lord Shortlands. 'This very morning, as the stable clock was striking seven –'

'If I don't do what he tells me to, he'll slice off my allowance. It's like in the Bible,' said Stanwood, searching for an illustration and recalling Augustus Robb's observations on the subject. 'You remember? Where the bozo said "Come" and they goeth.'

Lord Shortlands had now a complete, if muzzy, grip of the position of affairs.

'Ah, now I see. Now I understand. You are financially dependent on your father?'

'That's right.'

'As I am on my daughter Adela. Most unpleasant, being dependent on people.'

'You betcher.'

'Especially one's daughter. Adela – I wouldn't tell this to everyone, but I like your face – Adela oppresses me. You have heard of men being henpecked. I am chick-pecked. She makes me live all the time at my castle.'

'Have you a castle?'

'I have indeed. One of the worst. And she makes me live there. I feel like a caged skylark.'

'I feel like a piece of cheese. Run out of London just at the very moment when I want to be sticking to Eileen like a poultice, and chased off to this damned castle. A hell of a set-up, don't you think?'

Lord Shortlands, who had a feeling heart, admitted that his young friend's predicament was such as to extort the tear of pity.

'Though it is scarcely,' he went on to say, 'to be compared with the one in which I find myself. I'm just a toad beneath the harrow.'

'You said you were a skylark.'

'A toad, too.'

'Have you got to go to a castle?'

'I'm at a castle already. I told you that before.'

'Gee, that's tough.'

'You ... What was that expression you used just now? Ah, yes, "You betcher."'

'Must grind you a good deal, being at a castle already.'

'You betcher. But that, serious though it is, is not my principal trouble.'

'What's your principal trouble?'

Lord Shortlands hesitated for a moment. So far his British reserve had triumphed over a pint of champagne, a double whisky and splash and three McGuffy Specials, but now he felt it weakening. A brief spiritual conflict, and he, too, had decided to tell all.

'It is this. At my castle there is a cook.'

'Look, look, lookie, here comes cookie!'

'I beg your pardon?'

'Just a song I happened to remember.'

'I see. Well, as I was saying, at my castle there is a cook.'

'Another cook?'

'No, the same cook. And the fact is, well, I – er – I want to marry her.'

'Good for you.'

'You approve?'

'You betcher.'

'I am delighted to hear you say so, my dear boy. You know how much your sympathy means to me. Marry her, you suggest?'

'You betcher.'

'But here is the difficulty. My butler wants to marry her, too.'

'The butler at your castle?'

'You betcher. It is a grave problem.'

Stanwood knitted his brows. He was thinking the thing out.

'You can't both marry her.'

'Exactly.' This clear-sightedness delighted Lord Shortlands. An old head on young shoulders, he felt. 'You have put your finger on the very core of the dilemma. What do you advise?'

'Seems to me the cagey move would be to fire the butler,'

'Impossible. When I spoke of him as "my" butler, I used the word loosely. His salary is paid by my daughter Adela. Firing butlers is her prerogative, and she guards it jealously.'

'Gee, that's like it is with me and Augustus Robb. Well, then, you'll have to cut him out.'

'Easier said than done. He is a man of terrific personal attractions. His profile alone.... The only thing that gives me hope is that he bets.'

'Would he know anything good for Kempton Park next Friday?'

'Most unlikely. He seems to pick nothing but losers. That is why the fact that he is a betting man causes me to hope. He squanders his money, and Alice disapproves.'

'Who's Alice?'

'The cook.'

'The cook at your castle? The cook we've been talking about?'

'That very cook. She wants a steady husband. And she thinks me steady.'

'She does?'

'I have it from a reliable source.'

'Then you're set. It's in the bag. All you've got to do is keep plugging away and giving her the old personality. I think you'll nose him out.'

'Do you, my dear boy? You are certainly most comforting. But unfortunately there is one very formidable obstacle in my path. She won't marry anyone who cannot put up two hundred pounds to buy a public house.'

'Ah? So the real trouble is dough?'

'You betcher. In this world,' said Lord Shortlands weightily, 'the real trouble is always dough. All through my life I have found that out. And mine has been a long life. I'm fifty-two today.'

Stanwood started as if a chord in his soul had been touched. He threw back his head and began to sing in a booming bass:

> 'I'm fifty-two today,
> Fifty-two today.
> I've got the key of the door,
> Never been fifty-two before.

And Father says I can do as I like,
So shout Hip-hip-hooray,
He's a jolly good fellow,
Fifty-two –'

He broke off abruptly and pressed both hands to his temples. Too late he realized that the whole enterprise of throwing his head back and singing old music hall ballads, however apposite, was one against which his best friends would have warned him.

'If you'll excuse me,' he said rising, 'I think I'll just go to the washroom and put my head under the cold tap. Have you ever had that feeling that someone is driving white-hot rivets into your bean?'

'Not in recent years,' said Lord Shortlands, with a touch of wistfulness. 'As a young man –'

'Ice, of course, would be better,' said Stanwood, 'but you look so silly ordering a bucket of ice and sticking your head in it. But maybe cold water will do something.'

He tottered out, hoping for the best, and Lord Shortlands, allowing his lower jaw to droop restfully, gave himself up to meditation.

He thought of Mrs Punter, and wondered how she was enjoying herself with her relatives at Walham Green. He thought of Terry, and hoped she would buy a nice hat. He thought of ordering another McGuffy Special, but decided that it was not worth the effort. And then suddenly he found himself thinking of something else, something that sent an icy chill trickling down his spine and restored him to a sobriety which could not have been more complete if he had been spending the morning drinking malted milk.

Had he been wise, he asked himself, had he been entirely prudent in confiding to that charming young fellow, who had just gone out to put his head under the tap, the secret of his love? Suppose the thing were to come to Adela's ears?

A look of glassy horror came into Lord Shortlands's eyes. Perspiration bedewed his forehead, and the word 'Crikey!' trembled on his lips. From the very inception of his wooing he had been troubled by the thought of what the deuce would happen if Adela ever got to hear of it.

Then Reason reassured him. The young fellow and he were

just ships that pass in the night. They had met and spoken, and now they would part, never to meet again. There could be no possibility of the other ever coming into Adela's orbit. He had been alarming himself unnecessarily.

Comforted and relieved, but feeling an imperative need for an immediate restorative, he turned with the purpose of establishing communication with Aloysius McGuffy, and found that he was being scrutinized by a pair of extraordinarily good-looking twins, who on closer inspection coalesced into one extraordinary good-looking young man in a grey suit, who had come in unperceived and taken a seat at the adjoining table. And to his surprise this young man now rose and approached him with outstretched hand.

'How do you do?' he said.

Chapter 6

Lord Shortlands blinked.

'How do you do,' he replied cautiously. Sixteen years ago he had once been stung for five by an agreeable stranger who had scraped acquaintance with him in a bar, and he could not forget that he had at this moment nearly twelve pounds on his person. 'Be on the alert, Claude Percival John Delamere,' he was saying to himself.

'I have not got my facts twisted?' the other proceeded. 'You are Lord Shortlands?'

Though still wary, the fifth Earl saw no harm in conceding this. He said he was, and the young man said he had been convinced of it; he, the fifth Earl, having changed very little since the old days; looking, in fact, or so it seemed to him, younger than ever.

Lord Shortlands, though continuing to keep a hand on the money in his pocket, began to like this young man.

'You don't remember me. You wouldn't, of course. It's a long time since we met. Your son Tony brought me to Beevor for the summer holidays once, when we were boys together. Cardinal is the name.'

'Cardinal?'

'I mentioned that on the phone this morning, if you remember, but nothing seemed to stir. Nice running into one another like this. How is Tony?'

'He's all right. Cardinal? Out in Kenya, growing coffee and all that. Cardinal?' said Lord Shortlands, his McGuffy-Specialized brain at last answering the call. 'Why, you're the chap who's in love with my daughter Terry.'

The young man bowed.

'I could wish no neater description of myself,' he said. 'It cuts out all superfluities and gets right down to essentials. One of these days I shall be President of the United States, but I am quite content to live in history as the chap who was in love with your daughter Terry. It must be a very wonderful thing to have such a daughter.'

'Oh, decidedly.'

'Makes you chuck the chest out more than somewhat, I should imagine?'

'You betcher.'

'I'm surprised you don't go around singing all the time. It was a great relief to me when you told me she was still doing her hair the same way. It would be madness to go fooling about with that superb superstructure. And yet I don't know. I doubt whether any re-arrangement of the tresses could destroy their charm. The first time I saw her she had them down her back in pigtails, and I remember thinking the effect perfect.'

'Yes, Terry has pretty hair.'

'I would have said gorgeous. I love her eyes, too, don't you?'

Lord Shortlands said that he thought his daughter had nice eyes, and the young man frowned.

'Not "nice." If we are going to talk about Terry, we must take a little trouble to get the right word. Her eyes are heavenly. I don't suppose there's another pair of eyes like that in existence. How do you check up on her nose? That way it turns up slightly at the tip.'

'Ah,' said Lord Shortlands, wisely refraining from a more definite expression of opinion in the presence of this evidently meticulous critic, and the young man paused to light a cigarette.

Lord Shortlands goggled at him with a solemn intentness. He could see what Terry had meant about the fellow being good-looking. The word understated it. He was a sort of super-Spink. Sitting where he did, he presented his profile to Lord Shortlands, and the latter was able to study its clean-cut lines. There was no getting away from it. The chap began where Spink left off.

Mike Cardinal had finished lighting his cigarette and was ready to talk once more.

'Yes, she's got everything, hasn't she? I don't suppose you've the slightest conception of how I love that girl. What a great day that was when she came back into my life; on the hoof, as it were, and not merely as a golden, insubstantial memory. It happened quite by chance, and at a moment, oddly enough, when I was not thinking of her but of chump chops, Brussels sprouts and French fried potatoes. I was sauntering through the grill-room here, looking for a table, and I saw a friend of mine sitting with a girl and went over to exchange a word, and –'

'Yes, she told me.'

'Ah, she has been talking about me, has she? A promising sign. By the way, have I your permission to pay my addresses to your daughter? One likes to get these things settled.'

'Well, dash it, you have been paying your addresses to her.'

'Unofficially, yes. But unsuccessfully. And why unsuccessfully? Because unofficially.'

'Say that again,' said Lord Shortlands, whose mental powers were not at their keenest.

'What I mean is that I have not been going at this thing in the right way. I need official backing. If I had your approval of my suit, I feel sure I could swing the deal. A father's influence means so much. You could put in an occasional good word for me, guiding her mind in the right direction. Above all, you could invite me to Beevor for an indefinite stay, and in those romantic surroundings –'

'No, I couldn't. I can't invite people to Beevor.'

'Nonsense. A child could do it.'

'Well, I can't. My daughter Adela won't let me.'

'Ah? A nuisance, that. It's a pity I have never met Lady Adela.'

'Wasn't she at Beevor when you were there?'

'No.'

'Those were the days,' sighed Lord Shortlands.

Mike rose to a point of order. His voice, when he spoke, was a little stern.

'Then how about Stanwood Cobbold?'

'Eh?'

'It seems to me that your whole story about not being able to invite people to Beevor falls to the ground. I was round at his place just now, and his man told me a telegram had arrived for him from you, freely extending your hospitality. I shall be glad to hear what you have to say to that.'

'I never sent that telegram. It was Adela. Why should I want the chap messing around? He's probably a perisher.'

'Not at all.'

'Well, his father is.'

'Ah, there I cannot speak with firsthand knowledge. I have never met his father. But you'll like Stanwood. Everybody does. He's the best fellow that ever stepped, and I love him like a brother. When you get Stanwood, you've got something. However, to return to myself, I should have thought that, considering that I have already visited the castle and apparently gave satisfaction, seeing that nobody slung me out, Lady Adela would have stretched a point.'

'Not a hope. She never asks anyone down who doesn't write or paint or something. They have to be these bally artistic blighters.'

'Stanwood isn't an artistic blighter.'

'He's an exception.'

'I don't get in, then?'

'No, you don't.'

'Well, it's all very exasperating. You see how I'm handicapped. No wooer can possibly give of his best if he's in London and the divine object is in Kent and won't answer the telephone. Have you a vacancy for a butler?'

Lord Shortlands sighed wistfully.

'I wish I had. But it wouldn't be any use you coming to Beevor. Terry won't marry you.'

'She thinks she won't. But once let me get there –'

'There's some reason. She didn't tell me what.'

Mike frowned.

'The reason is that she's a little fathead and doesn't know what's good for her,' he said. 'It is that fathead streak that I am straining every nerve to correct. I keep pointing out to her that it's no use looking like an angel, if you can't spot a good man when you see one. And that she does look like an angel no one in his senses would deny. For the last five years I've been living in Hollywood, positively festooned with beautiful women, and I've never set eyes on one fit to be mentioned in the same breath with Terry. She stands alone.'

'Yes, Terry told me you worked in Hollywood. Motion picture agent or something, aren't you?'

'That's right.'

'Must make a good thing out of it, what?'

'Quite satisfactory. Have no fear that I shall not be able, when the moment comes, to support your daughter in the style to which she has become accustomed. But it is absolutely essential, as I say, that I come to Beevor, for this business of pressing my suit by mail and having her tell someone to say "She says she won't" on the telephone is getting me nowhere. Try to think of some method whereby I can be eased into the dear old place.'

Lord Shortlands thought hard. An obviously amiable and well-disposed son-in-law with a lucrative connexion in Hollywood was just what he had been scouring the country for for years. He was still thinking when Stanwood Cobbold returned, looking brighter and fitter. The cold-water cure had proved effective.

'Hiya, Mike,' he cried, in quite a buoyant tone.

'Hello, there,' said Mike. 'You look extraordinarily roguish. How come? I stopped in at your place on my way here, and Augustus Robb told me you were a sort of living corpse.'

'I had a Turkish bath, and I've just been putting my head under the cold tap.'

'I see. Do you know Lord Shortlands?'

'Never heard of the guy.'

'This is Lord Shortlands.'

'Oh, sure, I know him. We've just been chatting. He was telling me about his cook.'

'And this, Lord Shortlands, is the Stanwood Cobbold of whom you have heard so much; your forthcoming guest, who .... Why, what's the trouble?' asked Mike, concerned. Some powerful upheaval appeared to be taking place in the older man's system, manifesting itself outwardly in a sagging jaw and a popeyed stare of horror.

'Is your name Stanwood Cobbold?' cried Lord Shortlands, seeming to experience some difficulty in finding utterance.

'Sure. Why not? What's biting him, Mike?'

Mike was wondering the same thing himself. He hazarded a possible conjecture.

'I think it's joy. Augustus Robb tells me you are leaving today for Beevor Castle in the county of Kent. Lord Shortlands, who owns Beevor Castle, will consequently be your host. Apprised of this, he registers ecstasy. As who would not?'

Lord Shortlands was still finding it hard to speak.

'But this is terrible!'

'Oh, come. There's nothing wrong with Stanwood.'

'You see, I want to marry my cook –'

'Well, that's all right by me. How about you, Stanwood?'

'– and I told him. Suppose, when he gets to Beevor, he lets it out to my daughter Adela?'

'She would not be pleased?'

'She would make my life a hell on earth. Is he the sort of chap who's likely to go babbling?' asked Lord Shortlands, fastening his protruding eyes on Stanwood as if seeking to read his very soul.

'I fear he is.'

'Good Lord!'

'There is no vice in Stanwood Cobbold. His heart is the heart of a little child. But, like the little child whom in heart he so resembles, he has a tendency to lisp artlessly whatever comes into his head. His reputation is that of a man who, if there are beans to be spilled, will spill them with a firm and steady hand,

He has never kept a secret, and never will. His mother was frightened by a B.B.C. announcer.'

'Oh, my God!'

'Inevitably there will come a time at Beevor Castle when, closeted with Lady Adela and hunting around for some theme to interest, elevate and amuse, he will turn the conversation to the subject of you and the cook. He will mean no harm, of course. His only thought will be to make the party go.'

'Great heavens!'

'Most probably the disaster will occur at the dinner-table this very night. One can picture the scene. The fish and chips have been dished out, and Stanwood starts digging in. "Egad, Lady Adela," he says, speaking with his mouth full. "You have a darned good cook." "Glad you think so, Mr Cobbold. Eat hearty." "Is that the cook Lord Shortlands wants to marry?" says Stanwood. "I'm not surprised. I'd like to marry her myself." That's a thing you want to be prepared for.'

'This is frightful!'

'Yes, one can picture your embarrassment. That'll be the time to keep cool. But fortunately I have a suggestion to make which, if adopted, will, I think, ease the situation quite a good deal. How do you react to the idea of his staying in London and not going to Beevor at all?'

Stanwood frowned. He had been feeling so much better, and now all this.

'But I've got to go to Beevor, you poor fish. Father says so.'

Lord Shortlands, too, seemed displeased.

'Exactly. It is not kind, my dear fellow, to talk drivel at such a moment. Adela sent me in to fetch him. What's she going to say if I return alone?'

'You won't return alone. I shall be at your side. I ought to have mentioned that earlier.'

'You?'

'It seems the logical solution. I want to go to Beevor, Stanwood wants to remain in London, you want a guest who can be relied on not to introduce the cook *motif* into the conversation. The simple ruse which I have suggested would appear to make things all right for everybody.'

Lord Shortlands was a slow thinker.

'But Adela doesn't want you. She wants him.'

'Naturally in embarking on such an enterprise I should assume an incognito. The name Stanwood Cobbold suggests itself.'

Stanwood uttered a piercing cry of ecstasy. It made his head start aching again, but one cannot always be thinking of heads.

'Gosh, Mike, could we swing it?'

'It's in the bag.'

'This is genius.'

'You must expect that when you string along with me.'

'Gee, and it's only about half an hour since I was calling Eileen up and telling her I'd got to leave her. I must rush around and see her at once.'

'How about our lunch?'

'To hell with lunch.'

'And how about Augustus Robb?'

'To hell with Augustus Robb.'

'His heart was set on this visit.'

'To hell with Augustus Robb's heart and his lungs and his liver, too. If he starts acting up, I'll poke him in the eye,' said Stanwood, and departed like one walking on air.

Lord Shortlands, who could work things out if you gave him time, was beginning to get it now.

'You mean you'll come to Beevor instead of him?'

'Exactly.'

'Pretending to be him, and so forth?'

'That's right. It's a treat to see the way you're taking hold.'

'But, dash it.'

'Something on your mind?'

'How can you? Terry knows you. And, by Jove, now I remember, she knows him, too. Used to lunch with him and all that.'

'I had not overlooked the point you raise. I am taking it for granted that a daughter's love will ensure her silence.'

'That's true. Yes, I suppose it will.'

'It might, however, be as well to call her up and prepare her.'

'But she's here. Is it half past one?'

'Just on.'

'Then she'll be out in the lobby. I told her to be there at half past one.'

'This is glorious news. A chat with Terry is just what I wanted, to make my day. I have a bone to pick with that young half-wit. She and her "She says she won't's." Hello, what's this?'

A small boy in buttons had entered the bar. All the employees of Barribault's Hotel have sweet, refined voices. This lad's sweet, refined voice was chanting 'Lord Shortlands. Lord Shortlands.'

Lord Shortlands cocked an inquiring eye at Mike.

'He wants me.'

'Who wouldn't?'

'Here, boy.'

'Lord Shortlands, m'lord? Wanted on the telephone, m'lord.'

'Now, who the deuce can that be?' mused Lord Shortlands.

'Go and see,' suggested Mike. 'I, meanwhile, will be having the necessary word with Terry. Do you mind if I rub her turned-up little nose in the carpet?'

'Eh?'

' "She says she won't," indeed!' said Mike austerely.

Chapter 7

Barribault's Hotel being a favourite haunt of the wealthy, and the wealthy being almost uniformly repulsive, its lobby around the hour of one-thirty is always full of human eyesores. Terry in her new hat raised the tone quite a good deal. Or so it seemed to Mike Cardinal. She was sitting at a table near two financiers with four chins, and he made his way there and announced his presence with a genial 'Boo!' in her left ear. Having risen some six inches in a vertical direction, she stared at him incredulously.

'You!'

'You should have put your hand to your throat and rolled your eyeballs,' said Mike. 'It is the only way when you're saying "You!" Still, I know what you mean. I do keep bobbing up, don't I? One realizes dimly how Mary must have felt.'

'Yes, I think you must have lamb blood in you. Delighted to see you, of course.'

'Naturally.'

'But how did you know I was here?'

'Your father told me.'

'You've just met him?'

'Just now.'

'It's a small world, isn't it?'

'Not in the least. Why do you speak of it in that patronizing way? Because I met your father? We could hardly have helped meeting. He was in the bar, and I came in, and there we were, face to face.'

'Was he enjoying himself? Till then, I mean.'

'He seemed happy.'

'Not too happy?'

'Oh, no.'

'You see, today is his birthday, and he rather hinted that he intended to celebrate. I don't quite like this lounging in bars.'

'He has ceased to lounge. He was called to the telephone.'

'Called to the telephone?'

'Called to the telephone, Mister Bones. Why not?'

'But who could have been calling him?'

'I'm afraid I couldn't tell you. I'm a stranger in these parts myself.'

'Nobody knows he's here, I mean. Except the family at home, of course.'

'Then perhaps it was the family at home. Look, do you mind if we change the subject? I think we've about exhausted it. Let us speak of that letter I wrote you. Well-expressed, didn't you think? Full of good stuff? The phrases neatly turned?'

'Very.'

'So a friend of mine named Augustus Robb considered. I came in and found him reading it. A winner, he said cordially, and Augustus Robb is not a man who praises lightly. Personally, I thought it a composition calculated to melt a heart of stone. "That's going to drag home the gravy," I said to myself, as I licked the stamp. But I was wrong, it seems. Or did your father report you incorrectly when he said "She says she won't"?'

'No. That was what I told him to say.'

'Your idea being to break it gently?'

'You wouldn't have had me be abrupt?'

'Of course not. So you won't marry me?'

'No.'

'Somebody's got to.'

'Not me.'

'That's what you say now, but I don't despair.'

'Don't you?'

'Not by a jug full. Much may be done by persistence and perseverance. I shall follow you around a good deal and keep gazing at you with the lovelight in my eyes, and one of these days my hypnotic stare will do the trick. It's like a dog at meal time. You say to yourself "I will not feed this dog. It is not good for him," but he keeps his pleading eye glued on you, and you weaken. Talking of marrying, your father tells me he wants to marry the cook. I said he might.'

'Oh, Shorty! I knew something would happen if I let him run around loose in London with all that money in his pocket. Did he really get as confidential as that? You won't go spreading it about, will you?'

'My lips are sealed.'

'If my sister Adela ever heard about it, his life would not be worth a moment's purchase.'

'She shall never learn his secret from me. Clams take my correspondence course.'

'That's good. And now tell me how you come to be here. Lunching with some girl, I suppose?'

'Not at all. Stanwood Cobbold.'

'Really? Dear old Stanwood. Bless his heart.'

'Amen. He brought us together. Do you remember that day? You were sitting there in the grill-room, listening to him telling you about La Stoker, and I came along. "Good Lord," I said to myself. "I believe it's Terry!"'

'And was it?'

'Yes.'

'I don't call that much of a story.'

'It's a peach of a story. I don't know what more you want.'

'Has Stanwood told you that he's coming to Beevor?'

'He isn't.'

'Yes, he is. We're taking him back with us this afternoon. His father cabled Shorty, asking him to put Stanwood up.'

'I know all that. The old man wants to get him out of the orbit of the Stoker, who has just arrived in London. But you haven't got the scenario absolutely correct. To give you a complete grasp of it I shall have to go back to the beginning. I came here to meet Stanwood, and ran into your father. All straight so far?'

'Quite.'

'Good. Well, for awhile, as I told you, he appeared quietly happy. I introduced myself, and we chatted at our ease. About you, and how lovely your hair was and how your nose turned up at the tip and how I was going to marry you, and so on and so forth. All very pleasant and cozy. And then Stanwood blew in, and his happiness waned.'

'Didn't he like Stanwood?'

'That's just the trouble. He loved him not wisely but too well. Apparently they had met earlier in the proceedings and formed a beautiful friendship. You know those friendships where Friend A. can conceal nothing from Friend B., and vice versa.'

'You don't mean he –?'

'Exactly.'

'Oh, Shorty, Shorty, Shorty!'

'No doubt Stanwood began by telling your father all about the Stoker, and your father, not to be outdone in the courtesies, told Stanwood all about the cook. Not being aware who he was, of course. In these casual encounters in bars names are rarely exchanged. Until I introduced them, Stanwood had been to your father merely a pleasant stranger who looked like a hippopotamus.'

'He does look like a hippopotamus, doesn't he?'

'Much more than most hippopotamuses do.'

'Not that it matters.'

'Not in the least.'

'The important thing is, can he keep a secret? Because if he's coming to Beevor –'

'– he will meet your sister Adela. And if he mentions this little matter to your sister Adela, hell's foundations are going to quiver. Precisely. That was the reflection which cast a shadow on your father's sunny mood. He sought for reassurance, but I was not able to give him any. In the lexicon of Stanwood Cobbold, I was compelled to tell him, there is no such word as reticence. He is a beans-spiller of the first order. Over in America we seldom advertise in the papers now. If there is anything we want known, we just tell Stanwood. It's cheaper.'

'But this is frightful.'

'Exactly what your father said.'

'Oh, my goodness.'

'I'm not sure if he said that, too, but I think so. The drama gets you, does it? I thought it would. But it's all right. I've only been working up the agony in order to make the happy ending more of a punch.'

'Is there a happy ending?'

'There always is when I take things in hand. I found the solution first crack out of the box.'

'Are there no limits to the powers of this wonder man?'

'None have yet been discovered. My solution was a very simple one. I suggested that Stanwood should remain in London and that I should go to Beevor in his place.'

'As him do you mean?'

'As him,' said Mike.

He beamed at her in the manner of one expecting the approving smile and the word of praise, but Terry was looking thoughtful.

'I see.'

'Ingenious?'

'Very.'

'It's the only way out of what Augustus Robb would call the am-parce. I am taking it for granted, of course, that you will not gum the game by denouncing me.'

'Well, naturally. I can't let Shorty down.'

'Of course not. Stoutly spoken, young pipsqueak. Well, that's the scheme, and it seems to me ideal. Your sister wants to entertain Stanwood Cobbold, and she will get a far better Stanwood Cobbold than the original blue prints called for. Stanwood wants to stay in London, because of the Stoker. Your father wants him to stay in London, so that his fatal secret may be preserved. And I want to be at Beevor in order to buckle down to my wooing at close range. It is difficult to see how the set-up could be improved. We seem to have a full hand. As one passes through this world, one strives always to scatter light and sweetness and to promote the happiness of the greatest number, and here everybody will be pleased.'

'Except me.'

'Come, come. Is this the tone?'

'I repeat, except me.'

'Don't you want me at Beevor, Lady Teresa?'

'I do not, Mr Cardinal.'

'You say that now, but wait till I start growing on you. Wait till my beautiful nature begins to expand before your eyes like some lovely flower unfolding its petals. Don't you see what a wonderful opportunity this will be for you to become hep to my hidden depths?'

'You haven't any.'

'I have, too. Dozens.'

'I stick to it that I don't want you at Beevor.'

'Well, it's a mercy I'm coming there. How vividly I remember dear old Beevor, with all its romantic nooks and corners. A lovers' Paradise. Sauntering in the shrubberies, seated on the rustic benches, pacing the velvet lawns in the scented dusk and fishing for eels together in the moat, we shall soon get all this nonsense about not marrying me out of your head. "Golly," you'll say to yourself, "what a little mutt I must have been not to have recognized at the very outset that this bimbo was my destined mate!" And you will probably shed a tear or two at the thought of all the time you've wasted. Do you realize that we might have been an old married couple by now, if you had let yourself think along the right lines?'

'Aren't you keeping Stanwood waiting?'

'He's left. Our lunch is off. I shall take pot luck with you and your father.'

'You haven't been invited.'

'I don't need to be. I'm from Hollywood. Look, he approaches.'

Lord Shortlands was crossing the lobby towards them from the direction of the telephone booths, and so arresting was his aspect that Terry gave a little squeak of surprise.

'What on earth is the matter with him?'

The impression Mike Cardinal received was that someone had been feeding his future father-in-law meat, and he said so.

And certainly in Lord Shortland's demeanour there was a quite unusual effervescence. Though solidly built, he seemed to skip and amble. His whole appearance closely resembled that of Stanwood Cobbold immediately after taking the healing medicine which Augustus Robb had bought at the drug store. Stanwood's eyes had revolved in their sockets. His did the same. Stanwood had had the air of a man struck behind the ear by an unexpected thunderbolt. So had Lord Shortlands.

'Terry,' he cried, 'you know that album?'

He had to swallow once or twice before he could proceed.

'I've just been talking to Desborough on the telephone. He says he's found a stamp in it worth well over a thousand pounds!'

Book Two

Chapter 8

From down Westminster way there floated over London the sound of Big Ben striking half past two, and Augustus Robb came softly into the living-room of Number Seven, Bloxham House, Park Lane. He had just finished a late lunch, and was now planning to top it off with a good cigar from his employer's box. He was surprised and disconcerted, having made his selection, to observe Stanwood lying on the sofa.

'Why, 'ullo, cocky,' he said, hastily thrusting the corona into the recesses of his costume. 'I didn't 'ear you come in.'

Stanwood did not speak. His face was turned to the wall, and Augustus Robb, eyeing him, came to a not unnatural conclusion.

'Coo!' he exclaimed. 'What, *again*? You do live, chum. Only a few hours since you 'ad one of the biggest loads on I ever beheld in my mortal puff, and here you are once more, equally stinko. Beats me how you do it. Well, it's lucky for you you ain't in my old line of business, because there intemperance hampers you. Yus. I knew a feller once, Harry Corker his name was, Old Suction Pump we used to call him, got into a house while under the influence, caught hold of the safe as it came round for the second time, started twiddling the knobs, and first thing you know he'd got dance music from a Continental station. If he hadn't retained the presence of mind to dive through the window, taking the glass with him, he'd have been for it. Steadied him a good deal, that experience. Well, I suppose I'll have to step out and fetch along another bottle of that stuff. I'll tell the young fellow behind the counter to make it a bit stronger this time.'

Stanwood sat up. His features were drawn, but his voice was clear and his speech articulate.

'I'm not plastered.'

'Ain't you?' said Augustus Robb, surprised. 'Well, you look it. Country air's what you need. I've packed.'

'Then unpack.'

'What? Aren't we going to this Beevor Castle?'

'No,' said Stanwood, and proceeded to explain.

One points at Augustus Robb with pride. A snob from the crown of his thinly-covered head to the soles of his substantial feet, his heart had been set on going to stay at Beevor Castle. He had looked forward to writing letters to his circle of friends on crested stationery and swanking to them later about his pleasant intimacy with the titled and blueblooded, and, as he listened to Stanwood's story, he felt like a hornrimmed-spectacled Peri excluded from Paradise.

But his sterling nature triumphed over the blow. A few muttered 'Coo's,' and he was himself again. Of all the learned professions none is so character-building as that of the burglar. The man who has been trained in the hard school of porch climbing, where you often work half the night on a safe only to discover that all it contains is a close smell and a dead spider, learns to take the rough with the smooth and to bear with fortitude the disappointments from which no terrestrial existence can be wholly free.

But, though philosophic, he could not approve.

'No good's going to come of this,' he said.

'Why not?'

'Never does, cocky, from lies and deceptions. Sooner or later you'll find you've gone and got yourself into a nasty mess with these what I might call subterfuges. "Oh, what a tangled web we weave, when first we practise to deceive." I used to recite that as a nipper. Many a time I remember my old Uncle Fred giving me a bag of peppermints to stop. Said it 'ampered 'im in the digesting of his dinner. Used to keep the peppermints handy, in case I started. Well, if you're not stinko, what are you looking like that for?'

'Like what?'

'Like the way you are. You look like three penn'orth of last week's catsmeat,' said Augustus Robb, who was nothing if not frank.

In ordinary circumstances Stanwood might have hesitated to

confide his more intimate secrets to the flapping ears of one whose manner he sometimes found a little familiar and who, he suspected, needed but very slight encouragement to become more familiar still. But a great sorrow had just come into his life, earthquakes and black frosts had been playing havoc with his garden of dreams, and at such moments the urge to tell all to anyone who happens to be handy cannot be resisted.

'If you really want to know,' he said hollowly, 'my heart's broken.'

'Coo! Is it?' Augustus Robb was surprised and intrigued. 'Lumme, now that this Stoker jane of yours is in London and you 'aven't got to leave her, I'd have thought you'd have been as happy as a lark. What's gone wrong? Been playing you up, has she? Always the way with these spoiled public favourites. You young fellows will keep giving them flattery and adulation, when what they really need is a good clump over the ear-'ole, and that makes 'em get above themselves. Found somebody else, has she, and gone and handed you your hat? I thought something like that would happen.'

Stanwood groaned. He was finding his companion's attitude trying, but the urge to confide still persisted.

'No, it's not that. But I went to see her just now –'

'Shouldn't have done that, cocky. Rash step to take. Girls often wake up cross after a binge.'

'She wasn't cross. But she told me she had been thinking it over, and had made up her mind she wasn't going to get married again unless the fellow had money.'

'Mercenary, eh? You're well out of it, chum.'

'She's not mercenary, blast you.'

'Language!'

'It's just that she says she's tried it a couple of times, and it doesn't work. She says you can't stop marriage being a bust, if the wife has all the dough.'

Augustus Robb seated himself on the sofa and, having shifted his employer's knees to one side, for they were interfering with his comfort, put the tips of his fingers together like Counsel preparing to give an opinion in chambers.

'Well, she's quite right,' he said. 'You can't get away from that. I wouldn't have thought a Hollywood star would have had so much sense. Never does for the old man to have to keep running to the missus every time he wants a bob for a packet of gaspers or half a dollar to put on some 'orse he's heard good reports of. Prevents him being master in the 'ome, if you follow my meaning. It's 'appened in me own family. My Uncle Reginald –'

'Damn your Uncle Reginald!'

'Language again.' Augustus Robb rose, offended. 'Very well. I was going to tell you about him, and now I won't. But the fact remains she's perfectly correct. I'd have thought you'd have seen that for yourself. You don't want to be supported by your old woman, do you? Where's your self-respect?'

'To hell with self-respect!'

'Language once more. I wonder if you've ever considered the risk you're running of everlasting fire? Well, what are you going to do about it?'

'I don't know.'

'Nor me. Well, I'll tell you what I'll do, seeing that things has arrived at such a pass that it's only 'umane to relax the rules a bit. I'll fetch you a brandy and soda.'

'Make it a brandy straight.'

'All right, chum, if you prefer it. No use spoiling the ship for a ha'porth of tar.'

It was some little time before Augustus Robb returned, for a ring at the front door bell had delayed him. When he did so, he found his employer sitting up and taking nourishment in the shape of a cigarette.

'I'll tell you what I'm going to do,' said Stanwood, accepting the brandy gratefully. He had the air of one who has been thinking things over. 'I'm going to talk her out of it.'

Augustus Robb shook his head.

'Can't see how that's to be done,' he said. 'You aren't in the posish. It would mean pursuing 'er with your addresses; going to 'er and pleading with 'er, if you see what I mean, using all the eloquence at your disposal.'

'That's what I'm going to do.'

'No, you're not, chum. Talk sense. How can you pursue her with your addresses, if she's in London and you're in the country? It's the identical am-parce Mr Cardinal found him-

72

self up against, only there the little parcel of goods was in the country and 'im in London. Still, the principle's the same.'

Stanwood, though feeling better after the brandy, was still ill-disposed to listen to the gibberings of a valet who appeared to have become mentally deranged. He stared bleakly at Augustus Robb.

'What are you talking about? I told you I wasn't going to the country.'

'But you'll have to, chum, now this cable's arrived.'

'What cable?'

Augustus Robb slapped his forehead self-reproachfully.

'Forgot you 'adn't seen it. Be forgettin' me own 'ead next. It come while I was fetching you that brandy, and I was reading it in the 'all and left it on the hall table. It's from your Pop. There's been a new development.'

'Oh, my God! What's happened now?'

'It's about these photografts.'

'What photographs,'

'All right, all right, don't bustle me. I'm coming to that. It's a long cable, and I can't remember it all, but here's the nub. Your Pop, taking it for granted, as you might say, that you're going to this Beevor Castle, says he wants you to send along a lot of photographs of its interior, with you in 'em.'

'What!'

'Yus. Seems funny,' said Augustus Robb with an indulgent smile, 'anyone wanting photografts of a dial like yours, don't it? But there's a reason. He don't say so in so many words, but reading between the lines, as the expression is, it's obvious that why he wants 'em is so's he can show 'em around among his cronies in New York and stick on dog. See what I mean? He meets one of his gentlemen friends at the club or wherever it may be, and the gentleman friend says, "Tell me, cocky, what's become of that son of yours? Don't seem to have seen 'im around in quite a while." "Ho," says your Pop. "Ain't you 'eard? He's residing with this aristocratic English Earl at his old-world castle." "Coo!" says his pal. "An Earl?" "Yus," says your Pop. "One of the best of 'em, and the castle has to be seen to be believed. My boy's just sent me some photografts of the place. Look, this is 'im lounging in the amber droringroom, and 'ere's another where he's sauntering around the portrait gallery. Nice little place, ain't it, and they treat him like one of the family, he tells me." And then he puffs out his blinkin' chest and goes off to tell the tale to someone else. Sinful pride, of course, like Jeshurun who waxed fat and kicked, but there you are.'

A greenish pallor had manifested itself on Stanwood's face.

'Oh, gosh!'

'You may well say "Gosh!" though I'm not sure as I'd pass the expression, coming as it does under the 'ead of Language, or something very like it.'

'But how can I get photographs of the inside of this foul castle?'

'R. That's what we'd all like to know, isn't it? Properly up against it, you are, ain't you? The Wages of Sin you might call it. Seems to me the only thing you can do is 'urry and catch Mr Cardinal before he starts and tell him you're going to this Beevor Castle, after all. Look slippy, I should.'

Stanwood looked slippy. He was out of the flat in five seconds. A swift taxi took him to Barribault's Hotel. He shot from its interior and grasped the arm of the ornate attendant at the door, a man who knew both Mike and himself well.

'Say, listen,' he gasped. 'Have you seen Mr Cardinal?'

'Why, yes, sir,' said the attendant. 'He's just this minute left, Mr Cobbold. Went off in a car with an elderly gent and a young lady.'

It seemed to Stanwood that there was but one thing to do. He tottered to the small bar, and feebly asked Aloysius McGuffy for one of his Specials. As he consumed it, staring with haggard eyes into the murky future, he looked like something cast up by the tide, the sort of flotsam and jetsam that is passed over with a disdainful jerk of the beak by the discriminating seagull.

Chapter 9

The car rolled in through the great gates of Beevor Castle, rolled up the winding drive, crossed the moat and drew up at the front door: and Mike, looking out, heaved a sentimental sigh.

'How all this takes me back,' he said. 'It was here that I saw you for the first time.'

'Was it?' said Terry. 'I don't remember.'

'I do. A big moment, that. You were leaning out of that window up there.'

'The schoolroom.'

'So I deduced from the fact that there was jam on your face. It hinted at schoolroom tea.'

'I never had jam on my face.'

'Yes, you did. Raspberry jam. I loved every pip of it. It seemed to set off to perfection the exquisite fairness of your skin.'

Lord Shortlands heaved like an ocean billow, preparatory to alighting. For the last twenty miles he had been sitting in a sort of stupor, engrossed in thought, but before that, and during the luncheon which had preceded the drive, he had been very communicative. There was nothing now that Mike did not know concerning the Shortlands-Punter romance, and the rivalry, happily no longer dangerous, of Spink, the butler. He could also have passed an examination with regard to the stamp.

The stamp, Lord Shortlands had told him, not once but many times, was a Spanish 1851 *dos reales* blue unused. Desborough, whose industry and acumen could not in his opinion be over-praised, had happened upon it just as the luncheon gong was sounding, with such stirring effects on his morale that for the first time in his association with his wife, Lady Adela, he had become the dominant male, stoutly refusing to go to the table until he had telephoned the great news to his father-in-law. According to Desborough, a thousand pounds for such a stamp might be looked upon as a conservative figure. A similar one had sold only the other day for fifteen hundred.

'As far as I could follow him, there's an error in colour or something,' said Lord Shortlands, returning to the theme as the car stopped. He had mentioned this before, during lunch at least six times and in the earlier stages of the drive another four, but it seemed to him worth saying again. 'An error in colour. Those were the words he used. Why that should make it so valuable I'm blessed if I know.'

'From what I recall of my stamp-collecting days,' said Mike, 'an error in colour was always something to start torchlight processions about.'

'Used you to collect stamps?' asked Terry.

'As a boy. Why, don't you remember –'

'What?'

'I forget what I was going to say.'

'This is disappointing.'

'It was probably nothing of importance.'

'But one hangs on your lightest word.'

'I know. Still, it can't be helped. It may come back. It'll be something to look forward to.'

What he was looking forward to, Lord Shortlands said with a grim smile, was the meeting with the viper Spink. By this time, he explained, the news of his sudden accession to wealth must have seeped through to the Servants' Hall, and he made no attempt to conceal the fact that he was anticipating considerable entertainment from the sight of his rival's face, the play of expression on which would, no doubt, in the circumstances be well worth watching. He could hardly wait, he said. A mild and kindly man as a rule, Lord Shortlands could be a tough nut in his dealings with vipers.

It was consequently with keen disappointment that he stared at the small maid who had opened the door. To a man who has been expecting to see a butler with heart bowed down, small maids are a poor substitute.

'Hullo! Where's Spink?'

'Mr Spink's gone off on his motor cycle, m'lord.'

'Gone off on his motor cycle?' said Lord Shortlands, obviously disapproving of this athleticism. 'What's he gone off on his motor cycle for?'

But the butler, it appeared, was one of those strong, silent butlers. He had not revealed to the maid the motive behind the excursion.

'Oh? Well, all right. Just wanted to see him about something. It'll have to wait. Lady Adela in the drawing-room?'

'Yes, m'lord.'

'Then come along, Cobbold, my boy. I'll take you to her.'

The maid passed out of earshot, and Lord Shortlands seemed to preen himself.

'Notice how I called you Cobbold?'

'Very adroit.'

'Can't start too early.'

'The start is everything.'

'Don't go forgetting.'

'Trust me.'

'And you, Terry, don't you go forgetting.'

'I won't.'

'One false step, and ruin stares us in the face.'

'Right in the face. But isn't there something you're forgetting, Shorty?'

'Eh? What's that?'

'The possibility of Adela sticking to this stamp.'

Lord Shortlands gaped.

'Sticking to it? You mean keeping it?'

'That's what I mean. I feel I can speak freely before this synthetic Cobbold –'

'Do,' said Mike. 'Go right ahead. I like this spirit of wholesome confidence.'

'– because there isn't much about your private affairs you haven't already told him. He could write your biography by this time. Suppose she decides to set the stamp against services rendered?'

Lord Shortlands's jaw fell limply.

'She wouldn't do that?'

'She will. I can feel it in my bones.'

'And what bones they are!' said Mike cordially. 'Small and delicate. When I was a boy, I promised my mother I would never marry a girl who hadn't small, delicate bones.'

'You must go and look for one. You and I and Clare between us, Shorty, must owe Desborough well over a thousand pounds by this time for board and lodging, and it isn't a thing Adela is likely to have overlooked.'

'Then what the devil are we to do?'

'Would you care to hear my plan?' asked Mike, ever helpful.

'Have you a plan?'

'Cut and dried.'

'He always has,' said Terry. 'They call him the One-Man Brains Trust.'

'And not without reason,' said Mike. 'I'm good. Here is the procedure, as I see it. When we arrive in Lady Adela's presence, you introduce me to her. "Shake hands with Mr Cobbold" is a formula that suggests itself.'

'"Mitt Mr Cobbold" would be friendlier.'

'Much friendlier. And what happens then, you ask. I will tell you. I hold her hand as in a vice. While she is thus rendered powerless, your father snatches up the album and rushes out and hides it somewhere. This is what is called team work.'

Lord Shortlands's eyes did not readily sparkle, but they were sparkling now. As far as he was concerned, Mike had got one vote.

'What an admirable idea!'

'I told you I was good. With my other hand I could be choking her.'

'I don't think I'd do that.'

'It's how I see the scene. Still, just as you please. Tell me,' said Mike, the trend of the conversation and certain previous observations on the part of both his host and his host's youngest daughter having suggested a thought to him. 'If I am not intruding on delicate family secrets, is your sister Adela what is technically known as a tough baby?'

'None tougher. Her bite spells death.'

'I thought as much. Yet here I am, about to stroll calmly into her presence, impersonating an honoured guest, a thing which, if discovered, must infallibly bring her right to the boil. You must be admiring me a good deal.'

'Oh, I am.'

' "My hero!" you are possibly saying to yourself.'

'Those very words.'

'So I supposed. Women always admire courage. And how quickly admiration turns to love. Like a flash. It won't be long before you are weeping salt tears and asking me if I can ever forgive you for having tortured me with your coldness. A week at the outside. What is this door before which we have paused?'

'The drawing-room. You seem to have forgotten the geography of the house.'

'They didn't allow me in the drawing-room much, when I was here before. Rightly or wrongly, they considered that my proper place was in the tool shed, playing ha'penny nap with Tony and the second footman. All right, Lord Shortlands, lead on.'

Lord Shortlands led on.

There was a moment, when Mike caught his first glimpse of Lady Adela Topping, when even his iron courage faltered a trifle. He had been warned, of course. They had told him that the châtelaine of Beevor Castle was a tough baby. But he had not been prepared for anything quite so formidable as this. Lady Adela had just returned from the garden and was still holding a stout pair of shears, and the thought of what a nasty flesh wound could be inflicted with these had a daunting effect.

And apart from the shears he found her appearance intimidating. She was looking even more like Catherine of Russia than usual, and it is pretty generally agreed that Catherine of Russia, despite many excellent qualitites, was not everybody's girl.

However, he rallied quickly and played his part well in the scene of introduction, helped not a little by the fact that his hostess was showing her most affable and agreeable side. His spectacular good looks had made a powerful impression on the woman behind the shears, who noted with approval that Terry also was looking her best. It seemed to Lady Adela that it would be a very unusual young man who could fail to be attracted by so alluring a girl, and that Terry, for her part, unaccountable though she was in many ways, could scarcely remain indifferent for long to such outstanding physical qualitites in a man whose father was a millionaire. She was cordiality itself to Mike.

'So delighted that you were able to come, Mr Cobbold.'

'So kind of you to have me, Lady Adela.'

'I hope you will like it here. Terry must show you round after tea.'

'She was just suggesting it.'

'The rose garden –'

'She particularly mentioned the rose garden. She was telling me how romantic and secluded it was. "We shall be quite alone there," she said.'

'Your window looks out on it. You might show Mr Cobbold his room, Terry. There is just time before tea. He is in the Blue Room.'

The door closed behind Terry and Mike, and Lord Shortlands, who during these polished exchanges, had been shuffling his feet with some impatience, opened the subject nearest his heart.

'Where's that stamp?' he demanded.

'Stamp?' Lady Adela seemed to come out of a trance. In moving to the door Mike had shown his profile to her and she had been musing on it in a sort of ecstasy. Surely, she was feeling, a profile like that, taken in conjunction with a father's bank balance.... 'Oh, the stamp? You mean the one Desborough found.'

'Yes. I want it in my possession.'

'But it's not yours.'

'Yes, it is. Certainly it's mine.'

'Oh, of course, I had forgotten. You don't know. That wasn't your album. After lunch Clare started hunting around for things for her jumble sale, and she found yours at the back of one of the drawers of the desk in your study. It had your name on it, so there can't be any mistake. So the other one must belong to Spink.'

A nightmare feeling that the solid floor was slipping from under him gripped Lord Shortlands.

'Spink!'

The name Spink has qualities — that 's' at the beginning, which you can hiss, and that strong, culminating 'k' — which render it almost perfect for shouting at the top of his voice. It was at the top of his voice that Lord Shortlands had shouted it, and his daughter quivered as if he had hit her.

'Father! You nearly deafened me.'

'Spink?' repeated Lord Shortlands, a little more on the *piano* side, but still loudly.

'Yes. Desborough was talking about the stamp at lunch, and Clare was telling Mr Blair how she had found the album in a cupboard, and after lunch Spink came to me and explained that it was one which had been given him by Mr Rossiter, the son of those Americans who took the castle last summer. He said he had been looking for it everywhere.'

Lord Shortlands clutched for support at a chair. He was conscious of a feeling that it was very hard that a man with a high blood pressure should be subjected to this kind of thing. He could not forget that it was the death by apoplectic stroke of his Uncle Gervase that had enabled him to succeed to the title.

'Spink said that?'

'Yes.'

Lord Shortlands suddenly came to life.

'It's a ramp!' he cried passionately.

Every instinct told him that Mervyn Spink's story was a tissue, or, putting it another way, a farrago of falsehood. Do Americans who take castles for summers give butlers stamp albums? Of course they don't. They haven't any, to start with, and if they have they don't give them away. What on earth would they give them away for? And whoever heard of a philatelist butler? Preposterous, felt Lord Shortlands.

'It's a bally try-on!' he thundered.

'I don't know what you mean. Spink tells me he has collected stamps since he was a boy, and I see nothing improbable in his story. Anyhow, he claims the thing.'

'I don't care if he claims it till he's blue in the face.'

Lady Adela's eyebrows rose.

'Well, really, father, I can't see why you are making such a fuss.'

'Fuss!'

'I mean, it isn't as if there were any chance of it being yours. And it must belong to somebody, so why not Spink? No doubt Mr Rossiter did give it to him. It's just the sort of thing an American would do.'

'Well, I strongly protest against your handing this stamp over to Spink till he produces Rossiter. His statement is that Rossiter gave it to him. All right, then, let him produce Rossiter.'

'He's going to.'

A faint gleam of hope illuminated Lord Shortlands's darkness.

'Then you haven't given it to him?'

'Naturally not on his unsupported word. He says he thinks Mr Rossiter is in London, and he has gone up to try to find him. In the meantime the stamp will be quite safe. I have got it locked away. Ah, tea,' said Lady Adela welcomingly.

Lord Shortlands, though generally fond of his cup at this hour, exhibited no corresponding elation. He was staring before him with unseeing eyes and wishing that the kindly Aloysius McGuffy could have been at his side, to start shaking up six or seven of his justly famous Specials.

Chapter 10

A song on his lips and the sparkle of triumph in his eye, opening his throttle gaily and tooting his horn with a carefree exuberance, Mervyn Spink sped home from London on his cycle, his air that of a man who sits on top of the world. Only the necessity of keeping both hands on the handlebars prevented him patting himself on the back.

The world was looking very beautiful to Mervyn Spink. He gazed at the blue skies, the fleecy clouds, the fluttering butterflies, the hedgerows bright with wild flowers and the spreading fields of wheat that took on the appearance of velvet rubbed the wrong way as the light breeze played over them, and approved of them all, in the order named. He did not actually sing 'tra la', but it was a very close thing. In the whole of Kent at that moment you could not have found a more cheerio butler.

The sight of Lord Shortlands standing in the road outside the castle gates increased his feeling of *bien être*. He had been looking forward to meeting Lord Shortlands. A nasty knock, he felt correctly, this stamp sequence would be for his rival, and he wished to gloat on his despair. Mervyn Spink was a man who believed in treating rivals rough.

He braked his motor cycle, removed trousers seat from saddle and alighted.

'Ah, Shortlands,' he said.

Lord Shortlands started. His face, already mauve, took on a deeper shade, and his eyes seemed to be suspended at the end of stalks, like those of a snail or prawn.

'How dare you address me like that?'

A frown marred the alabaster smoothness of Mervyn Spink's brow.

'We'd better get this settled once and for all, Shortlands,' he said coldly. 'Want me to call you "m'lord", do you? Well, if we were the other side of those gates, I'd call you "m'lord" till my eyes bubbled. But when I'm off duty and we meet in the public highway, I am no longer your employee.'

It was a nice piece of reasoning, well expressed, but Lord Shortlands continued dissatisfied:

'Yes, you are.'

'No, I'm not. We're man and man. If you think otherwise, you can complain to her ladyship. It'll mean telling her the whole story and explaining just how matters stand between us, but I don't mind that, if you don't.'

The purple flush died out of Lord Shortlands's face. A man with his consistently high blood pressure could not actually blench, but he came reasonably near to doing so. The picture those words had conjured up had made him feel as if his spine had been suddenly removed and the vacancy filled with gelatine. His manner, which had had perhaps almost too much in it of the medieval Earl dealing with a scurvy knave or varlet, changed, taking on the suggestion of a cushat dove calling to its mate.

'Well, never mind, Spink. Quite all right. The point is – er – immaterial.'

'Okey-doke, Shortlands.'

'Just a technicality. And now what's all this about that stamp?'

'What about it?'

'My daughter tells me you've claimed it.'

'I have.'

'Says you say you were given it by this fellow Rossiter. I don't believe it,' cried Lord Shortlands, recapturing something of the first fine careless rapture of his original manner. The spirit of his fighting ancestors was once more strong within him, and if he had been Lady Adela Topping herself he could not have been more resolutely determined to stand no nonsense. 'It's a bally swindle!'

It seemed for an instant as though Mervyn Spink, in defiance of the first rule laid down by the Butlers' Guild for the guidance of its members, was about to laugh. But he managed to check the impulse and to substitute for the guffaw a quiet smile.

'Listen,' he said. 'I'll tell you something.'

Until now we have seen this butler only at his best, a skilful carrier of malted milk and a man whose appearance would have shed lustre on a ducal home; his only fault, as far as we have been able to ascertain, the venial one of liking to have an occasional ten bob on the two-thirty. He now strips the mask from his face and stands revealed as the modern Machiavelli he was. The typewriter falters as it records his words, and even Lord Shortlands, though he had known all along that dirty work was in progress in some form or other, found himself stunned and amazed.

'You're quite right, Shortlands. It *is* a bally swindle, and what are you going to do about it? Nothing. Because you can't.'

He was right, and Lord Shortlands realized it. However bally the swindle, he could make no move to cope with it. His fear of his daughter Adela held him gagged and bound. Tortured by the humiliating sense of impotence, he uttered a wordless sound at the back of his throat. Augustus Robb, in a similar situation, would have said 'Coo!' Both would have meant the

84

same thing. 'Young Rossiter didn't give me that album. I've never seen the thing in my life. But I've a nephew on the stage who plays character parts, and doesn't stick at much so long as he knows there's something in it for him. Well, he's going to play another character part tomorrow. I've just been to see him, and we've fixed everything up.'

He paused for an instant, his face darkening a little. The only flaw in his contentment was the lurking feeling that a shade more energy on his part during the initial bargaining might have resulted in his nephew closing for fifty quid, instead of sticking out, as he had done, for ten down and a further ninety on the completion of the deal. But a man about to collect fifteen hundred can afford to be spacious, and he had brightened again when he resumed his remarks.

'I'm telling her ladyship that I had the good luck to catch Mr Rossiter on the eve of his departure for France, and that he'll be delighted to stop off at the castle tomorrow, on his way to Dover, and substantiate my claim. You'll be seeing him about lunch time. So there you are. All nice and smooth, I call it.'

Lord Shortlands did not reply. He turned and started to totter home. Mervyn Spink wheeled his motor cycle beside him.

'Beautiful evening, m'lord,' he said deferentially. They had passed through the gates. 'Weather keeps up nicely, m'lord.'

He contemplated his companion's face with all the pleasure he had known he was going to feel at the sight of it. Lord Shortlands was looking like Stanwood Cobbold on the morning after. Transferring his gaze to the local flora and fauna, Mervyn Spink felt more uplifted than ever. He drew satisfaction from the lilac bush that blossomed to the left and from the bird with the red beak which had settled on a tree to the right. And perhaps the best proof of his exalted frame of mind is that he found something exhilarating even in the appearance of Cosmo Blair, the playwright, who came towards them at that moment, smoking a cigarette. For this gifted man, though the author of half a dozen dramas which had brought him pots of money both in England and in the United States, was in no sense an eyeful. The normal eye, resting upon Cosmo Blair, was apt to blink and turn away.

Successful playwrights as a class are slender. Vertically there may be quite a lot, though not more than their admirers desire, of Terence Rattigan and, in a greater degree, of Ian Hay, but you can hardly see them sideways. Cosmo Blair struck a new note by being short and tubby. Lord Shortlands had called him a pot-bellied perisher; and though the fifth Earl was prejudiced, his young guest having an annoying habit of addressing him as 'My dear Shortlands', and contradicting every second thing he said, it must be admitted that there was something in the charge.

He scanned the pair through a glistening eyeglass.

'Ah, my dear Shortlands.'

Lord Shortlands uttered a sound like a cinnamon bear with a bone in its throat.

'Ah, Spink.'

'Good evening, sir.'

'Been out for a ride?'

'Yes, sir.'

'Nice evening.'

'Extremely, sir.'

'Oh, by the way, Spink,' said Cosmo Blair.

He, too, was feeling serene and contented. There had been crumpets for tea, dripping with butter, as he liked them, and after tea he had read his second act again to Clare. Her outspoken admiration had been very pleasant to him, inducing a sensation of benevolence towards his fellows, and this benevolence had been increased by the beauty of the Spring evening. He looked at Mervyn Spink and was glad that it was within his power to do him a kindness.

'By the way, Spink, you remember asking me the other day to do something for that nephew of yours, the actor? Roland Winter, didn't you say his name was?'

'Roland Winter, yes, sir.'

'Is he fixed up just now?'

'No, sir. He is at present at liberty.'

'Well, I've got something for him in this thing I'm writing. It's an odd thing, my dear Shortlands,' said Cosmo Blair, drawing at his cigarette, 'how one forgets people. This nephew of our good friend Spink. I've been trying ever since he spoke to me to think why the name Roland Winter was familiar, and I only remembered this afternoon. I had him in a show of mine last year, and he was quite –'

He had been about to say 'good', but the word changed on his lips to a startled exclamation. The motor cycle had fallen from Mervyn Spink's nerveless fingers with a crash.

'You know my nephew, sir?'

'Oh, rather. Tall, thin chap with a slight squint and a funny-shaped mouth. Red hair hasn't he got? Yes, now I recall it, red hair. Well, tell him to go and see Charlie Cockburn at the St George's. I'll drop Charlie a line.'

Cosmo Blair went on his way, conscious of a good deed done, and Lord Shortlands uttered an explosive 'Ha!'

'Now how about it, you Spink?' he cried exultantly.

Mervyn Spink did not speak. His face was very sad.

'If this blighter Blair knows your blighted nephew so well,' proceeded Lord Shortlands, elaborating his point and making it clear to the meanest intelligence, 'how the dickens do you propose to introduce him into the place as this blighted Rossiter? You're pipped, Spink. Your whole vile scheme strikes a snag.'

Mervyn Spink did not deign to reply. Sombrely he picked up the motor cycle, sombrely mounted it, sombrely opened the throttle and rode off in the direction of the village.

His heart, so light before, was heavy now. He looked at the blue skies and fleecy clouds and took an instant dislike to them. He resented the presence of the fluttering butterflies. The fields of wheat jarred upon his eye. There are few things which more speedily modify the Pippa Passes outlook on life of a butler who has been congratulating himself on having formulated a cast-iron scheme for putting large sums of money in his pocket than the discovery that that scheme, through the most capricious and unforeseeable of chances, has come unstuck.

'Hell!' mused Mervyn Spink, brooding darkly.

At the post office he alighted and dispatched a telegram to his nephew, briefly cancelling all arrangements; then rode sombrely back to the castle and sought refuge in the seclusion of his pantry.

He had been sitting there for some little time, feeling with the poet that of all sad words of tongue or pen the saddest are these: It might have been – when the bell of Lady Adela's room rang.

Bells must be answered, though the heart is aching.

'M'lady?'

'Oh, Spink, Mr Cobbold has arrived. Will you go and see that he has everything he wants.'

'Very good, m'lady.'

'Did you find Mr Rossiter?'

'No, m'lady. I regret to say that the gentleman is not at the moment in London.'

'But you will be able to get in touch with him?'

'No doubt, m'lady.'

Mervyn Spink departed on his errand. He experienced no soaring of the spirits at the prospect of renewing his acquaintance with one with whom his relations had once been cordial. During their association in Mr Ellery Cobbold's palatial home at Great Neck he had found Stanwood a pleasant and congenial companion, practically a buddy; for Stanwood, a gregarious soul, had often dropped in on him for a drink and a chat, and on several occasions they had attended prize fights together.

But as he approached the Blue Room his heart was still heavy.

Chapter 11

In the Blue Room, Mike, dressed and ready for dinner, was thoroughly approving of his quarters. To Lord Shortlands, that modern Prisoner of Chillon, everything connected with Beevor Castle might be the abomination of desolation, but to Mike, coming to it with a fresh eye, the Blue Room seemed about as satisfactory a Blue Room as a man could wish for.

Its windows, as his hostess had stated, looked out upon the rose garden and beyond it on a pleasing panorama of woods and fields, rooks cawing in the former, rabbits moving briskly to and fro in the latter, and its interior was comfortable, even luxurious. He particularly liked the easy chair. Too often in English country house bedrooms the guest finds himself fobbed off with something hard and upright, constructed to the order of some remote ancestor by the upholsterer of the Spanish Inquisition, but this one invited repose.

He was reclining in it with his feet on the table, thinking long, lingering thoughts of Terry, when his reverie was interrupted. The door had opened, to reveal a handsome stranger, from his dress and deportment apparently the castle butler. He eyed him with interest. This, then, was the Spink whose rivalry had caused Lord Shortlands so much concern, the cork-drawing Adonis who had threatened at one time to play the Serpent in his lordship's Garden of Eden. He could understand how any Earl might have feared such a man.

'Good evening, sir.'

'Good evening.'

On Spink's mobile lips, in spite of his heaviness of heart, there had appeared a faint, respectful smile; the smile of a butler who sees that an amusing blunder has been made by those higher up. G.H.Q. had told him that he would find Stanwood Cobbold in the Blue Room. This was unquestionably the Blue Room, but the man before him was not his old buddy.

'Excuse me, sir, I must have misunderstood her ladyship. I supposed her to say that Mr Cobbold was occupying this apartment.'

'I'm Mr Cobbold.'

Butlers do not start. Spink merely rippled a little.

'Mr Stanwood Cobbold?'

'That's right.'

There was a short pause. Then Spink said: 'Indeed sir?'

It is a very unintelligent butler who, expecting to see in a Blue Room a Stanwood Cobbold with a face like a hippopotamus and finding himself confronted by one with a face like a Greek god, does not suspect that there is funny business afoot. To Spink, who was highly intelligent, the very air seemed thick with funny business, and his eye grew stern and bleak.

And simultaneously there came to him, for his was a mind

that worked like a steel spring where his financial interests were concerned, the thought that here was where he might be able to do something towards repairing the ruin of his fortunes. Young men who come to castles calling themselves Stanwood Cobbold when they are not Stanwood Cobbold do not do so without an important reason, and a butler who knows their secret may reasonably expect to exact the price of his silence. It seemed to Mervyn Spink that things were looking up.

'I wonder if I might make an observation, sir?'

'Go ahead.'

'I would merely wish to remark that I know Mr Stanwood Cobbold extremely well.'

Mike saw that he had made a mistake about that easy chair. He had supposed it comfortable, and in reality it was red-hot. He left it quickly.

'You do?'

'Yes, sir. I was for nearly a year in the employment of Mr Cobbold senior at his home in Great Neck, Long Island, and saw Mr Stanwood daily.'

Mike ran a finger around the inside of his collar. It had seemed, when he put it on, a well-fitting collar, but now it felt unpleasantly tight.

'This opens up a new line of thought,' he said.

'I fancied it might, sir.'

'A new and very interesting line of thought.'

'Yes, sir.'

The fact that he was still calling him 'Sir' suggested to Mike that the other had not, as a lesser butler would have done, leaped immediately to the conclusion that he was visiting Beevor Castle in the hope of making away with the spoons. No doubt some subtle something in his appearance, some touch of natural dignity in his bearing, had caused the man to reject what on the face of it would have been the obvious explanation of his presence.

This encouraged him. He would have been the last person to dispute that the situation still presented certain embarrassing features, but the thought came to him, remembering that all men have their price, that it might be possible by exploring every avenue to find some formula that would be acceptable to both parties. There were, in short, in the Blue Room at that moment two minds with but a single thought.

He proceeded to try to pave the way to an understanding.

'Your name is Spink, I believe?'

'Yes, sir.'

'Then sit down at this table, Spink. It is, you will notice, a round table, always essential on these occasions. Now, first and foremost, Spink, we must keep quite cool.'

'Yes, sir.'

'We must not lose our heads. We must get together over the round table and thresh this thing out quietly and calmly in a spirit of mutual cooperation.'

'Yes, sir.'

'I will begin by conceding a point. I am not Stanwood Cobbold.'

'No, sir.'

'Very good. We make progress. The question now arises, Who *am* I? Any suggestion?'

'I am not aware of your surname, sir, but I would hazard the conjecture that your first name is Michael.'

'This is uncanny.'

'I would also hazard the conjecture that you are a friend of Mr Stanwood, and that you obtained his permission to impersonate him here because you desired to be in the society of Lady Teresa.'

'How do you do it? With mirrors?'

Mervyn Spink smiled gently.

'A letter recently arrived for Lady Teresa, couched in impassioned terms and signed "Mike".'

'Good God! She didn't show it around?'

'No, sir. A member of the domestic staff came upon it while accidentally glancing through the contents of her ladyship's dressing-table and, having perused it, reported its substance to the Servants' Hall.'

A pretty blush suffused Mike's cheeks. He ground his teeth a little.

'He did, did he?'

'She, sir. It was one of the maids. I rebuked her.'

You didn't wring her neck?'

'That did not occur to me, sir.'

'You missed a bet. Did she enjoy it?'

'No, sir. I chided her severely.'

'I mean the letter. It entertained her?'

'Yes, sir.'

'Fine. One likes to feel that one's letters have given pleasure. Augustus Robb thought it good, too. He looked it over before it left.'

'Sir?'

'A London critic. You haven't met him. If you ever do, introduce him to the maid. They will want to swap views on my literary style. Well, seeing that you are so well-informed, I will admit that I did come here for the reason you suggest. So where do we go from here? My name, by the way, is Cardinal.'

'I have often heard Mr Stanwood speak of you, sir.'

'Very likely. We're old friends. And you're right in supposing that I have his full sympathy and approval in the venture which I have undertaken. He was all for it.'

'It is the attitude which one would have expected in Mr Stanwood. He has a big heart and would, of course, do all that lay in his power to further a friend's romance. But you were saying, sir –'

'Yes, let's get back to it. Where do we go from here?'

'Sir?'

'Come, come, Spink, use the bean. The first essential, as you must see for yourself, is the ensuring of your silence. One word from you to the lady up top, and I am undone.'

'Yes, sir.'

'How is this silence to be contrived?'

'Well, sir, if I might make the suggestion –'

'You have the floor.'

'– I would propose that we came to some amicable arrangement.'

'Of a financial nature?'

'Precisely, sir.'

Mike drew a breath of relief. It was as he had hoped. They had explored every avenue, and here came the formula, hot from the griddle. He beamed upon Mervyn Spink, as the inhabitants of Ghent no doubt beamed upon the men who brought the good news to that city from Aix.

'Now you're tooting. Now the fog of misunderstanding is dissipated and we can talk turkey. How do you react to the idea of a tenner?'

'Unenthusiastically, sir.'

'Ten pounds is nice sugar, Spink.'

'Inferior to two hundred, sir.'

There was a pause. Mike laughed.

'Funny how one's ears play one tricks. It sounded to me for a moment as though you had said two hundred. Something to do with the acoustics, no doubt.'

'That was the sum I mentioned, sir.'

Mike clicked his tongue.

'Now listen, Spink. Your comedy is good, and we all enjoy a little wholesome fun, but we mustn't waste time. Twenty was what you meant, wasn't it?'

'No, sir. Two hundred. Mr Stanwood has frequently spoken of the large income which you make in the exercise of your profession in Hollywood, and I am sure you will feel that two hundred pounds is a small price to pay for the privilege of making an extended stay at the castle. Judging by the tone of your letter.'

'I wouldn't harp too much on that letter. I might plug you in the eye.'

'Very good, sir.'

'Already I feel a strong urge in that direction.'

'I am sorry to hear that, sir.'

'Two hundred pounds!'

'I require the sum for a particular purpose, sir.'

'I know.'

'His lordship has confided in you, sir?'

'From soup to nuts. And that's another thing that gives me pause. Apart from the disagreeableness of having to cough up two hundred pounds there is the Lord Shortlands angle. This is going to be tough on him. It will dish his hopes and dreams.'

'Into each life some rain must fall.'

'Eh?'

'I was merely wishing to indicate, sir, that you cannot make an omelette without breaking eggs.'

'Is this a time to talk of omelettes, Spink? You realize, of course, that you are a lop-eared blackmailer?'

'Yes, sir.'

'And you don't shudder?'

'No, sir.'

'Then there is no more to be said.'

'You will find pen and ink on the writing-table, sir.'

Mike made his way slowly to the writing-table, and took pen in hand.

'Well, it's a comfort to think that this sort of thing is bound to grow on you and that eventually you will get it in the neck,' he said. 'I can read your future like a book. Before long another opportunity of stinging some member of the general public will present itself, and you will be unable to resist it. And after that you will go on and on, sinking deeper and deeper into the mire of crime. The appetite grows by what it feeds on, Spink.'

'Yes, sir.'

'You don't feel like pulling up while there is yet time?'

'No, sir.'

'Just as you say. Let us hurry on, then, to the melancholy end. You will, as I say, go on and on, blackmailing the populace like nobody's business, until one day you make that false step which they all make and – bingo! – into the dock for yours, with the judge saying, "Well, prisoner at the bar, it's been nice knowing you –" And then off to the cooler for an exemplary sentence. I shall come on visiting days and make faces at you through the bars.'

'I shall be delighted to receive you, sir.'

'You won't be when you see the faces. What's the date?'

'The twelfth of May, sir.'

'And your first name?'

'Mervyn, sir.'

'A sweet name.'

'So my mother felt, sir.'

'Can you think of your mother at a moment when you are gouging a stranger, scarcely an acquaintance, for two hundred of the best and brightest?'

'Yes, sir.'

'Ponder well, Spink. She is looking down on you from heaven –'

'She lives in East Dulwich, sir.'

'Well, from East Dulwich, then. It makes no difference to my argument. She is looking down on you from East Dulwich –'

'If you would kindly make the cheque open –'

'All right. Here you are.'

'Thank you, sir.'

'Yes, she is –'

Mike paused. Somebody had knocked on the door.

'Come in.'

Lady Adela entered.

'I thought I would come and see if you were all right, Mr Cobbold,' said Lady Adela brightly. 'Are you quite comfortable?'

'Very, thank you.'

'I suppose you and Spink have been having a talk about old times? He tells me he used to be your father's butler. Did you find Mr Cobbold just the same, Spink?'

There were things about Mervyn Spink which many people did not like, but he always gave value for money.

'Just the same, m'lady. The sight of him brought back many happy memories. Mr Stanwood was always very kind to me during the period of my sojourn in the United States of America, m'lady.'

From down the corridor came the plaintive note of a husband in distress. Desborough Topping, hampered by lumbago, was experiencing a difficulty in tying his tie. Like a tigress hearing the cry of her cub, Lady Adela hurried from the room.

'Thank you, Spink,' said Mike.

'Not at all, sir.'

'That handsome testimonial should fix me nicely.'

'Yes, sir.'

'I wish there was something I could do for you in return.'

Mervyn Spink smiled benevolently.

'You have done something, sir.'

'The cheque? You feel satisfied?'

'Entirely, sir.'

'Well, that's fine. But you're easily pleased. That cheque's no good. You will have noted that it is signed "Michael Cardinal", which will cause the bank to sling it back at you like a bouncer ejecting a cash customer. For you were mistaken in supposing Michael to be my Christian name. It is Mycroft, like Sherlock Holmes's brother, and that is my official signature. You see what I mean?'

Mervyn Spink reeled. His clean-cut face twisted. If he had had a moustache, he would have looked like a baffled baronet.

'I'll go straight to her ladyship –'

'And tell her that you were mistaken in stating that I was the Stanwood Cobbold who was so kind to you during the period of your sojourn in the United States of America? I wouldn't. It would mean a good deal of tedious explaining. No, no, I think we may look on the incident as closed. This is a glad day for your mother, Spink. The son she loves has been saved from the perpetration of a crime at which her gentle spirit would have shuddered. If you ask me,' said Mike, 'my bet is that she'll go singing about East Dulwich.'

Chapter 12

Lord Shortlands was beginning to perk up. For a father whose daughter treats him as a problem child, and is inclined at the slightest offence to stand him in the corner and stop his pocket money, it must always be a matter of extreme delicacy and danger to introduce into that daughter's home a changeling in place of the guest she is expecting to entertain, and during the early stages of Mike's stay at Beevor Castle the fifth Earl, fully appreciating this, had run the gamut of the emotions.

At first fear had reigned supreme, causing him to start at sudden noises and to understand with a ghastly clarity what must have been the feelings of that Damocles of whom he had read in his school days. Then gradually hope had come stealing in, stiffening the jellied backbone. But it was only on the evening of the third day, as he sat in his study before dinner prodding the ribs of his dog Whiskers, happily cured of his recent indisposition, that he was able to view the position of affairs with any real confidence. It seemed to him that, as far as the great imposture was concerned, things had settled down nicely.

With regard to the activities of the viper Spink, he continued to feel apprehensive. So far, that snakelike man had been foiled, but he feared for the future. Butlers, he knew, though crushed to earth, will rise again, and he shuddered to think how nearly Mervyn Spink had triumphed already. If it had not been for the quick brainwork of his young friend Cardinal, he realized, this would have been a big weekend for vipers.

Mike's description of his duel with Mervyn Spink had thrilled Lord Shortlands to the core. He had no words to express his admiration for the splendid qualities which this beardless youth had displayed in circumstances which might well have proved too much for a veteran strategist, and more and more did it seem to him inexplicable that his daughter Terry, wooed by such a suitor, should not scoop him in with a cry of joy and grapple him to her soul with hoops of steel.

He looked at Terry meditatively, planning the word in season. She had come in a few moments before and was assisting him in his kindly attentions to the dog Whiskers by tickling the latter's stomach.

'Terry,' he said.

But, before he could proceed further, the door had opened and Mike was standing on the threshold.

A gentle glow permeated Mike's system, as he surveyed the charming domestic scene. His future wife, his future father-in-law, and his future dog by marriage, all on the spot and doing their stuff before him. What could be sweeter? It pained him to have to break up the pretty picture, but he had come to impart news, and it must be imparted.

'Good evening, good evening, Lord Shortlands,' he said. 'Though I'm not sure I like that "Lord Shortlands". If you're going to be my father-in-law, I really ought to begin calling you something not quite so formal. "Pop" or "Dad" or something. In this connexion, I find Desborough Topping a disappointing guide. I had hoped to pick up some hints from him.

but he doesn't seem to call you anything, except occasionally "Er". I don't like "Er".'

'Adela wanted Desborough to call Shorty "Pater",' said Terry.

'I don't like "Pater", either.'

'Nor did Desborough. It was too much for him. So now he just coughs.'

'Coughing should be well within my scope.'

Lord Shortlands had a better idea.

'Call me "Shorty", as Terry does.'

'You solve the whole difficulty,' said Mike gratefully. 'I doubt if coughing would have been really satisfactory. In constant association with a roupy son-in-law, a father-in-law's love falters and dies. Too tedious, always having to be passing the lozenges. Well, Shorty, you are doubtless wondering what brings me here, intruding on your privacy.'

'My dear fellow!'

'Intruding, I repeat. No need to tell me I am butting in. But the fact is, I bring news. And not too good news, I'm afraid. Hang on to your chair.'

In spite of the fact that his mind, such as it was, was a good deal easier than it had been, it took very little to alarm Lord Shortlands nowadays. At these ominous words he quivered like a blancmange and, as Mike had advised, clutched the arms of his chair in a fevered grip.

'Has Adela found out?' he gasped.

'No, no, no. Not quite so bad as that, It has to do with Stanwood Cobbold. I regret to have to inform you that dear old Stanwood is in our midst.'

As far as a man can reel who is seated in an armchair, Lord Shortlands reeled.

'You don't mean that?'

'I do. Stanwood is here. Himself. Not a picture.'

Terry squeaked.

'Here in the house?'

'Not actually in the house, no. He is at present infesting the local inn. He sent me a note from there this afternoon, asking me to go and confer with him. But he speaks of paying us a visit.'

The dog Whiskers indicated with a gesture that there was still an area of his person which had not been attended to, but Lord Shortlands was in no mood now for massaging dogs.

'My God! He'll meet Adela!'

Mike said that that was precisely the thought which he, too, found disturbing.

'And if he does, and she asks him who he is, you can bet that his instant reply will be "Stanwood Cobbold, ma'am". He would never let slip such a gorgeous opportunity of spilling the beans. So I did my best to make him see how essential it was that he should remain at the inn and not move a step in this direction. I assured him that the finest brains at the castle would be strained to their utmost capacity to find a solution for his problem. You see, what has happened is that his father has cabled telling him to send along a number of photographs of the interior of the house with himself prominently displayed in the foreground.'

'Good God!'

'The cable apparently arrived the day we left London, and Stanwood has been pondering ever since on what was to be done about it. Last night he got the bright idea that if he came down here, I would be able to sneak him into the place in the early morning and act as his photographer. He has brought a camera.'

Lord Shortlands writhed like a wounded snake, and Terry squeaked again.

'The early morning?' moaned Lord Shortlands. 'Fatal!'

'The very worst time,' agreed Terry. 'The place will be seething with housemaids –'

'Who'll take him for a burglar –'

'And scream –'

'Thus bringing Lady Adela to the spot with her foot in her hand and putting us right in the soup,' said Mike. 'That was the very picture that rose before my eyes when he outlined the scheme. But cheer up. There's nothing to be worried about.'

It was a well-intentioned remark, but Terry appeared to take exception to it. Her squeak this time was one of justifiable indignation, and provoked a thoughtful comment from Mike.

'Tell me,' he said. 'How do you manage to produce that

extraordinary sound? It's like a basketful of puppies. I wouldn't have thought the human voice could have done it.'

Terry was not to be lured into a discussion on voice production.

'What do you mean by scaring us stiff like that, and then saying there's nothing to be worried about?'

'There isn't. Have I ever let you down?'

'You've never had the chance.'

'No, that's true. But I should have thought you would have realized by this time that there is no am-parce so sticky that the Cardinal brain cannot make it play ball. I have the situation well in hand.'

'You haven't thought of something?'

'Of course I've thought of something.'

'Then I think you might have told us before, instead of giving us heart failure. Shorty has high blood pressure.'

'Very high,' said Lord Shortlands. 'Runs in the family.'

Mike saw their point.

'Yes, I suppose you're right. I was to blame. I don't know if you've noticed that I have a rather unpleasant habit of painting a set-up in the darkest colours in order to make the joy-bells, when they ring, sound louder. It has got me a good deal disliked.'

'I don't wonder.'

'It's the artist in me. I have to play for Suspense. But you are waiting for the low-down. Here it comes. Is it not a fact that on Saturday afternoons throughout the Spring and Summer months this historic joint is thrown open to the general public on payment of an entrance fee of a bob a nob?'

'Why, of course!'

'Don't say "Of course" in that light way. You wouldn't have thought of it in a million years.'

'Stanwood can come with the crowd –'

'Complete with camera.'

'He can get all the photographs he wants.'

'Without incurring the least suspicion.'

'But how about Spink? He shows them round.'

'Disregard Spink. He can't do a thing. We have the Indian sign on him. Spink is as the dust beneath our chariot wheels.'

Terry drew a deep breath.

'You know, you're rather wonderful.'

'Why "rather"?'

'Have you told Stanwood?'

'Not yet. The brain-wave came after I had left him. I propose to look in on him tomorrow morning and set his mind at rest. He seemed a little feverish, when we parted. That's the trouble with Stanwood. He worries. He lets things prey on his mind. And now ought we not to be making our way to the drawing-room? I should imagine that your sister Adela is a woman who throws her weight about a good deal, if people are late for dinner.'

Lord Shortlands started.

'Has the gong gone?'

'Not yet. But it's past eight.'

'Come on, come on, come on!' cried Lord Shortlands, stirred to his depths, and was out of the room in two impressive leaps.

Mike and Terry followed more slowly.

'Did you know,' said Mike, 'that a flea one-twelfth of an inch long, weighing one eighty-thousandth of an ounce, can broad jump thirteen inches?'

'No,' said Terry.

'A fact, I believe. Watching your father brought it to my mind. He's very agile.'

'Well, you scared him. He's frightened to death of Adela.'

'I don't blame him. If the Cardinals knew what fear is, I should be frightened of her myself. As hard an egg as ever stepped out of the saucepan.'

'You ought to see her doing her imitation of an angry headmistress.'

'Well worth watching, I imagine. Odd how different sisters can be. I can't imagine you scaring anyone. Yours is a beautiful nature; kind, sweet, gentle, dovelike, the very type of nature that one wants to have around the house. Will you marry me?'

'No.'

'I think you're wrong. One of these days, when we are walking down the aisle together, with the choir singing "The Voice

that Breathed O'er Eden", I shall remind you of this. "Aha!"
I shall say. "Who said she wouldn't marry me?" That'll make
you look silly.'

They caught Lord Shortlands up at the drawing-room door,
and soothed him into something resembling calm. The gong,
they pointed out, is the acid test as to whether you are in time
for or late for dinner, and the gong had not yet sounded.

So firmly based on reason was their argument that the fifth
Earl was able to enter the room with almost a swagger. It sub-
sided a little as he saw that they were the last arrivals, but he
still maintained a fairly firm front.

'Hullo, hullo,' he said. 'Dinner's a bit late, isn't it?'

There was no frown on Lady Adela's face. She appeared
quite amiable.

'Yes' she said. 'I told Spink to put it back ten minutes.
We're waiting for Mr Rossiter.'

At the moment of his entry Lord Shortlands had paused at
an occasional table and picked up a china ornament, in order
to fortify his courage by fiddling with it. At these words, it
slipped from his grasp, crashing to ruin on the parquet floor.

'Rossiter!'

'Yes. I wish you wouldn't break things, Father.'

At another moment, Lord Shortlands would have wilted at
the displeasure in his daughter's voice, and would probably
have thrown together some hasty story about somebody having
joggled his arm. But now he had no thought for such minor
matters.

'Rossiter?' he cried. 'How do you mean Rossiter?'

'Apparently Mr Rossiter has been staying at the inn in the
village for the fishing. Quite a coincidence that he should have
been there just when Spink was trying to find him. Spink happened to go to the inn this evening, and met him. Of course, I
asked him to come to the castle.'

The door opened, and Mervyn Spink appeared. His eye, as it
rested upon Lord Shortlands, had in it a lurking gleam.

'Mr Rossiter,' he announced.

Stanwood Cobbold walked into the room, tripping over a
rug, as was his habit when he entered rooms.

Chapter 13

'It's no good looking to me for guidance, my dear Shorty,' said Mike. 'I'm sunk.'

He spoke in response to a certain wild appeal in the other's eye, which he had just caught. Dinner was over, and a council of three had met in Lord Shortlands's study to discuss the latest development. Its president was pacing the floor with his hands behind his back, occasionally removing them in order to gesticulate in a rather frenzied manner. Mike and Terry, the remaining delegates to the conference, were seated. The dog Whiskers was present, but took no part in the proceedings. He was trying to locate a flea which had been causing him some annoyance.

'Sunk,' Mike repeated. 'I am stunned, bewildered and at a loss. *Bouleversé*, if you would like a little French.'

Lord Shortlands groaned, and flung his arms up like a despairing semaphore. He was thinking of Mervyn Spink's face as he had seen it during the recent meal. For the most part, as befitted a butler performing his official duties, it had been impassive: but once, on Lady Adela asking Mr Rossiter if he remembered having given her head of staff his stamp album, and Mr Rossiter, who seemed a nervous young man, inclined to start violently and try to swallow his uvula when spoken to, upsetting his glass and replying 'Oh, sure,' it had softened into a quick smile. And in the gesture with which the fellow had offered him the potatoes there had been something virtually tantamount to a dig in the ribs. It had gone through Lord Shortlands like a knife through butter.

'No,' said Mike, proceeding, 'it's no use my trying to pretend that I am hep. I am not hep. What is all this Rossiter stuff?'

Terry clicked her tongue impatiently, like a worried school-mistress with a child of slow intelligence.

'Weren't you listening when Adela said that to Stanwood at dinner?'

'Said what?'

'About the album.'

'I'm sorry. I missed it.'

'Well, Spink is pretending that the album was given him by the son of some Americans named Rossiter, who took the castle last summer –'

'The viper!' interpolated Lord Shortlands.

'– and somehow, I can't imagine how, he has got Stanwood to say he is Mr Rossiter. And when Adela asked him if he had given Spink the album, he said he had. Now do you see?'

Mike whistled. Lord Shortlands, whose nervous system had been greatly impaired by the night's happenings, asked him not to whistle, and Mike said that he would endeavour not to do so in future but that this particular whistle had been forced from him by the intense stickiness of the situation.

'I should say I do see,' he said. 'Has Spink got the stamp, then?'

'No, not yet. He came to the drawing-room after dinner and asked for it, but Adela said that it would be much better for her to keep it till Desborough was well enough to go to London. She said he would be able to get a better price than Spink could, because he knows the right people to go to.'

'Very shrewd.'

'Spink argued a bit, but Adela squashed him.'

'Good for her. Well, this is fine. This gives us a respite.'

Lord Shortlands was not to be comforted.

'What's the good of a respite? What the dickens does it matter if the fellow gets the thing tonight or the day after tomorrow?'

'The delay, my dear Shorty, is of the utmost importance. It means everything. I have a plan.'

'He has a plan,' said Terry.

'I have a plan,' said Mike. 'No need to be surprised. You know my lightning brain. In the interval which elapses before Desborough Topping's lumbago slackens its grip and he is able to travel, we will act. Boys and girls, we are going to pinch this stamp.'

'What!'

'Pinch it,' said Mike firmly. 'Swipe it. Obtain possession of it by strong-arm tactics. Up against this dark and subtle butler, we cannot afford to be too nice in our methods. He has raised the banner with the strange device "Anything goes". Let that slogan be ours.'

Terry was a girl who believed in giving praise where praise was due, even though there was the risk that such praise might increase the tendency of its recipient to get above himself.

'What a splendid idea. How nice it is to come across someone with a really criminal mind. I suppose this is one of those hidden depths of yours that you were speaking of?'

'That's right. I'm full of them.'

Lord Shortlands's conscience appeared to be less elastic than his daughter's. Where she had applauded, he fingered the chin dubiously.

'But I can't go about pinching things.'

'Why not?'

'Well, dash it.'

'Oh, Shorty.'

'No, he's quite right,' said Mike. 'I see what he means. He shrinks from smirching the old escutcheon, and I honour him for his scruples. But have no qualms, my dear Shorty. In pinching this stamp you will simply be restoring it to its rightful owner. That album belongs to Terry.'

Terry shook her head.

'Well meant, but no good. Shorty knows I haven't collected stamps since I was in the schoolroom.'

'It was in the schoolroom that you collected this one. I was on the point of mentioning it when we were getting out of the car the day I arrived, only Shorty was so sure the thing was his that I hadn't the heart to. Throw your mind back. A rainy afternoon eight years ago. You were sitting at the schoolroom table, covered with glue, poring over your childish collection. I entered and said: "Hello, looking at your stamps?" You came clean. Yes, you said, you were looking at your stamps. "You don't seem to have many," I said. "Would you like mine?" adding that I had recently been given an album full of the dam' things as a birthday present by an uncle who wasn't abreast of affairs and didn't know that it was considered bad form at the dear old school to collect stamps. A pastime only fit for kids.'

'Oh, golly. Yes, I remember now.'

'I thought you would. So I wrote for it and presented it to you.'

'Little knowing that it was a gold mine.'

'It would have made no difference if I had known. We Cardinals are like that. Lavish to those we love. You can imagine what excellent husbands we make.'

'Well, we Cobbolds have scruples about accepting gifts worth hundreds of pounds from young men who look like Caesar Romero.'

'I don't look in the least like Caesar Romero. And I don't see what you can do about it. You took it.'

'I can give it back.'

'A happy way out of the difficulty would be to turn it over to Shorty.'

'That's a wonderful idea. Yes, I'll do that. So you see the stamp does belong to you, Shorty,' said Terry. 'Thank the gentleman, dear.'

'Thanks,' said Lord Shortlands dazedly. Things were happening a little too rapidly tonight for his orderly mind, and he had the sense of having been caught up in a cyclone. He was also conscious of a lurking feeling that there was a catch somewhere, if only he could pin it down.

'You are now able,' said Mike, pointing out the happy ending, 'to tie a can to your spiritual struggles. Your conscience, satisfied that it is being asked to do nothing raw, can spit on its hands and charge ahead without a tremor. Or don't you agree with me?'

'Oh, quite. Oh, certainly. But –'

'Now what?'

'Well, dash it, this stamp's worth fifteen hundred pounds, Desborough says. I can't take fifteen hundred pounds from you, Terry.' This was not actually the catch Lord Shortlands was trying to pin down – that still eluded him – but it was a point that needed to be touched on. 'If you could let me have two hundred as a loan –'

'Nonsense, darling. What's mine is yours.'

'Well, it's extremely kind of you, my dear. I hardly know what to say.'

'Mike's the one you ought to be grateful to.'

'I am. His generosity is princely.'

'Yes,' said Mike. 'What an extraordinarily fine fellow this chap Cardinal is turning out to be. But let's stick to business. The proposal before the meeting is that we pinch this stamp before Spink can get his hooks on it. Carried unanimously, I fancy? Yes, carried unanimously. It only remains, therefore, to decide on the best means to that end. It should not be difficult. A little cunning questioning of Desborough Topping will inform us where Lady Adela is keeping the thing. No doubt in the drawer of her escritoire or somewhere. Having ascertained this, we procure a stout chisel and go to it.'

'But –'

'Now, don't *make* difficulties, Shorty darling,' said Terry maternally. 'You must see that this is the only way. I'll go and question Desborough cunningly.'

She went out, and Lord Shortlands continued to exhibit evidence of the cold foot and the sagging spine. Mike looked at. him solicitously.

'I still note a faint shadow on your brow, Shorty,' he said. 'What seems to be the trouble? Not the conscience again?'

Lord Shortlands had found the catch.

'But, my dear fellow, if Adela finds the drawer of her escritoire broken open and the stamp gone, she'll suspect me.'

'Well, what do you care? You'll simply laugh at her. "What are you going to do about it?" you will say, adding or not adding "Huh?" according to taste. And she will bite her lip in silence.'

'Silence?' said Lord Shortlands dubiously.

'She won't have a thing to say. What can she say?'

'H'm,' said Lord Shortlands, and so joyless was his manner . that Mike felt constrained to pat him on the back.

'Tails up,' he urged.

Lord Shortlands's manner continued joyless.

'It's all very well to say "Tails up". I don't like it. Apart from anything else, I don't believe I could ever bring myself to break open an escritoire drawer with a chisel. *Anybody's* escritoire drawer.'

'My dear Shorty, is that what's worrying you? I shall attend to that, of course.'

'You will?'

'Naturally. It's young men's work.'

'Well, I'm very much obliged to you.'

'Not at all.'

'I wish to goodness Terry would marry you. She'll never get a better husband.'

'Keep telling her that. It's exactly what I've always felt. Has she given you any inkling as to what seems to be the difficulty?'

'Not the slightest.'

The door opened. Terry had returned. She sat down, and Mike noticed that her manner, which had been one of radiant confidence, was now subdued. Lord Shortlands would have noticed it, too, had he been in better condition tonight for noticing things.

'Well?' said Mike.

'Well?' said Lord Shortlands.

'Well,' said Terry. 'I saw Desborough.'

'Did you find out what you wanted?'

'I found out something I didn't want.'

'Less of the mysterious stuff.'

Terry sighed.

'I was only trying to break it gently. If you must have it, Desborough suspects Stanwood.'

'Suspects him?' cried Lord Shortlands.

'What of?' said Mike.

'Of not being Rossiter.'

'But Spink has given him the okay.'

'Yes, and that has made Desborough suspect Spink, too. He thinks it's a plot. "After all," he said, "what do we really know of Spink?" and he quoted authorities to show that in nine cases out of ten the butler at a country house turns out to be one of the Black Onion gang or something. I wish he hadn't read so many detective stories.'

'But what on earth has made him suspect Stanwood?'

'He took him off after dinner to talk stamps, and of course Stanwood knew nothing about stamps and gave it away in the first minute. The way Desborough has figured it out is that Stanwood and Spink are working together to loot the house.

What a pity it is that Stanwood looks so like something out of a crook play. I never saw anything so obviously criminal as his face during dinner.'

'So what steps is he planning to take?'

'I don't know. But a step he has taken is to put the stamp in an envelope and lock it up in the safe.'

There was a silence.

'In the safe?' said Mike at length.

'Yes.'

'Is there a safe?'

'Yes. In the library.'

'Of all silly things to have in a house! Well, this, I admit, is a development which I had not foreseen. I shall have to leave you for a while and ponder apart. You will find me in my room, if you want me. Safes, forsooth!' said Mike bitterly, and went out with knitted brow.

It was clear to him that he had here one of those brainteasers which Sherlock Holmes used to call three-pipe problems, and he made his way to the Blue Room to get his smoking materials.

As he entered, the vast form of Stanwood Cobbold rose from the easy chair.

Chapter 14

Stanwood was not looking his best. Dinner, with its enforced propinquity to a hostess who had scared the daylights out of him at first sight, and the subsequent *tête-à-tête* with Desborough Topping had taken their toll. There had been moments in his life when, with representatives of Notre-Dame and Minnesota walking about on his face or pressing the more jagged parts of their persons into his stomach, Stanwood Cobbold had experienced a certain discomfort, but nothing in his career to date had ever reduced him to such a ruin of a fine young man as the ordeal which had been thrust upon him tonight. Gazing at him, you would have said that his soul had passed through the furnace, and you would have been perfectly correct. Mike's first act, before asking any questions, was to hurry to the chest of drawers, take out a flask and press it upon his friend.

'Thanks,' said Stanwood, handing it back empty. 'Gosh, I needed that. I've had one hell of a time, Mike.'

Mike, having satisfied the humane side of his nature, was now prepared to be stern.

'Well, you asked for it.'

'Who's the little guy with the nose-glasses?'

'Desborough Topping, your hostess's husband.'

'He's been talking stamps to me,' said Stanwood, with a reminiscent shudder.

'Well, what did you think he would do? If you horn into a house pretending to be a stamp collector, and that house contains another stamp collector, you must expect to be talked stamps at.'

'It's the darnedest thing. I don't believe I ever met anyone before who collected stamps. I thought only sissies did. And now I don't seem to meet anyone who doesn't. Kind of looney set-up, don't you think?'

Mike was not to be diverted into an academic discussion of the looniness of the conditions prevailing at Beevor Castle.

'What the devil did you come here for? I told you to stay at the inn till you heard from me.'

'Sure, I know. But I had a feeling that you weren't going to deliver. Seemed to me you had lost your grip. So when Spink came along with his proposition, I was ready to do business.'

'How did you meet Spink?'

'He blew in just after you had left, and we got together. We had known each other before. We used to be buddies over on the other side. He was father's butler.'

'So he told me.'

'Well, I gave him the low-down about the cable and the photographs and asked him if he had anything to suggest, and he said it was a pip. All I had to do was to say I was this bozo Rossiter, and I was set. I would have the run of the joint, and we could fix up the photographs any time that suited me. Naturally I said Check, and he went to the 'phone and called Her Nibs up, and she told him to tell me to come along and join the gang.'

'What did he say about the album?'

'Nothing much. Just that he wanted it.'

'You bet he wanted it. There's a stamp in it worth fifteen hundred pounds.'

'Gosh! Really?'

'Which belongs to Terry. Of course, she can't prove it, and of course Spink, now that you've gone and butted in, can. What you've done, you poor mutt, is to chisel that unhappy child out of fifteen hundred smackers. A girl who has eaten your salt.'

'I don't get this.'

'I'll explain it in words of one syllable,' said Mike, and proceeded to do so. When he had finished, it was plain that Stanwood was feeling the bitter twinges of remorse. You could see the iron twisting about in his soul.

'Why the hell didn't you wise me up about this before?' he said, aggrieved.

'How was I to know you were going to go haywire and come to the castle?'

'Let's get this straight. If Spink has this stamp, old Shortlands won't be able to marry that cook of his.'

'No.'

'Spink will buy her with his gold.'

'Yes.'

Stanwood wagged his head disapprovingly.

'No nice cook ought to marry a man like Spink. Funny I never got on to him. I always thought him a swell guy. I used to go to his pantry dying of thirst, and he would dish out the life saver. How was I to know he was a fiend in human shape? If a fellow's a fiend in human shape,' said Stanwood, with a good deal of justice, 'he ought to act like one. Well, it's pretty clear what your next move is, Mike, old man. Only rough-stuff will meet the situation. You want to chuck all the lessons you learned at mother's knee into the ashcan and get tough. You'll have to swipe that stamp.'

'Yes, I thought of that. But it's locked up in a safe.'

'Then bust the safe.'

'How?'

'Why, get Augustus Robb to do it, of course.'

Mike started. An awed look had come into his face; the sort of look which members of garrisons beleaguered by savages give one another when somebody says: 'Here come the United States Marines.'

'Good Lord! I'd clean forgotten that Augustus used to be a burglar.'

'It'll be pie to him.'

'Did you bring him with you?'

'Sure.'

'Stanwood, old man,' said Mike in a quivering voice, 'I take back all the things I said about you. Forget that I called you a dish-faced moron.'

'You didn't.'

'Well, I meant to. You may have started badly, but you've certainly come through nicely at the finish. Augustus Robb! Of course. The hour has produced the man. It always does. Excuse me a moment. I must go and tell the boys in the back room about this.'

But as he reached the door it opened, and Terry came in, followed by Lord Shortlands.

'We couldn't wait any longer. We had to come and see if you had. . . . Oh, hullo, Stanwood.'

'Hello, Terry. Hiya, Lord Shortlands.'

Terry's eye was cold and reproachful.

'You've made a nice mess of things, Stanwood.'

'Yay. Mike's been telling me. I'm sorry.'

'Too late to be sorry now,' said Lord Shortlands sepulchrally.

His despondency was so marked that Mike thought it only kind to do something to raise his spirits. The method he chose was to utter a piercing 'Whoopee!' It caused Lord Shortlands to leap like a gaffed salmon and Terry to quiver all over.

'Good news,' he said. 'Tidings of great joy. The problem is solved.'

'What!'

'I have everything taped out. It turns out, after all, to be extraordinarily simple. We bust the safe.'

Terry closed her eyes. She seemed in pain.

'You see, Shorty. He always finds the way. We bust the safe.'

112

Lord Shortlands was feeling unequal to the intellectual pressure of the conversation.

'Can you – er – bust safes?'

'Myself, no. But I have influential friends. We send for Augustus Robb.'

'Augustus Robb?'

'Who is this mysterious Augustus Robb you're always talking about,' asked Terry.

'My man,' said Stanwood. 'He's downstairs with the rest of the help.'

'And before he got converted at a revival meeting,' said Mike, 'he used to be a burglar.'

Terry's face had lost its drawn look. It had become bright and animated.

'How absolutely marvellous! Was he a good burglar?'

'One of the very best. There was a time, he gave me to understand, when the name of Robb was one to conjure with in the Underworld.'

'Rather a good name for a burglar – Robb.'

'I told him that myself, and I thought it very quick and clever of me. Very quick and clever of you, too. If you're as good as that, we shall have many a lively duel of wit over the fireside. According to Augustus, the same crack has been made by fifty-six other people, but I don't see that that matters. You and I can't expect to be the only ones in the world with minds like rapiers.'

'But if he's got religion, he'll probably have a conscience.'

'We shall be able to overcome it. He will see the justice of our cause, which, of course, sticks out like a sore thumb, and, apart from that, he's a snob. He will be quite incapable of resisting an Earl's appeal. Have you a coronet, Shorty?'

'Eh? Coronet? Oh, yes, somewhere about.'

'Then stick it on when you're negotiating with him, with a rakish tilt over one eye, and I don't think we shall have any trouble.'

But there was no time to secure this adventitious aid. He had scarcely finished speaking when a hearty fist banged on the door, a hearty voice cried 'Hoy!' and the man whom the hour had produced appeared in person.

'Well, cocky. I just came to see how you was getting al – Why, 'ullo,' said Augustus Robb, pausing on the threshold and surveying the mob scene before him. 'I didn't know you had company, chum. Excuse me.'

He made as if to withdraw, but Mike, leaping forward, seized his coat in a firm grip.

'Don't be coy, Augustus. Come right in. You're just the fellow we want. Your name was on our lips at that very moment, and we were on the point of sending the bloodhounds out in search of you. So you've got to Beevor Castle, after all?'

'Yus, though it went against my conscience.' Augustus Robb drew Mike aside and spoke in a hoarse whisper. 'Do they know about it?'

'Oh, yes. All pals here.'

'That's all right, then. Wouldn't have wanted to make a bloomer of any description. Nice little place you've got here,' said Augustus Robb, speaking less guardedly. 'Done you proud, ain't they? Where does that window look out on? The rose garden? Coo! Got a rose garden, 'ave they? Every luxury, as you might say. Well, enjoy it while you can, chum. It won't be long before you're bunged out on your blinkin' ear.'

'Why do you strike this morbid note?'

'Just a feeling I 'ave. The wicked may flourish like a ruddy bay tree, as the Good Book says, but they always cop it in the end.'

'You rank me among the wicked?'

'Well, you're practisin' deceit, ain't you? Living a lie, I call it. There's a tract I'd like you to read, bearing on that, only coming away in a hurry I left me tracts behind.' Augustus Robb cocked an appreciative eye at Terry and, placing a tactful hand before his mouth, spoke out of the corner of the latter in his original hoarse whisper. 'Who's the little bit of fluff?' he asked.

'You recall me to my duties as a host, Augustus,' said Mike. 'Come and get acquainted. Stanwood, of course, you know. But I don't think you have met Lord Shortlands.'

'How do you do, Mr Robb?'

'Pip-pip, m'lord,' said Augustus Robb, visibly moved.

114

'Welcome – ah – to Beevor Castle.'

'Thanks, m'lord. Seems funny bein' inside here, m'lord. Only seen the place from the outside before, m'lord. Cycled here one Bank Holiday, when I was a lad. Took sandwiches.'

'It must have seemed strange, too,' said Mike, 'coming in by the door. Your natural impulse, I imagine, would have been to climb through the scullery window.'

Augustus Robb, displeased, pleaded for a little tact, and Mike apologized.

'Sorry. But it's a subject we shall be leading up to before long. And this is Lord Shortlands's daughter, Lady Teresa Cobbold, whose name will be familiar to you from my correspondence. Thank you, Augustus,' said Mike, acknowledging the other's wink and upward jerk of the thumbs. 'I'm glad you approve. Do sit down. You will find this chair comfortable.'

'Have a cushion, Mr Robb,' said Terry.

'A cigar?' said Lord Shortlands.

'I'd offer you a drink,' said Mike, 'but Stanwood has cleaned me out.'

Too late, he saw that he had said the wrong thing. Augustus Robb, the ecstasy of finding himself in such distinguished company having induced in him a state of mind comparable to the Nirvana of the Buddhists, had been leaning back in his chair with a soft, contented smile on his lips. This statement brought him up with a jerk, his face hard.

'Ho! So you've been drinking again, have you?' he observed austerely, giving Stanwood a stern look. 'After all I said. All right, I wash me 'ands of you. If you want a 'obnailed liver, carry on, cocky. And if eventually you kick the bucket, what of it? I don't care. It's a matter of complete in-bleedin'-difference to me.'

This generous outburst brought about one of those awkward pauses. Mike looked at Lord Shortlands. Terry looked at Stanwood. She also frowned significantly, and Stanwood took the hint. His was not a very high I.Q., but even he had realized the vital necessity of conciliating this man.

'Gee, Augustus, I'm sorry.'

Augustus Robb sucked his front tooth.

'I'm sure he won't do it again, Mr Robb.'

Augustus Robb preserved an icy silence.

'Augustus,' said Mike gently, 'Lady Teresa Cobbold is speaking to you. She is, of course, the daughter of the fifth Earl of Shortlands, connected on her mother's side with the Byng-Brown-Byngs and the Foster-Frenches. The Sussex Foster-Frenches, not the Devonshire lot.'

It was as if Augustus Robb had come out of a swoon and was saying 'Where am I?' He blinked at Terry through his horn-rimmed spectacles, seeming to drink in her Byng-Brown-Byng-ness, and looked for a moment as if he were about to rise and bow. The cold sternness died out of his eyes, and he inclined his head forgivingly.

'Right ho. Say no more about it.'

'That's the way to talk. Everything hotsy-totsy once more? Fine. Sure you're quite comfortable, Augustus?'

'Another cushion, Mr Robb?' said Terry.

'How's the cigar?' said Lord Shortlands.

And Stanwood, showing an almost human intelligence, muttered something about how he had long thought of taking the pledge and would start looking into the matter tomorrow.

'Well, Augustus,' said Mike, satisfied with the success of the preliminary operation and feeling that brass tacks could now be got down to, 'as I was saying, you couldn't have come at a more fortunate moment. I did mention that his name was on our lips, didn't I?'

'You betcher,' said Stanwood.

'You betcher,' said Lord Shortlands.

'We were saying such nice things about you, Mr Robb,' said Terry. She knew she was being kittenish, but there are moments when a girl must not spare the kitten.

Augustus Robb choked on his cigar. His head was swimming a little.

'The fact is, Augustus, we are in a spot, and only you can get us out of it. When I say "us", I allude primarily to the fifth Earl of Shortlands, whose family, as you probably know, came over with the Conqueror. You have it in your power to do the fifth Earl of Shortlands a signal service, and one which he will never forget. Years hence, when he drops in at the

116

House of Lords, he will find himself chatting with other Earls – and no doubt a few Dukes – and the subject of selfless devotion will come up. Stories will be swapped, here an Earl speaking of some splendid secretary or estate agent, there a Duke eulogizing his faithful dog Ponto, and then Lord Shortlands will top the lot with his tale of you. "Let me tell you about Augustus Robb," he will say, and the Dukes and Earls will listen spell-bound. "Coo!" they will cry, when he has finished. "Some fellow, that Augustus Robb. I'd like to meet him."'

Augustus Robb took off his horn-rimmed spectacles and polished them. His head was swimming more than ever, and his chest had begun to heave. His was a life passed mainly in the society of men who spoke what came into their simple minds, and the things that came into their simple minds were nearly always rude. It was not often that he was able to listen to his sort of thing.

'In a nutshell,' said Mike, 'Lord Shortlands is being beset by butlers. Have you met the butler here, the man Spink?'

A shudder ran through Augustus Robb.

'Yus,' he said. 'Have you?'

'I have indeed.'

'And prayed for him?'

'No, I haven't got around to that yet.'

'I'm surprised to hear it. I wouldn't have thought you could have been in his presence five minutes without being moved to Christian pity.'

'You find him a hard nut?'

'A lost scoffer,' said Augustus Robb severely, 'whose words are as barbed arrows winged with sinfulness. If ever there was an emissary of Satan with side whiskers, it's him.'

He had got what is called in Parliamentary circles the feeling of the House. It would scarcely have been possible for these words to have gone better. Lord Shortlands snorted rapturously. Stanwood said: ''At's the stuff!' Terry lit up the speaker's system with a dazzling smile, and Mike patted him on the back.

'That's great,' said Mike. 'If that's the way you feel, we can get down to cases.'

In Augustus Robb's demeanour, as he listened to the story of the stamp, there exhibited itself at first only a growing horror. Three times in the course of the narrative he said 'Coo!' and each time, as the inkiness of the butler's soul became more and more plain to him, with a greater intensity of repulsion. There seemed no question that Mike was holding his audience, and had its sympathy.

But when, passing from his preamble, he went on to outline what it was that Augustus Robb was expected to do, the other's aspect changed. It was still instinct with horror, but a horror directed now not at Mervyn Spink but at one whom it was evident that he had mentally labelled as The Tempter. He rose, swelling formidably.

'What! You're asking me to bust a pete?'

'A safe,' corrected Lord Shortlands deferentially.

'Well, a pete is a safe, ain't it?'

'Is it?'

'Of course it is,' said Mike. 'Safes are always called petes in the best circles. Yes, that's the scheme, Augustus. How about it?'

'No!'

Mike blinked. The monosyllable, spoken at the fullest extent of a good man's lungs, had seemed to strike him like a projectile.

'Did you say No?'

'Yus, no.'

'But it'll only take a few minutes of your time.'

'No, I tell you. A thousand times no.'

'Not even to oblige an Earl?'

'Not even to oblige a dozen ruddy Earls.'

Mike blinked again. He glanced round at his colleagues, and drew little comfort from their deportment. Lord Shortlands was looking crushed and desolate. Terry's eyes were round with dismay. Stanwood Cobbold seemed to be grinding his teeth, which of course is never much use in a crisis of this sort.

'I had not expected this, Augustus,' said Mike reproachfully.

'You knew I was saved, didn't you?'

'Yes, but can't you understand that this is a far, far better thing that we are asking you to do than you have ever done? Consider the righteousness of our cause.'

'Busting a pete is busting a pete, and you can't get away from it.'

'You aren't forgetting that Lord Shortlands's ancestors came over with the conqueror?'

For an instant Augustus Robb seemed to waver.

'This won't please the Foster-Frenches.'

The weakness passed. Augustus Robb was himself again.

'That's enough of that. Stop tempting me. Get thou behind me, Satan, and look slippy about it. Why don't you get behind me?' asked Augustus Robb peevishly.

'And how about the Byng-Brown-Byngs?' said Mike.

Stanwood exploded like a bomb. For some moments he had been muttering to himself, and it had been plain that he was not in sympathy with the conscientious objector.

'What's the good of talking to the fellow? Kick him!'

Mike started. It was a thought.

'Egad, Stanwood, I believe you've got something there.'

'Grab him by the scruff of the neck and bend him over and leave the rest to me.'

'Wait,' said Mike. 'Not in thin evening shoes. Go and put on your thick boots. And you, Terry, had better be leaving us. The situation is one which strong men must thresh out face to face. Or, perhaps, not face to face exactly –'

Augustus Robb had paled. He was essentially a man of peace.

'If there's going to be verlence –'

'There is.'

It was Stanwood who had spoken. In his manner there was no trace now of his former meek obsequiousness. It had all the poised authority which had been wont to mark it in the days when, crouched and menacing, he had waited to plunge against the opposing line.

'You betcher there's going to be verlence. I'll give you two seconds to change you mind.'

Augustus Robb changed it in one.

'Well, right ho,' he said hastily. 'If you put it that way, chum, I suppose I've no option.'

'That's the way to talk.'

'Well spoken, Augustus.'

'But you're overlooking something. It's years since I bust a pete.'

'No doubt the old skill still lingers.'

'As to that, I wouldn't say it didn't. But what you've omitted to take into account, cockies,' said Augustus Robb with gloomy triumph, 'is me nervous system. I'm not the man I was. I wouldn't 'ave the nerve to do a job nowadays without I took a gargle first. And I can't take a gargle, because gargling's sinful. So there you are. It's an am-parce.'

Terry smiled that winning smile of hers.

'You wouldn't mind taking a tiny little gargle to oblige me, Mr Robb?'

'Yus, I would. And it wouldn't be tiny, either. I'd need a bucketful.'

'Then take a bucketful,' said Lord Shortlands.

It was a good, practical suggestion, but Augustus Robb shook his head.

'Those boots, Stanwood,' said Mike. 'Be as quick as you can.'

Augustus Robb capitulated. He had never actually seen Stanwood on the football field, but his imagination was good and he could picture him punting.

'Well, all right. 'Ave it your own way, chums. But no good's going to come of this.'

'Splendid, Augustus,' said Mike. 'We knew you wouldn't fail us. How about tools?'

'I'll have to go to London and fetch 'em, I suppose.'

'You still have the dear old things, then?'

'Yus. I 'adn't the 'eart to get rid of 'em. They're with a gentleman friend of mine that lives in Seven Dials. I'll go and get 'em. More trouble,' said Augustus Robb, and, moving broodingly to the door, was gone.

'Stanwood!' cried Terry. 'You're marvellous! How did you think of it?'

'Oh, it just came to me,' said Stanwood modestly.

'In these delicate negotiations,' explained Mike, 'it often happens that, where skilled masters of the spoken word fail to bring home the bacon, success is achieved by some plain, blunt,

120

practical man who ignores the niceties of diplomacy and goes straight to the root of the matter. The question now arises. How do we procure the needful? We can't very well raid the cellar. It seems to me that the best plan will be for me to run up to London tomorrow with Augustus and lay in supplies.'

'Get plenty,' advised Stanwood.

'I will.'

'And of all varieties,' added Lord Shortlands, who in matters like this was a farseeing man. 'There's no telling what the chap will prefer. Many people, for instance, dislike the taste of whisky. I have never been able to see eye to eye with them, but it is an undoubted fact. Get a good representative mixed assortment, my boy, and put it in my room. He will need a quiet place in which to prepare himself. And anything that's left over,' said Lord Shortlands, a sudden brightness coming into his eyes, 'I can use myself.'

Chapter 15

In every human enterprise, if success is to be achieved, there must always be behind the operations the directing brain. In the matter of breaking open the library safe at Beevor Castle and abstracting the Spanish 1851 *dos reales* stamp, blue unused, it was Mike who had framed the plan of campaign and issued the divisional orders.

These were as follows:

1. *Zero hour to be 1.30 a.m.*

Start the attack earlier, Mike had pointed out, and it might find members of the household awake. Start it later, and it cut into one's night too much. He wanted his sleep, he said, and Lord Shortlands said he wanted his, too.

2. *All units to assemble in the study at 1.15 a.m.*

Because they had to assemble somewhere, and it would be wisest if Augustus Robb, before repairing to the library, were to remove a pane of glass from the study window and make a few chisel marks on the woodwork, thus conveying the suggestion that the job had been an outside one. This ruse was strongly approved of by Lord Shortlands, who did not conceal his opinion that the more outside the job could be made to look, the better.

3. *Lord Shortlands to be O. C. Robb.*

His task was to smuggle Augustus Robb into his bedroom and there ply him with drink until in his, Augustus's, opinion his nerve was back in the mid-season form of the old days. He would then conduct him to the study, reporting there at one-fifteen. This would allow five minutes for a pep talk from the General in charge of operations, eight minutes for the breaking of the window and the chisel marks, and two for getting upstairs. A margin would also be left for kicking Augustus Robb, should he render this necessary by ringing in that conscience of his again.

4. *Stanwood was to go to bed.*

And darned well stay there. Because though it was impossible to say offhand just how, if permitted to be present, he would gum the game, that he would somehow find a way of doing so was certain.

5. *Terry was to go to bed, too.*

Because in moments of excitement she had that extraordinary habit of squeaking like a basketful of puppies, and in any case in an enterprise of this kind girls were in the way. (Seconded by Lord Shortlands, who said that in the mystery thriller which Desborough Topping had given him for his birthday the detective had been seriously hampered in his activities by the adhesiveness of a girl named Mabel, who had hair the colour of ripe wheat.)

6. *Terry was to stop arguing and do as she was told.*

Discussion on this point threatened for a time to become acrimonious, but on Mike challenging her to deny that her hair was the colour of ripe wheat she had been obliged to yield.

Nevertheless, as the clock over the stables struck the hour of

122

one, Terry was lying on the sofa in the study, reading the second of the three volumes of a novel entitled *Percy's Promise*, by Marcia Huddlestone (Popgood and Grooly, 1869). She had found it lying on the table and had picked it up for want of anything better. She was looking charming in pyjamas, a kimono and mules.

At three minutes past the hour Lord Shortlands entered, looking charming in pyjamas, a dressing gown and slippers. His eyes, as always in times of emotion, were protruding, and at the sight of his daughter they protruded still further.

'Good Lord, Terry! What are you doing here?'

'Just reading, darling, to while away the time.'

'But Cardinal said you were to go to bed.'

'So he did, didn't he? Bless my soul, what a nerve that young man has, to be sure. Bed, indeed! Well, you certainly have got a frightful collection of books, Shorty. There wasn't anything in your shelves published later than 1870.'

'Eh? Oh, those aren't mine,' said Lord Shortlands. He spoke absently. While he deplored his child's presence, it had just occurred to him what an admirable opportunity this was for speaking that word in season. 'My old uncle's.'

'Did he like Victorian novels?'

'I suppose so.'

'I believe you do, too. This one was lying on the table, obviously recently perused.'

'Young Cardinal borrowed it, and returned it this afternoon. He said it had given him food for thought. I don't know what he meant. Terry,' said Lord Shortlands, welcoming the cue, 'I've been thinking about young Cardinal.'

'Have you, angel? He rather thrusts himself on the attention, doesn't he?'

'He's a smart chap.'

'Yes. I suppose he would admit that himself.'

'Look at the way he baffled Spink.'

'Very adroit.'

'Brave as a lion, too. Faces Adela without a tremor.'

'What's all this leading up to, darling?'

'Well, I was – er – wondering if by any chance you might be beginning to change your mind about him.'

'Oh, I see.'

'Are you?'

'No.'

'Ho,' said Lord Shortlands, damped.

There was a pause. The thing was not going quite so well as the fifth Earl had hoped.

'Why not?'

'There's a reason.'

'I'm dashed if I can see what it is. I should have thought he would have been just the chap for you. Rich. Good looking. Amusing. And loves you like the dickens. You can tell that by the way he looks at you. It's a sort of – how shall I describe it? –'

'A sort of melting look?'

'That's right. You've got it first shot. A sort of melting look.'

'And your complaint is that it doesn't melt me?'

'Exactly.'

'Well, I'll tell you something, Shorty. I am by no means insensible, as the heroine of *Percy's Promise* would say, to this look you mention. It may interest you to know that it goes through me like a burning dart.'

'It does?' cried Lord Shortlands, greatly encouraged. This was more the sort of stuff he wanted to hear.

'It seems to pump me full of vitamins. It makes me feel as if the sun was shining and my hat was right and my shoes were right and my frock was right and my stockings were right, and somebody had just left me ten thousand a year.'

'Well, then.'

'Not so fast, my pet. Wait for the epilogue. But all the same I'm not going to let myself fall in love with him. I don't feel that I have exclusive rights in that look of his.'

'I don't follow you.'

'I fancy I have to share it with a good many other girls.'

'You mean you think he's one of these – er – flibberty-gibbets?'

'Yes, if a flibbertygibbet is a man who can't help making love to every girl he meets who's reasonably pretty.'

'But he says he's loved you since you were fifteen or whatever it was.'

124

'He has to say something, to keep the conversation going.'

'But what makes you feel like that about him?'

'Instinct. I think young Mike Cardinal is a butterfly, Shorty, the kind that flits from flower to flower and sips. I strongly suspect him of having been flitting and sipping this very afternoon. Did you see him when he came back from the great city?'

'No. I was giving Whiskers his run.'

'Well, I did. We had quite a chat. And the air for yards about him was heavy with some strange, exotic scent, as if he had been having his coat sleeve pawed at for hours by some mysterious exotic female. I'm not blaming him, mind you. It's not his fault that he looks like a Greek god. And if women chuck themselves at his feet, it's only natural that he should pick them up. Still, you can understand my being a little wary. He thrills me, Shorty, but all the time there's a prudent side of me, a sort of Terry Cobbold in spectacles and mittens, that whispers that no good ever comes of getting entangled with Greek gods. I mistrust men who are too good-looking. In short, my heart inclines to Mike Cardinal, but my head restrains me. I suppose I feel about him pretty much as Mrs Punter feels about Spink.'

Lord Shortlands puffed unhappily.

'Well, I think you're making a great mistake.'

'So do I – sometimes.'

'About that scent. He probably rubbed up against some woman.'

'That is what I fear.'

'You ought to marry him.'

'Why do you want me to so much?'

'Well, dash it, I like the chap.'

'So do I.'

'And have you considered what's going to happen after this fellow Robb has got that stamp? I get married and go off and leave you here alone with Adela – if, as you say, and I think you're right, Clare's going to collar Blair. You'll hate it. You'll be miserable, old girl. Why don't you marry the chap?'

The picture he had drawn of a Shorty-less Beevor Castle had not failed to make its impression on Terry. It was something she had not thought of. She was considering it with a frown, when the door opened and Mike came in.

Mike was looking tense and solemn. He was a young man abundantly equipped with what he called *sang froid* and people who did not like him usually alluded to as gall, but tonight's operations were making him feel like a nervous impresario just before an opening. In another quarter of an hour the curtain would be going up, and the sense of his responsibility for the success of the venture weighed upon him. At the sight of Terry and of a Lord Shortlands unaccompanied by Augustus Robb he started visibly.

'What are you doing here?' he demanded sternly. 'You're supposed to be in bed.'

'I know. I got up. I want to watch. I've never seen a pete busted before.'

'One wishes to keep the women out of this.'

'Well, one won't.'

'Now I know what the papers mean when they talk about the headstrong modern girl.'

'Avid for sensation.'

'Avid, as you say, for sensation. Well, it's lucky you're going to get an indulgent husband.'

'Am I?'

'I think so. I've got a new system. Where's Augustus?'

'Up in Shorty's room, I suppose.'

'Then why aren't you with him, Shorty? Staff work, staff work. We must have staff work.'

Lord Shortlands spoke plaintively.

'He told me to go away. I didn't want to, but he said my watching him made him nervous. He seems a very highstrung sort of chap.'

'How was he getting on?'

'All right, it seemed to me.'

'Well, you had better go and fetch him.'

'Can't you?'

'No. I want to have a word with Terry.'

Lord Shortlands, on whom the strain was beginning to tell, ran a fevered hand through his grizzled hair, and whispered something about wishing he could have a drink.

126

This surprised Mike.

'Haven't you had one? Didn't you share Augustus's plenty?'

'He wouldn't let me. He said it was sinful. And, when I pressed the point, he threatened to bounce a bottle on my head. I would give,' said Lord Shortlands spaciously, 'a million pounds for a drink.'

'I can do you one cheaper than that,' said Mike. 'Skim up to my room, feel at the back of the top right-hand drawer of the chest of drawers, and you will find a flask full of what you need. Help yourself and leave twopence on the mantelpiece.'

He went to the door and closed it after his rapidly departing host.

'Alone at last,' he said.

Terry's gentle heart had been touched by a father's distress.

'Poor old Shorty!'

'Yes.'

'He really isn't fit for this sort of thing.'

'No.'

'His high blood pressure –'

Mike took her gently by the elbow and led her to a chair. He deposited her lovingly in its depths and seated himself on the arm.

'When I said "Alone at last",' he explained, 'I didn't mean that now was our chance to discuss Shorty's blood pressure. The time to do that will be later on, when we are sitting side by side before the fire in our little home. "Let's have a long talk about Shorty's blood pressure," you will say, and I shall reply, "Yes, let's." But for the moment there are weightier matters on the agenda paper. When I came into the room just now, I overheard your father make a very pregnant remark.'

'Eavesdropping, eh?'

'I see no harm in dropping a few eaves from time to time. People do it behind screens on the stage, and are highly thought of. He was saying: "Why don't you marry the chap, you miserable little fathead?"'

'He didn't call me a fathead.'

'He should have done. Was he alluding to me?'

'He was.'

'What a pal! How did the subject come up?'

'He had been asking me why I wouldn't marry you.'

'Now, there's a thing I've been trying to figure out for weeks, and I believe I've got it. I see you've been reading *Percy's Promise*. I skimmed through it last night, and it has given me food for thought. It has suggested to me this new system of which I spoke just now. I see now that I have not been handling my wooing the right way.'

'No?'

'No. I have been too flip. Amusing, yes. Entertaining, true. But too flip. They did these things better in 1869. Have you got to the part where Lord Percy proposes to the girl in the conservatory?'

'Not yet.'

'I will read it to you. Try to imagine that it is I who am speaking, because he puts in beautiful words just what I want to say. Ready?'

'If you are.'

'Then here we go. "It has been with a loving eye, dearest of all girls, that I have watched you grow from infancy to womanhood. I saw how your natural graces developed, and how by the sweetness of your disposition you were possessing yourself of a manner which I, who have seen courts, must be allowed to pronounce perfect. It is not too much to say that I am asking a gift which any man, of whatever exalted rank, would be proud to have; that there is no position, however lofty which you would not grace; and that I yield to no one in the resolution make that home happy which it is in your power to give me. You slightest wish shall be gratified, your most trifling want shall be anticipated." How's that?'

'It's good.'

'Let's try some more. "Dearest, you are breaking a heart that beats only for you, I know that I am not one for whom nature has made a royal road to the hearts of women. You would feel for me if you knew the envy with which I regard those who are so favoured. If I do not look, if I do not speak as a lover ought to do, it is not, heaven knows, because love is wanting. The pitcher may be full of good wine, but for that very reason it flows with difficulty. It is hard indeed that eloquence should be denied to one who is pleading for his very

128

life. I love you, I love you, I love you. Dearest, can you never love me?'" I don't know why he beefed about not being eloquent. Some steam there. How's it coming? Are you moved?'

'Not much.'

'Odd. Percy's girl was. It was at that point that he swung the deal. "'You do not answer,' he cried, drawing her close to him, 'but your silence speaks for you as sweetly as any words. May I take my happiness for granted, love? Your cheek is white, but I will change that lily to a rose.' So saying, he pressed his lips to hers and she, with a low, soft cry, half sigh, half sob, returned his kiss. And thus they plighted troth." You can't get around a definite statement like that. Boy got girl. No question about it. But in my case Boy doesn't?'

'No.'

'You didn't give a low, soft cry, half sigh, half sob, without my noticing it?'

'No.'

'Then I think I see where the trouble lies. Percy, according to the author, had a "flowing beard," which he appears to have acquired – honestly, one hopes – at the early age of twenty-four. We shall have to wait till I have a flowing beard. It would seem to be an essential. I'll start growing one tomorrow.'

'I wouldn't. Shall I tell you why I'm not moved?'

'It's about time you made some official pronouncement.'

'Well. . . . Have you go to sit on the arm of this chair?'

'Not necessarily. I just wanted to be handy, in case the moment arrived for changing that lily to a rose. However, I will move across the way. Now, then.'

Terry hesitated.

'Proceed,' said Mike encouragingly.

'It's going to sound rather crazy, I'm afraid.'

'Never mind. Start gibbering. Why won't you marry me?'

'Well, if you really want to know, because you're too frightfully goodlooking.'

'Too – what?'

'Too dazzlingly handsome. I told you it was going to sound crazy.'

There was a long silence. Mike seemed stunned.

'Crazy?' he said at length. 'It's cuckoo. Girls have been slapped into padded cells for less. You wouldn't call me handsome?'

'You're like something out of a super-film. Haven't you noticed it yourself?'

'Never. Just a good, serviceable face, I should have said.'

'The face that launched a thousand ships. Go and look in the glass.'

Mike did so. He closed one eye, peered intently and shook his head.

'I don't get it. It's a nice face. A kind face. A face that makes you feel how thoroughly trustworthy and reliable I am. But nothing more.'

'It's the profile that stuns. Look at yourself sideways.'

'What do you think I am? A contortionist?' Mike moved away from the mirror. His air was still that of a man who is out of his depth. 'And that's really why you won't marry me?'

'Yes.'

'Well, I was expecting something pretty unbalanced, but nothing on this stupendous scale. You surpass yourself, my young breath-taker. I think I see what must have happened. Leaning out of that schoolroom window during your formative years, you overbalanced and fell on your fat little head.'

'It's nice of you to try to find excuses.'

'It's the only possible explanation. My child, you're *non compos*.'

'It isn't *non compos*-ness. It's prudence.'

'But what have you got against goodlooking men?'

'I mistrust them.'

'Including me?'

'Including you.'

'Then you're a misguided little chump.'

'All right, I'm a misguided little chump.'

'My nature is pure gold, clear through.'

'That's your story?'

'And I stick to it. You won't change your mind?'

'No.'

Mike breathed a little stertorously.

'I suppose it would be a breach of hospitality if I socked my hostess's sister in the eye?'

130

'The county would purse its lips.'

'Darn these hidebound conventions. Well how much of a gargoyle has a man got to be before you will consider him as a mate? If I looked like Stanwood –?'

'Ah!'

'Well, I don't suppose I shall ever touch that supreme height. But if I pursue the hobby of amateur boxing, to which I am greatly addicted, it is possible that some kindly fist may some day bestow on me a cauliflower ear or leave my nose just that half inch out of the straight which makes all the difference. If I come to you later with the old beezer pointing sou'-sou'-west, will you reconsider?'

'I'll give the matter thought.'

'We'll leave it at that, then. All this won't make any difference to my devotion, of course. I shall continue to love you.'

'Thanks.'

'Quite all right. A pleasure. But I do think Shorty ought to kick in three guineas and have your head examined by some good specialist. It would be money well spent. Ah, Shorty,' said Mike, as the fifth Earl entered, looking much refreshed. 'Glad to see you once more my dear old stag at eve. Do you know what your daughter Teresa has just been telling me? She says she won't marry me because I'm too good looking.'

'No!'

'Those were her very words, spoken with a sort of imbecile glitter in her eyes. The whole thing is extraordinarily sad. But why are you still alone? What have you done with Augustus?'

'I can't find him.'

'Wasn't he in your room?'

'No. He's gone.'

'Perhaps he went to the library,' suggested Terry.

Mike frowned.

'I guess he did. I never saw such an undisciplined rabble in all my life. I wish people would stick to their instructions and not start acting on their own initiative.'

'Too bad, Sergeant-Major.'

'Well, what's the good of me organizing you, if you won't stay organized? Let's go to the library and look.'

Terry's theory was proved correct. The missing man was in

131

the library. He was tacking to and fro across the floor with a bottle of *crème de menthe* in his hand.

He greeted them, as they entered, with a rollicking 'Hoy!'

Chapter 16

'Rollicking', indeed, was the only adjective to describe Augustus Robb's whole deportment at this critical moment in his career. That, or its French equivalent, was the word which would have leaped to the mind of the stylist Flaubert, always so careful in his search for the *mot juste*. His face was a vivid scarlet, his eyes gleaming, his smile broad and benevolent. It needed but a glance to see that he was full to the brim of goodwill to all men.

'Come in, cockies,' he bellowed, waving the bottle spaciously, and the generous timbre of his voice sent a chill of apprehension through his audience. In the silent night it had seemed to blare out like the Last Trump.

'Sh!' said Mike.

'Sh!' said Lord Shortlands.

'Sh!' said Terry.

A look of courteous surprise came into the vermilion face of the star of the night's performance.

'' 'Ow do you mean, Sh?' he asked, puzzled.

'Not so loud, Augustus. It's half past one.'

'What about it?'

'You'll go waking people.'

'Coo! That's right. Never thought of that,' said Augustus Robb. He put the bottle to his lips, and drank a deep draught. 'Peppermint, this tastes of,' he said. This was the first time he had come in contact with *crème de menthe*, and he wished to share his discoveries with his little group of friends. 'Yus, pep-hic-ermint.'

It had become apparent to Mike that in framing his plans he had omitted to guard against all the contingencies which might lead to those plans going awry. He had budgeted for an Augustus Robb primed to the sticking point. That the other, having reached his objective, might decide to push on further he had not foreseen. And it was only too manifest that he had done so. Augustus Robb, if not actually plastered, was beyond a question oiled, and he endeavoured to check the mischief before it could spread.

'Better give me that bottle, Augustus.'

'Why?'

'I think you've had enough.'

'Enough?' Augustus Robb seemed amazed. 'Why, I've only just started.'

'Come on, old friend. Hand it over.'

A menacing look came into Augustus Robb's eyes.

'You lay a finger on it, cocky, just so much as a ruddy finger, and I'll bounce it on your head.' He drank again. 'Yus, peppermint,' he said. 'Nice taste. Wholesome, too. I always liked peppermints as a nipper. My old Uncle Fred used to give me them to stop me reciting "Oh, what a tangled web we weave, when first we practise to deceive." Which is what you're doing, chum,' said Augustus Robb, regarding Mike reproachfully. 'Acting a lie, that's what it amounts to. Ananias and Sapphira.'

Lord Shortlands plucked at Mike's elbow. His manner was anxious.

'Cardinal.'

'Hullo?'

'Do you notice anything?'

'Eh?'

'I believe the fellow's blotto.'

'I believe he is.'

'What shall we do?'

'Start operations without delay, before he gets worse. Augustus.'

' 'ULLO?'

'Sh,' said Mike.

'Sh,' said Lord Shortlands.

'Sh,' said Terry.

Their well-meant warning piqued Augustus Robb. That menacing look came into his eyes again.

'What you saying Sh for?' he demanded, aggrieved. 'You

keep on saying Sh. Everybody says Sh. I've 'ad to speak of this before.'

'Sorry, Augustus,' said Mike pacifically. 'It shan't occur again. How about making a start?'

'Start? What at?'

'That safe.'

'What safe?'

'The safe you've come to open.'

'Oh, that one?' said Augustus Robb, enlightened. 'All right, cocky, let's go. 'Ullo.'

'What's the matter?'

'Where's me tools?'

'Haven't you got them?'

'Don't seem to see 'em nowhere about.'

'You can't have lost them.'

Augustus Robb could not concede this.

'Why can't I have lost them? Plumbers lose their tools, don't they? Well, then. Try to talk sense, chum.'

'Perhaps you left them in Shorty's room, Mr Robb,' suggested Terry.

'Now, don't *you* go making silly remarks, ducky. I've never been there.'

'My father's room.'

Augustus Robb turned to the fifth Earl, surprised.

'Is your name Shorty?'

'Shorty is short for Shortlands,' Mike explained.

'Shorty short for Shortlands,' murmured Augustus Robb. Then, as the full humour of the thing began to penetrate, he repeated the words with an appreciative chuckle rather more loudly; so loudly, indeed, that the fifth Earl rose a full six inches in the direction of the ceiling and, having descended, clutched at Mike's arm.

'Can't you stop him making such a noise?'

'I'll try.'

'Adela is not a heavy sleeper.'

Mike saw that he had overlooked something else in framing his plans. Lady Adela Topping should have been given a Mickey Finn in her bedtime glass of warm milk. It is just these small details that escape an organizer's notice.

134

'I think he's subsiding,' he said. And indeed Augustus Robb, who had been striding about the room with an odd, lurching movement, as if he were having leg trouble, had navigated to a chair and was sitting there, looking benevolent and murmuring 'Shorty short for Shortlands' in a meditative undertone, like a parrot under a green baize cloth. 'Rush along and see if those tools are in your room.'

Lord Shortlands rushed along, and a strange silence fell upon the library. Augustus Robb had stopped his soliloquy, and was sitting with bowed head. As he raised it for a moment in order to refresh himself from the bottle, Terry touched Mike's arm.

'Mike.'

'Yes, love?'

'Look,' whispered Terry, and there was womanly commiseration in her voice. 'He's crying!'

Mike looked. It was even as she had said. A tear was stealing down behind the hornrimmed spectacles.

'Something the matter, Augustus?' he asked.

Augustus Robb wiped away the pearly drop.

'Just thinking of 'Er, cocky,' he said huskily.

' 'Er?'

'The woman I lost, chum.'

Mike felt profoundly relieved.

'It's all right,' he whispered to Terry, 'The quiet, sentimental stage.'

'Oh, is that it?'

'That's it. Let us hope it persists, because the next one in rotation is the violent. I didn't know you'd lost a woman, Augustus. Where did you see her last?'

'I didn't. She wasn't there.'

'Where?'

'At the blinking registry office. I suppose it's never occurred to you, cocky, to ask yourself why I'm a solitary chip drifting down the river of life, as the saying is. Well, I'll tell you. I was once going to marry a good woman, but she didn't turn up.'

'That was tough.'

'You may well say it was tough.'

'What a shame, Mr Robb.'

'And *you* may say "What a shame, Mr Robb," ducky. No, she didn't turn up. I'd confessed my past to her the night before, and she had seemed to forgive, but she must have slep' on it and changed her mind, because the fact remains that I waited a couple of hours at the Beak Street registry office and not a sign of her.'

'An unpleasant experience. What did you do?'

'I went and had a sarsaparilla and a ham sandwich and tried to forget. Not that I ever 'ave forgot. The memory of her sweet face still gnaws my bosom like a flock of perishing rats.'

Mike nodded sympathetically.

'Women are like that.'

The slur on the sex offended Augustus Robb's chivalry.

'No, they aren't. Unless they are, of course,' he added, for he was a man who could look at things from every angle. 'And yet sometimes,' he said, finishing the *crème de menthe* thoughtfully, 'I wonder if maybe she wasn't a mere tool of Fate, as the expression is. You see, there's a Beak Street registry office and a Meek Street registry office, and a Greek Street registry office, and who knows but what she may have gone and got confused? What I mean, how am I to know that all the time I was waiting at Beak Street she mayn't have been waiting at Meek Street?'

'Or Greek Street.'

'R. It's the sort of thing might easily happen.'

'Didn't you think of asking her?'

'Yus. But too late. The possibility of there having been some such what you might call misunderstanding didn't occur to me till a week or two later, and when I nipped round to her lodgings she'd gorn, leaving no address. And a couple of days after that I had to go to America with an American gentleman who I'd took service with, so there we were, sundered by the seas. Sundered by the ruddy seas,' he added, to make his meaning clearer. 'And I've never seen her since.'

A silence fell. Mike and Terry, disinclined for chatter after the stark human story to which they had been listening, sat gazing at Augustus Robb in mute sympathy, and Augustus Robb, except for an occasional soft hiccough, might have been a statue of himself, erected by a few friends and admirers.

Presently he came to life, like a male Galatea.

'Broke my blinking 'eart, that did,' he said. 'If I was to tell you how that woman could cook steak-and-kidney pudding, you wouldn't believe me. Melted in the mouth.'

'It's a tragedy,' said Terry.

'You're right, ducky. It's a tragedy.'

'You ought to have told it to Shakespeare,' said Mike. 'He could have made a play out of it.'

'R,' said Augustus Robb moodily. He removed his hornrimmed spectacles in order to wipe away another tear, and, re-placing them, looked at his young companions mournfully. 'Yus, it's a tragedy right enough. Lots of aching 'earts you see around you these days. Something chronic. Which reminds me. 'Ow's your business coming along, Mr Cardinal? You and this little party. Thought quite a bit about that, I 'ave. Ever tried kissing her? I've known that to answer.'

Terry started, and there came into her face a flush which Mike found himself comparing, to the latter's disadvantage, to the first faint glow of pink in some lovely summer sky. He asked himself what Lord Percy would have done at such a mo-ment. The answer came readily. He would have spared the loved one's blushes, turning that rose back again to a lily.

'Let's talk about something else,' he suggested.

Augustus Robb's brow darkened. He twitched his chin petu-lantly.

'I won't talk about something else. I don't want any pie-faced young Gawd-'elp-uses tellin' me what to talk about.'

'Read any good books lately, Augustus?'

'Whippersnappers,' said Augustus Robb, after a pause, as if, like Flaubert, he had been hunting for the *mot juste,* and was about to dilate on the theme when Lord Shortlands re-entered, announcing that he had been unable to find the tools.

Augustus Robb turned a cold eye upon him.

'What tools?'

'Your tools.'

Augustus Robb stiffened. It was plain that that last unfortu-nate dip into the *crème de menthe* bottle had eased him im-perceptibly from the sentimental to the peevish stage of intoxication, accentuating his natural touchiness to a dangerous degree.

He directed at Lord Shortlands a misty, but penetrating, stare.

'You let me catch you messing about with my tools, and I'll twist your head off and make you swallow it.'

'But you told me to go and look for them,' pleaded Lord Shortlands.

'I never!'

'Well, he did,' said Lord Shortlands.

Augustus Robb transferred his morose gaze to Mike.

'What's it got to do with him, may I ask?'

'I thought it wisest to start hunting around, Augustus. We want those tools.'

'Well, we've got 'em ain't we? They're under the sofa, where I put 'em, ain't they? Fust thing I done on enterin' this room was to place my tools neatly under the sofa.'

'I see. Just a little misunderstanding.'

'I don't like little misunderstandings.'

'Here you are. All present and correct.'

Augustus Robb took the bag of tools absently. He was glaring at Lord Shortlands again. For some reason he seemed to have taken a sudden dislike to that inoffensive peer.

'Earls!' he said disparagingly, and it was plain that, by some process not easily understandable, the *crème de menthe* had turned this once staunch supporter of England's aristocracy into a republican with strong leanings towards the extreme left. 'Earls aren't everything. They make me sick.'

'Earls are all right, Augustus,' said Mike, trying to check the drift to Moscow.

'No, they ain't,' retorted Augustus Robb hotly. 'Swanking about and taking the bread out of the mouths of the widow and the orphan. And, what's more, I don't believe he's a ruddy Earl at all.'

'Yes, he is. He'll show you his coronet tomorrow, and you can play with it, Augustus.'

'Mr Robb.'

'I'm sorry.'

'You well may be. Augustus, indeed! If there's one thing I

don't 'old with, it's familiarity. I've had to speak to young Cobbold about that. I may not be an Earl, but I have my self-respect.'

'Quite right, Mr Robb,' said Terry.

'R,' said Augustus Robb.

Lord Shortlands, as if feeling that it had taken an embarrassing turn, changed the conversation.

'I stopped outside Adela's door and listened,' he said to Mike. 'She seemed to be asleep.'

'Good.'

'Who's Adela?' asked Augustus Robb.

'My daughter.'

Augustus Robb frowned. He knew that for some reason his mind was slightly under a cloud, but he could detect an obvious misstatement when he heard one.

'No, she ain't. This little bit is your daughter.'

'There are three of us, Mr Robb,' explained Terry. 'Three little bits.'

'Ho,' said Augustus Robb in the manner of one who, though unconvinced, is too chivalrous to contradict a lady. 'Well, let's all go up and 'ave a talk with Adela.'

'Later, don't you think?' suggested Mike, touched by Lord Shortlands's almost animal cry of agony. 'After you've attended to that safe. It's over by the window.'

'To the right of the window,' said Terry.

'Over there by the window, slightly to the right,' said Lord Shortlands, clarifying the combined message beyond the possibility of mistake.

'R,' said Augustus Robb, comprehending. 'If you'd told me that before, we shouldn't have wasted all this . . . OUCH!'

His three supporters leaped like one supporter.

'Sh!' said Mike.

'Sh!' said Lord Shortlands.

'Sh!' said Terry.

Augustus Robb glared balefully.

'You say, 'Sh' again, and I'll know what to do about it. Touch of cramp, that was,' he explained. 'Ketches me sometimes.'

He heaved himself from his chair, the bag of tools in his

139

hand. After doing a few simple calisthenics to prevent a recurrence of the touch of cramp, he approached the safe and tapped it with an experimental forefinger. Then he sneered at it openly.

'Call this a safe?'

The loftiness of his tone encouraged his supporters greatly. Theirs was the lay outlook, and to them the safe appeared quite a toughish sort of safe. It was stimulating to hear this expert speak of it with so airy a contempt.

'You think you'll be able to bust it?' said Mike.

Augustus Robb gave a short, amused laugh.

'Bust it? I could do it with a sardine opener. Go and get me a sardine opener,' he said, jerking an authoritative thumb at Lord Shortlands, whom he seemed to have come to regard as a sort of plumber's mate. 'No, 'arf a mo'.' He scrutinized the despised object more closely. 'No, it ain't sporting. Gimme a hairpin.'

Lord Shortlands, frankly unequal to the situation, had withdrawn to the sofa, and was sitting on it with his head between his hands. Mike, too, was at a loss for words. It was left to Terry to try to reason with the man of the hour.

'Don't you think you had better use your tools, Mr Robb?' she said, smiling that winning smile of hers. 'It seems a pity not to, after you went to all the trouble of going to London for them.'

Augustus Robb, though normally clay in the hands of pleading Beauty, shook his head.

'Gimme a hairpin,' he repeated firmly.

There came to Mike the realization of the blunder he had made in not permitting Stanwood Cobbold to take part in these operations. With his direct, forceful methods, Stanwood was just the man this crisis called for. He endeavoured to play an understudy's role, though conscious of being but a poor substitute.

'That'll be all of that,' he said crisply and authoritatively. 'We don't want any more of this nonsense. Cut the comedy, and get busy.'

It was an error in tactics. The honeyed word might have

140

softened Augustus Robb. The harsh tone offended him. He drew himself up haughtily.

'So that's the way you talk, is it? Well, just for that I'm going to chuck the ruddy tools out of the ruddy window.'

He turned and raised the hand that held the bag. He started swinging it.

'Mike!' cried Terry.

'Stop him!' cried Lord Shortlands.

Mike sprang forward to do so. Then suddenly he paused.

The reason he paused was that he had heard, from the corridor outside, a female voice uttering the words 'Who is there?' and it had chilled him to the marrow. But it was an unfortunate thing to have done, for it left him within the orbit of the swinging bag. Full of hard instruments with sharp edges, it struck him on the side of the face, and he reeled back. The next moment there was a crash, sounding in many of its essentials like the end of the world. Augustus Robb had released the bag, and it had passed through the window with a rending noise of broken glass. A distant splash told that it had fallen into the moat.

'Coo!' said Augustus Robb, sobered.

Terry gave a cry.

'Oh, Mike! Are you hurt?'

But Mike had bounded from the room, banging the door behind him.

Chapter 17

To the little group he had left in the library this abrupt departure seemed inexplicable. Intent on their own affairs, they had heard no female voice in the corridor, and for some moments they gazed at each other in silent bewilderment.

Lord Shortlands was the first to speak. More and more during the recent proceedings he had been wishing himself elsewhere, and now that the chief executive had created a deadlock by recklessly disposing of his tools there seemed nothing to keep him.

'I'm going to bed,' he announced.

'But what made him rush off like that?' asked Terry.

Augustus Robb had found a theory that seemed to cover the facts.

'Went to bathe his eye, ducky. Nasty one he stopped. Only natural his first impulse would be to redooce the swelling. Coo! I wouldn't have had a thing like that happen for a hundred quid.'

'Oh, Shorty, do you think he's hurt?'

Lord Shortlands declined to be drawn into a discussion of Mike's injuries. He liked Mike, and in normal circumstances would have been the first to sympathize, but there had just come to him the stimulating thought that, even after Augustus Robb had had his fill, there must still be quite a bit of the right stuff in his room, and he yearned for it as the heart yearns for the waterbrooks. With the golden prospect of a couple of quick ones before him, it is difficult for an elderly gentleman with high blood pressure, who has been through what the fifth Earl of Shortlands had so recently been through, to allow his mind to dwell on the black eyes of young men who are more acquaintances than friends.

'Good night,' he said, and left them.

Augustus Robb continued to suffer the pangs of remorse.

'No, not for a thousand million pounds would I 'ave 'ad a thing like that 'appen,' he said, regretfully. 'When I think of all the blokes there are that I'd enjoy dotting in the eye, it do seem a bit 'ard that it 'ad to be Mr Cardinal who copped it. A gentleman that I 'ave the highest respect for.'

Terry turned on him like a leopardess.

'You might have killed him!'

'I wouldn't go so far as to say that, ducky,' Augustus Robb demurred. 'Just a simple slosh in the eye, such as so often occurs. 'Owever, I'm glad to see you takin' it to 'eart so much, because it shows that love has awakened in your bosom.'

Terry's indignation had waned. Her sense of humour was seldom dormant for long.

'Does it, Mr Robb?'

142

'Sure sign, ducky. You've been acting silly, trying to 'arden your heart to Mr Cardinal like Pharaoh in the Good Book when all those frogs come along.' He raised the *crème de menthe* to his lips and lowered it disappointedly. ' 'Ullo, none left.'

'What a shame.'

'Peppermint,' said Augustus Robb, sniffing. 'Takes me back, that does. Years ago, before you were born or thought of, my old Uncle Fred –'

'Yes, you told me.'

'Did I? Ho. Well, what was we talking about?'

'Frogs.'

'We wasn't, neither. I simply 'appened to mention frogs in passing, like. We was talking about 'ardening 'earts, and I was saying the love had awakened in your bosom. And 'igh time, too. Why don't you go after Mr Cardinal and give him a nice big kiss?'

'That would be a good idea, you think?'

'Only possible course to pursue. He loves you, ducky.'

'What a lot you seem to know about it all. Did he confide in you? Oh, I was forgetting. You read that letter of his.'

'That's right. Found it lying on his desk.'

'Do you always read people's private letters?'

'Why, yus, when I get the chanst. I like to keep abreast of what's going on around me. And I take a particular interest in Mr Cardinal's affairs. There's a gentleman that any young woman ought ot be proud to hitch up with. A fine feller, Mr Cardinal is. What they call in America an ace.'

'Did you like America, Mr Robb?'

'Why, yus, America's all right. Ever tasted corn beef hash?'

'No.'

'You get that in America. And waffles.'

'Tell me all about waffles.'

'I won't tell you all about waffles. I'm telling you about Mr Cardinal. The whitest man I know.'

'Do you know many white men?'

Augustus Robb fell into a brief reverie.

'And planked shad,' he said, coming out of it. 'You get that

143

in America, too. And chicken Maryland. R, and strorberry shortcake.'

'You seem very fond of food.'

'And I'm very fond of Mr Cardinal,' said Augustus Robb, not to be diverted from his theme. 'I keep tellin' young Cobbold he ought to try and be more like 'im. Great anxiety that young Cobbold is to me. His Pop put him in my charge, and I look upon him as a sacred trust. And what 'appens? 'Arf the time he's off somewhere getting a skin full, and the other 'arf he's going about allowing butlers to persuade him to say his name's Rossiter.'

'I didn't know Stanwood drank so very much.'

'Absorbs the stuff like a thirsty flower absorbs the summer rain, ducky. Different from Mr Cardinal. Always moderate 'e is. You could let Mr Cardinal loose in a distillery with a bucket in 'is hand, and he'd come out clear-eyed and rosy-cheeked and be able to say "British Constitution" without 'esitation. Yus, a splendid feller. And that's what makes it seem so strange that a little peanut like you keeps giving him the push.'

'Aren't you getting rather rude, Mr Robb?'

'Only for your own good, ducky. I want to see you 'appy.'

'Oh? I beg your pardon.'

'Granted. You'd be very 'appy with Mr Cardinal. Nice disposition he's got.'

'Yes.'

'Always merry and bright.'

'Yes.'

'Plays the ukelele.'

'You're making my mouth water.'

'*And* kind to animals. I've known Mr Cardinal pick up a pore lorst dog in the street and press it to his bosom, like Abraham – muddy day it was, too – and fetch it along to young Cobbold's apartment and give it young Cobbold's dinner. Touched me, that did,' said Augustus Robb, wiping away another tear. 'Thinkin' of bein' kind to dorgs reminds me of 'Er,' he said, in explanation of this weakness. 'She was always very kind to dorgs. And now 'ow about going after him and givng him that kiss and telling him you'll be his?'

'I don't think I will, Mr Robb.'

144

'Aren't you going to be his?'

'No.'

'Now, don't you be a little muttonhead, ducky. You just 'op along and . . . Oh, 'ullo Mr Cardinal.'

Terry gave a cry.

'Oh, Mike!'

And Augustus Robb, with a sharp 'Coo!' stared aghast at his handiwork. Mike's left eye was closed, and a bruise had begun to spread over the side of his face, giving him the appearance of a man who has been stung by bees.

'Coo, Mr Cardinal, I'm sorry.'

Mike waved aside his apologies.

'Quite all right, Augustus. Sort of thing that might have happened to anyone. Where's Shorty?'

'Gone to bed,' said Terry. She was still staring at his battered face, conscious of strange emotions stirring within her. 'Why did you rush off like that?'

'I heard your sister Adela out in the corridor.'

'Oh, my goodness!'

'It's all right. I steered her off.'

'What did you say to her?'

'Well, I had to think quick, of course. She was headed for the scene of disturbance, and moving well. She asked me what went on, and, as I told you, I had to think quick. You say Shorty's gone to bed? I'm glad. Let him be happy while he can. Poor old Shorty. The heart bleeds.'

'Do go on. What did you say?'

'I'll tell you. I mentioned, I believe, that I had to think quick?'

'Yes, twice.'

'No, only once, but then, like lightning. Well, what happened was this. It seemed to me, thinking quick, that the only way of solving the am-parce was to sacrifice Shorty. Like Russian peasants with their children, you know, when they are pursued by wolves and it becomes imperative to lighten the sledge. It would never have done for your sister to come in here and find Augustus, so I told her that Shorty was in the library, as tight as an owl and breaking windows. "Look what he's done to my eye," I said. I begged her to leave the thing to me. I said I would get him to bed all right. She was very grateful. She thanked me, and said what a comfort I was, and pushed off. You don't seem very elated.'

'I'm thinking of Shorty.'

'Yes, he is a little on my mind, too. I told you that my heart bled for him. Still, into each life some rain must fall. That's one of Spink's gags. Another is that you cannot make an omelette without breaking eggs.'

'I suppose not. And, of course, you had to think quick.'

'Very quick. I feel sure that Shorty, when informed of all the circumstances, will applaud.'

'If not too heartily.'

'If, as you say, not too heartily. He will see that I acted for the best.'

'Let's hope that that will comfort him when he meets Adela tomorrow. And now what do we do for that eye of yours?'

'I was about to take it to bed.'

'It wants bathing in warm water.'

'It wants 'avin' a bit of steak put on it,' said Augustus Robb with decision. His had been a life into which at one time injured eyes had entered rather largely. 'You trot along to the larder, ducky, and get a nice piece of raw steak. Have him fixed up in no time.'

'I think you're right,' said Mike.

'I know I'm right. You can't beat steak.'

'Cruel Sports of the Past – Beating the Steak. I hate to give you all this trouble.'

'No trouble,' said Terry, and departed on her errand of mercy.

Augustus Robb surveyed the eye, and delivered an expert's verdict.

'That's a shiner, all right, chum.'

'It is, indeed, Augustus. I feel as if I'd got mumps.'

'Pity it 'ad to come at a time like this.'

'You consider the moment ill chosen?'

'Well, use your intelligence, cocky. You want to look your best before 'Er, don't you? Women don't like seein' a feller with a bunged-up eye. Puts them off of him. May awake pity, per'aps, but not love. I could tell by the way the little bit of fluff was talkin' just now –'

146

'By "little bit of fluff" you mean –?'

'Why, 'Er.'

'I see. Would it be possible for you, Augustus, in speaking of Lady Teresa Cobbold, not to describe her as a little bit of fluff?'

'Well, if you're so particular. So what was I saying? Ho, yus. When I suggested to her that she should ... Coo! That eye's getting worse. Deepenin' in colour. Reminds me of one a feller give me in our debating society once, when I was speaking in the Conservative interest, him being of Socialistic views ... Where was I?'

'I don't know.'

'I do. I was starting to tell you the advice I give that little bit of fluff.'

'Augustus!'

'Mind you, I can fully understand your being took with 'er. Now I've seen 'er, I can appreciate those sentiments of yours in that letter. She's a cuddly little piece.'

Mike sighed. He had hoped to be able to get through the evening without recourse to Stanwood Cobbold methods, but it was plain that only these methods would serve here.

'Augustus,' he said gently.

' 'Ullo?'

'Doing anything at the moment?'

'No.'

'Then just turn around, will you?'

'Why?'

'Never mind why. I ask this as a favour. Turn around, and bend over a little.'

'Like this?'

'That's exactly right. There!' said Mike, and kicked the inviting target with a vigour and crispness of follow-through which would have caused even Stanwood to nod approvingly.

'Hoy!' cried Augustus Robb.

He had drawn himself to his full height, and would probably have spoken further, but at this moment Terry came in, carrying a bowl of warm water and a plate with a piece of steak on it.

'Here we are,' she said. 'You look very serious, Mr Robb.'

Augustus Robb did not reply. His feelings had been wounded to the quick, and he was full of thoughts too deep for utterance. Adjusting his hornrimmed spectacles and giving Mike another long, silent, reproachful look, he strode from the room. Terry gazed after him, perplexed.

'What's the matter with Mr Robb?'

'I have just been obliged to kick him.'

'Kick him? Why?'

'He spoke lightly of a woman's name.'

'No!'

'I assure you.'

'How is he as a light speaker?'

'In the first rank. He sullied my ears by describing you as a cuddly little piece.'

'But aren't I?'

'That is not the point. If we are to be saved from the disruptive forces that wrecked Rome and Babylon, we cannot have retired porch climbers speaking in this lax manner of girls who are more like angels than anything. It strikes at the very root of everything that makes for sane and stabilized government, "Cuddly little piece", indeed!'

'Bend your head down,' said Terry. She dabbed at his eye with the sponge. 'You know, you're going to be sorry for this.'

'Not unless you drip the water down my neck.'

'For kicking poor Mr Robb, I mean. He's your staunchest friend and firmest supporter. Before you came in, he was urging me to marry you.'

'What!'

'I told you you would be sorry.'

'I'm gnawed by remorse. How can I ever atone? Tell me more.'

'He was very emphatic. He said you were the whitest man he knew, and expressed himself as amazed that a little peanut like me should spurn your suit.'

'God bless him! To think that foot of mine should have jolted that goldenhearted trouser seat. I will abase myself before him tomorrow. But isn't it extraordinary –'

'Don't wiggle. The water's going down your neck.'

'I like it. But isn't it extraordinary how everyone seems to want you to marry me? First Shorty, and now Augustus. It's what the papers call a widespread popular demand. Don't you think you ought to listen to the voice of the People?'

'Now the steak. I'll tie it up with your handkerchief.'

Mike sighed sentimentally.

'How little I thought in those lonely days in Hollywood that a time would come when I would be sitting in your home, with you sticking a steak on my eye!'

'Were you lonely in Hollywood?'

'Achingly lonely.'

'Odd.'

'Not at all. You were not there.'

'I mean, that isn't Stanwood's story. He said you were never to be seen without dozens of girls around you, like the hero of a musical comedy.'

Mike started.

'Did Stanwood tell you that?'

'Yes. He said that watching you flit through the night life of Hollywood always brought to his mind that old song "Hullo, hullo, hullo, it's a different girl again!"'

There came to Mike, not for the first time, the thought that Stanwood Cobbold ought to be in some kind of home.

'Wasn't he right? Didn't you ever go out with girls?'

It is difficult to look dignified with a piece of steak on your left eye, but Mike did his best.

'I may occasionally have relaxed in feminine society. One does in those parts. But what of it?'

'Oh, nothing. I just mentioned it.'

'Hollywood is not a monastery.'

'No, so I've heard.'

'It's a place where women are, as it were, rather thrust upon you. And one has to be civil.'

'There. That's the best I can do. How does it feel?'

'Awful. Like some kind of loathsome growth.'

'I wish you could see yourself in the glass.'

'You're always wanting me to see myself in the glass. Do I look bad?'

'Repulsive. Like a wounded gangster after a beer war.'

'Then now is obviously the moment to renew my suit. You

149

said, if you remember, that if ever there came a time when my fatal beauty took a toss –'

'It's only temporary, I'm afraid. Tomorrow, if you keep the steak on, you'll be just as dazzling as ever. I'll say good night.'

'You would say some silly thing like that at a moment like this. I'm going to keep you here till breakfast time, unless you're sensible.'

'In what way sensible?'

'You know in what way sensible. Terry, you little mutt, will you marry me?'

'No.'

'But why not?'

'I told you why not.'

'I wrote that off as pure delirium. Girls don't turn a man down just because he has regular features.'

'This one does.'

'But you know I love you.'

'Do I?'

'You ought to by this time. You're the only girl in the world, as far as I'm concerned.'

'Not according to Stanwood. He was most explicit on the point. Dozens of them, he told me, night after night, each lovelier than the last and all of them squealing "Oh, *Mike*, darling!"'

'Curse Stanwood! The sort of man who ought to be horse-whipped on the steps of his club.'

'The only trouble is that if you horse-whipped Stanwood on the steps of his club, he would horse-whip you on the steps of yours.'

'I know. That's the catch. It's all wrong that fellows who talk the way Stanwood Cobbold does should be constructed so large and muscular. It doesn't give the righteous a chance.'

'Tell me about these girls.'

'There's nothing to tell. I used to go dancing with them.'

'Ah!'

'You needn't say "Ah!" If you want to dance, you've got to provide youself with a girl, haven't you? How long do you think it would take the management at the Trocadero to bounce a fellow who started pirouetting all over the floor

150

by himself? They're extraordinarily strict about that sort of thing.'

'What's the Trocadero?'

'A Hollywood haunt of pleasure.'

'Where you took your harem?'

'Don't call them my harem! They were mere acquaintances; some merer than others, of course, but all of them very mere. I wish you would expunge Stanwood's whole story from your mind.'

'Well, I can't. I think perhaps I had better tell you something.'

'More delirium?'

'No, not this time. It's something that may make you understand why I'm like this. You asked me yesterday what I had got against men who were too goodlooking, and I said I mistrusted them. I will now tell you why. I was once engaged to one.'

'Good Lord! When?'

'Not so long ago. When I was in that musical comedy. He was the juvenile. Geoffrey Harvest.'

Mike uttered a revolted cry.

'My God! That heel? That worm? That oleaginous louse? Whenever I went to the show, I used to long to leap across the footlights and crown him.'

'You can't deny that he was handsome.'

'In a certain ghastly, greasy, nausea-promoting way, perhaps.'

'Well, that's the point I'm trying to make. I thought him wonderful.'

'You ought to be ashamed of yourself.'

'I am.'

'A juvenile! You fell for a juvenile! And not one of those song-and-hoofing juveniles, whom you can respect, but the kind that looks noble and sings tenor. I am shocked and horrified, young Terry. Whatever made you go and do a fatheaded thing like that?'

'I told you. His beauty ensnared me. But the scales fell from my eyes. He turned out to be a flibbertygibbet.'

'A what was that once again?'

'Shorty's word, not mine.'

'Where does Shorty pick up these expressions?'

'It means a man who can't resist a pretty face. After I had caught him not resisting a few, I broke off the engagement. And I made up my mind that I would never, never, never let myself be swept off my feet by good looks again. So now you understand.'

Mike was struggling with complex emotions.

'But what earthly right have you coolly to assume that I'm like that?'

'Just a woman's intuition.'

'You're all wrong.'

'Perhaps. But there it is. I can't risk it. I couldn't go through it all again. I simply couldn't. You've no idea how a girl feels when she falls in love with a man who lets her down. It's horrible. You suffer torments, and all the while you're calling yourself a fool for minding. It's like being skinned alive in front of an amused audience.'

'I wouldn't let you down.'

'I wonder.'

'Terry! Come on. Take a chance.'

'You speak as if it were a sort of game. I'm afraid I'm rather Victorian and earnest about marriage. I don't look on it as just a lark.'

'Nor do I!'

'You seem to.'

'Why do you say that?'

'Well, don't you think yourself that your attitude all through has been a little on the flippant side?'

Mike beat his breast, like the Wedding Guest.

'There you are! That's it! I felt all along that that was the trouble. You think I'm not sincere, because I clown. I knew it. All the time I was saying to myself "Lay off it, you poor sap! Change the record," but I couldn't. I had to clown. It was a kind of protective armour against shyness.'

'You aren't telling me you're shy?'

'Of course I'm shy. Every man's shy when he's really in love. For God's sake don't think I'm not serious. I love you. I've always loved you. I loved you the first time I saw you.'

Terry, darling, do please believe me. This is life and death.'

Terry's heart gave a leap. Her citadel of defence was crumbling.

'If you had talked like that before –'

'Well, it's not too late, is it? Terry, say it's not too late. Because it will be, if you turn me down now. This is my last chance.'

'What do you mean?'

'I've got to go.'

'Go?'

'Back to Hollywood.'

A cold hand seemed to clutch at Terry's heart. She stared at him dumbly. He had been striding about the room, but now he was at her side, bending over her.

'Oh, Mike,' she whispered.

'Next week at the latest. I found a cable waiting for me in London this afternoon. They want me at the office. The head man's ill, and I've got to go back at once. We shall be six thousand miles apart, and not a chance of ever getting together again.'

'Oh, Mike,' said Terry.

Into Mike's mind there flashed a recent remark of Augustus Robb's. Turning the conversation to the affairs of him, Mike, and what he described as 'this little party', Augustus Robb had asked the pertinent question 'Ever tried kissing her?' adding the words 'I've known that to answer.'

True, Augustus Robb had been considerably more than one over the eight when he had thrown out this *obiter dictum*, but that did not in any way detract from the value of the pronouncement. Many a man's brain gives of its best and most constructive only when it has been pepped up with *crème de menthe*, and something seemed to tell Mike that in so speaking the fellow had been right.

'Terry, darling!'

He took Terry in his arms and kissed her, and it was even as Angustus Robb had said.

It answered.

Book Three

Chapter 18

Stanwood Cobbold sat up in bed and switched on the light. He looked at his watch. The hour was some minutes after two.

Stanwood was a young man whom prolonged association with football coaches had trained to obey orders, and when Mike had told him to go to bed and stay there he had done so without demur. It had pained him to be excluded from the night's doings, but he was fairminded and could quite appreciate the justice of his friend's statement that, if permitted to be present, he would infallibly gum the game. Looking back on his past, he realized that he always had gummed such games as he had taken part in, and there seemed no reason to suppose that he would not gum this one.

But now that he had woken at this particular moment, he could see no possible harm in getting up and stepping along to the library in order to ascertain if all had gone according to plan. By now, if they had run to schedule, the operations must be concluded, and he was consumed with curiosity as to how it had all come out. He also wanted to get a flash of Augustus Robb. A lit-up Augustus Robb should, he considered, provide a spectacle which nobody ought to miss.

He knew where the library was. It was thither that the little guy with the nose-glasses had taken him after dinner to talk about stamps. Slipping on a dressing-gown, he made his way down a flight of stairs and along a passage. A chink of light beneath the door told him that the room was still occupied, and he entered expecting to find a full gathering – a little apprehensive, too, lest that full gathering might turn on him and give him hell for intruding. His mental attitude, as he went in, resembled that of a large, wet dog which steals into a drawing-room, unable to resist the gregarious urge to join the party but none too sure of its welcome.

He was relieved to find only Terry present. She was sitting in a deep chair, apparently wrapped in thought.

'Hiya,' he said in what, if questioned, he would have described as a cautious whisper.

Terry came out of her meditations with a leap and a squeak. She had stayed on after Mike had left to take the basin and plate back to the kitchen. She had promised him that she would go to bed immediately, but she had not done so, for she was loath to break the magic spell which was upon her. Stanwood's voice, which was like the sudden blaring of a radio when you turn the knob too far, gave her a painful shock.

'Stanwood!' she said severely. 'What do you mean by yelling like that?'

'I was whispering,' said Stanwood, aggrieved.

'Well, whisper a bit more *piano*. Come and sit on the sofa and murmur in my ear.'

Stanwood tripped over a rug and upset a small table and came to rest at her side.

'Everything okay?' he murmured hoarsely.

'Yes, wonderful,' said Terry, with shining eyes.

Stanwood was well pleased. The success or non-success of the expedition could not affect him personally, but it had had his sympathy and support.

'That's good. Then Augustus brought home the bacon all right?'

'What?'

'He got the stamp?'

'Oh, the stamp?' It came to Stanwood as a passing thought that his companion seemed a little distrait. 'No, he didn't. There was a hitch.'

'A hitch?'

'Yes. You see that broken window? Mr Robb threw his tools through it, and they are now at the bottom of the moat.'

Stanwood inspected the window. He had been thinking he felt a draught, but had put it down to his imagination.

'What made him do that?' he asked, interested.

'Fretfulness. Mike spoke crossly to him, and it hurt his feelings.'

'Gee! He must have been sozzled.'

'He was.'

'I wish I'd seen him.'

'It was a very impressive spectacle.'

Stanwood found a variety of emotions competing for precedence within him – pity for Lord Shortlands, who had not got his stamp; regret that he himself should have come too late to see Augustus Robb with so spectacular a bun on; but principally bewilderment. He could not square this record of failure with the speaker's ecstatic mood and her statement that conditions were wonderful.

'But you said everything was okay.'

'So it is. Have you ever felt that you were floating on a pink cloud over an ocean of bliss?'

'Sure,' said Stanwood. This illusion had come to him twice in his life; once when Eileen Stoker, knocking the ash off her cigarette, had told him that she would be his, and once, a few years earlier, on the occasion when his inspired place kick had enabled his University to beat Notre-Dame 7–6 in the last half-minute.

'Well, that's how I'm feeling. I'm going to marry Mike, Stanwood.'

'You are? But I thought –'

'So did I. But I changed my mind.'

'Good for you.'

'You're pleased?'

'You betcher.'

There was a silence. Terry, floating on that pink cloud, was thinking her own thoughts with a light in her eyes and a smile on her parted lips, and Stanwood was experiencing once again the surge of relief which had swept over him on the morning when Augustus Robb had first revealed Mike Cardinal's love for a girl who was not Eileen Stoker. As then, he felt that a great weight had been removed from his mind.

'I'm tickled to death,' he said, resuming the conversation after time out for silent rejoicing. 'And I'll tell you why. This removes old Mike from circulation. Great relief, that is.'

'What do you mean?'

'Well, you know how it is when a guy that's as good-looking as he is is knocking around. You get uneasy.'

'Why?'

'Well, you never know what may not happen. I had the idea that he was making a play for Eileen.'

The pink cloud failed to support Terry. It shredded away beneath her, and she plunged into the ocean. And it was not, as she had supposed, an ocean of bliss, but a cold, stinging ocean, full of horrible creatures which were driving poisoned darts into her.

'Don't be an idiot,' she said, and her voice sounded strange and unfamiliar in her ears.

Stanwood proceeded. He was feeling fine.

'It was at that party of mine that I first got thinking that way. I gave a party for Eileen when she hit London, and Mike was there with his hair in a braid, and he seemed to me to be giving her quite a rush. I don't know if you've ever noticed that way he's got of looking at girls? I'd call it a sort of melting look. . . . Yes?'

'Nothing.'

'I thought you spoke.'

'No.'

'Well, he seemed to me to be giving her that look a good deal during the doings, and I didn't like it much. Of course, he had known her in Hollywood –'

'Were they good friends?'

'Oh, sure. Well, that was that, and when she sprang that thing on me –'

'What thing?' said Terry dully.

'Didn't I tell you about that? Why, no, of course, I didn't get the chance. She suddenly told me she wasn't going to marry me unless I could get me some money. Said she'd tried it before, marrying guys with no money, and it hadn't worked out so good. So it was all off, she said, if I couldn't deliver. Well, that sounded straight enough, but tonight, as I was dropping off to sleep, it suddenly struck me that maybe it was just a bit of boloney.'

'Boloney?'

'The old army game,' explained Stanwood. 'I thought she might be simply playing me up. You see, I remembered her and Mike at that party, and I knew what Mike's like with girls, and I sort of wondered if they mightn't have fallen for each other and this was just her way of easing me out. That's why it's so great to hear that you and he have fixed it up. Because if he's that way with you, he can't be that way with her, can he?'

Terry found herself unable to subscribe to this simple creed. It appeared to satisfy Stanwood, who had an honest and guile-less mind, but she shivered. There had risen before her eyes the wraith of Geoffrey Harvest, that inconstant juvenile. He, though ostensibly 'that way' with her, had never experienced the slightest difficulty in being 'that way' with others. Some-thing seemed to stab at her heart, and with a little cry she bur-ied her face in her hands.

'Here! Hey!' said Stanwood. 'What goes on?'

The minds of men like Stanwood Cobbold run on conven-tional lines. Certain actions automatically produce in them cer-tain responses. When, for instance, they find themselves in the society of an old crony of the opposite sex and that crony suddenly gives a gurgle like a dying duck and buries her face in her hands, the Stanwood Cobbolds know what to do. They say 'Here! Hey! What goes on?' and place their arm in a brotherly fashion about her waist.

It was as Stanwood was adjusting this brotherly arm that a voice spoke in his rear.

'Mr ROSSITER!'

Lady Adela Topping was standing in thè doorway, surveying the scene with what was only too plainly a disapproving eye.

When a woman of strict views comes into her library at half past two in the morning to inspect the damage created there by a supposedly inebriated father and finds her youngest sister, towards whom she has always felt like a mother, seated on the sofa in pyjamas and a kimono with a young man in pyjamas and a dressing-gown; and when this young man has his arm, if not actually around her waist, as nearly so as makes no matter, it is understandable that she should speak like Mrs Grundy at her most censorious. It was thus that Lady Adela had spoken, and Stanwood, who until her voice rang out had been unaware that she was a pleasant visitor, rose from his seat as if a charge of trinitrotoluol had been touched off under him.

'Gosh!' he exclaimed.

It was a favourite monosyllable of his, but never had he spoken it with such a wealth of emphasis. His emotions were almost identical with those which he had experienced one November afternoon when an opposing linesman, noticing that the referee was looking the other way, had driven a quick fist into his solar plexus. For an instant he was incapable of further speech, or even of connected thought. Then, his brain clearing, he saw what he had to do.

In the code of the Stanwood Cobbolds of this world there is a commandment which stands out above all others, written in large letters, and those letters of gold. It is the one that enacts that if by his ill-considered actions the man of honour has compromised a lady he must at once proceed, no matter what the cost, to de-compromise her.

He did not hesitate. Tripping over the skirt of his dressing-gown and clutching at a pedestal bearing a bust of the late Mr Gladstone, and bringing pedestal and bust with a crash to the ground, he said with quiet nobility:

'It's all right, ma'am. We're engaged!'

As a general rule, given conditions such as prevailed in the library of Beevor Castle at two-thirty on this May morning, no better thing than this can be said. Such a statement clears the air and removes misunderstandings. It smoothes the frown from the knitted brow of censure and brings to the tightened lips of disapproval the forgiving smile. But on this occasion something went wrong with the system, and what caused this hitch was Lady Adela's practical, common-sense outlook.

'Engaged?' she echoed, not in the least soothed; in fact, looking more like Mrs Grundy than ever. 'Don't talk nonsense. How can you be engaged? You met my sister for the first time at dinner tonight.'

Then, suddenly, as she paused for a reply, there came to her the recollection of certain babblings which Desborough had inflicted upon her in the privacy of her bedroom that night, while she was creaming her face. Some story about this Mr Rossiter of Spink's being an impostor; a view, if she recollected rightly, which he had based on the fact that the other had displayed an ignorance about stamps.

At the time she had scouted the notion, it being her habit to scout practically all her husband's notions. But now, gazing at Stanwood, she found herself inclining to a theory which at the time when it was placed before her she had dismissed as absurd. A moment later, she was not merely inclining, she had become that theory's wholehearted supporter. Foreign though it was to her policy to admit that Desborough could ever be right about anything, she knew that in this single instance he had not erred.

Nearly a year had passed since, in exile at Harrogate, she had read the second of those reports which she had ordered Mervyn Spink to send her each month, telling of the progress of events at the castle during her absence, but now a sentence in it came vividly to her mind. Mervyn Spink, in his running commentary, had stated that, owing to having broken his spectacles and so rendered it difficult for him to see where he was going, young Mr Rossiter had had the misfortune to collide with and destroy the large Chinese vase in the hall.

His spectacles!

She fixed Stanwood with a burning eye, which, much as he would have preferred to do so, he could not avoid.

'Where are your spectacles?' she demanded.

'Ma'am?' ,

'Do you wear spectacles?'

'No, ma'am.'

'Then WHO ARE YOU?'

'Stanwood Cobbold, ma'am,' said Stanwood, even as Mike had predicted. Beneath that eye he was incapable of subterfuge.

Lady Adela gasped. Whatever she had expected to hear, it was not this.

'Stanwood Cobbold?'

'Yes, ma'am.'

Lady Adela, as so often happens in these knotty cases, decided to take a second opinion.

'Is this Mr Cobbold, Terry?'

'Yes.'

'Then who – WHO – is the other one?'

'He is a friend of Stanwood's. His name is Cardinal.'

A bright flush came into Lady Adela's face. No hostess can

be expected to enjoy this sort of thing, and she was the type of hostess who enjoys it least.

'Then why did he come here, saying he was you?' she demanded, turning that incandescent eye upon Stanwood again

Stanwood cleared his throat. He untied the knot of the cord of his dressing-gown and re-tied it. He passed a hand over his chin, then ran it down the back of his head.

'Well, it was this way –' he began, and so evident was it to Terry that he was about to relate in full detail the story of Lord Shortlands and his cook that she intervened hurriedly.

'Stanwood had some very important business that kept him in London –'

'Yay,' said Stanwood, grateful for this kind assistance.

'– so he couldn't come, and – and Mr Cardinal made a sort of bet that he could come instead –'

'Yay,' said Stanwood, well pleased with the way the story was shaping.

'– and not be found out . . .'

She paused. It may have been owing to Stanwood's interpolations, but the story sounded to her thin. She passed it under swift review. Yes, thin.

'It was a sort of joke,' she said lamely.

Earls' daughters do not snort, but Lady Adela came very near to doing so.

'A joke!'

'And then Stanwood found that he was able to come, after all . . .'

Terry paused again.

'So he came,' she said.

To her amazement she saw that her sister's stony gaze was softening. It was as if a sweeter, kindlier Lady Adela Topping had been substituted for that forbidding statue of sternness and disapproval. The châtelaine of Beevor Castle was actually smiling.

'I think I can guess why he did that,' she said archly, and again Terry marvelled. She had never seen Adela arch before. 'You found you couldn't keep away from Terry, Mr Cobbold? Wasn't that it?'

Stanwood was in poor shape, but he was still equal to saying 'Yay,' so he said it.

'And Spink suggested your pretending to be Mr Rossiter?'

'Yay.'

'I shall speak to Spink in the morning,' said Lady Adela, with a return of her earlier manner. 'And to this Mr Cardinal, too. Well, I ought to be very angry with you, Mr Cobbold.'

'Yay.'

'But I feel I can't be. And now you had better go to bed.'

'Yay.'

'I would like a word with Terry. Good night.'

'Yay,' said Stanwood, and withdrew in disorder.

The word his hostess had with Terry was brief.

'Well, really, Terry!' she said.

Terry did not speak.

'You are the most extraordinary girl. Behaving like this. Still, I won't scold you. I'm so delighted.'

Lady Adela folded her sister in a loving embrace. She gave her a long, lingering, congratulatory kiss.

'Desborough says his father's worth MILLIONS!' she said.

Chapter 19

The sunshine of another balmy day gilded the ancient walls of Beevor Castle. Nine mellow chimes sounded from the clock over the stables. And Lord Shortlands, entering the breakfast-room, heaved a sigh as he saw Desborough Topping seated at the table. He had hoped for solitude. Sombre though his thoughts were, he wanted to be alone with them.

'Oh, hello,' said Desborough Topping. 'Good morning.'

'Good morning,' said Lord Shortlands.

He spoke dully. He was pale and leaden-eyed and looked like a butler who has come home with the milk, for he had had little sleep. Few things are less conducive to slumber than the sudden collapse of all one's hopes and dreams round about bedtime, and when Augustus Robb in that unfortunate moment of pique had hurled his bag of tools into the moat, he had ruined the fifth Earl's chances of a good night's rest. From two o'clock onwards the unhappy peer had tossed on his pillow, dozing only in snatches and waking beyond hope of further repose at about the hour when the knowledgeable bird is starting wormwards.

'Nice day,' said Desborough Topping. 'Don't touch the bacon,' he advised. 'That girl's scorched it again.'

'Oh?' said Lord Shortlands. A tragedy to his son-in-law, who liked his bit of bacon of a morning, the misadventure left him cold.

'To a cinder, darn her. Thank goodness Mrs Punter comes back this afternoon.'

A look of infinite sadness came into Lord Shortlands's eyes. He was aware of Mrs Punter's imminent return, and last night had hoped to have been able to greet her with the news that he had become a man of capital. Augustus Robb had shattered that dream. He helped himself to coffee – black coffee, but no blacker than his thoughts of Augustus Robb.

Breakfast at Beevor Castle was a repast in the grand old English manner, designed for sturdy men who liked to put their heads down and square their elbows and go to it. It was open to Lord Shortlands, had he so desired, to start with porridge, proceed to kippers, sausages, scrambled eggs and cold ham, and wind up with marmalade: and no better evidence of his state of mind can be advanced than the fact that he merely took a slice of dry toast, for he was a man who, when conditions were right, could put tapeworms to the blush at the morning meal. His prowess with knife and fork had often been noted by his friends. 'Shortlands,' they used to say, 'may have his limitations, but he *can* breakfast.'

He finished his coffee and refilled his cup. Desborough Topping, who had been foritfying himself with scrambled eggs, rose and helped himself to ham from the sideboard.

'Young Cobbold just left,' he said, returning to the table.

'Oh?'

'Yes. Hurried through his breakfast. Said he had to get in to London early.'

'Oh?'

'Probably wanted to have that eye of his seen to.'

Lord Shortlands was not a quickwitted man, but even he could see that he must know nothing of Mike's eye.

'What eye?'

'He has a black eye.'

'How did he get that?'

'Ah, that's what I'd like to know, but he didn't tell me. I said to him, "That's a nasty eye you've got," and he said, "Into each life some nasty eyes must fall." Evasive.'

'Perhaps he bumped into something.'

'Maybe.'

Desborough Topping applied himself to his ham in silence for a space.

'But what?'

'What?'

'That's what I said – What? What could he have bumped into?'

Lord Shortlands tried to think of some of the things with which a man's eye could collide.

'A door?'

'Then why not say so?'

'I don't know.

'Nor me. Mysterious.'

'Most.'

'There's a lot of things going on in this house that want explaining. Did you hear a crash in the night?'

'A crash?'

'It woke me up.'

Lord Shortlands was in a condition when he would have found any breakfast table conversation trying, but he found this one particularly so.

'No. I – ah – heard nothing.'

'Well, there was a crash. Around two in the morning. A sort of crashing sound, as if something had – er – crashed. I heard it distinctly. And that's not the only thing I'd like to have explained. Look,' said Desborough Topping, peering keenly through his pince-nez like Scotland Yard on the trail, 'what do you make of that guy that calls himself Rossiter?'

Lord Shortlands licked his lips. This is a phrase that usually denotes joy. In this instance, it did not. He prayed for something to break up this *tête-à-tête*, and his prayer was answered. The voice of Cosmo Blair, raised in song, sounded from without. The door opened, and Clare entered, followed by the eminent playwright.

'Ah, my dear Shortlands.'

'Good morning, Father.'

'Good morning,' said Lord Shortlands, feeling like the man who, having got rid of one devil, was immediately occupied by seven others, worse than the first. When he had prayed for something to interrupt his chat with Desborough Topping, he had not been thinking of Cosmo Blair.

His spirit drooped still further. Those of Cosmo Blair, on the other hand, appeared to be soaring. Lord Shortlands had never seen the fellow so effervescent.

'Did you hear a crash last night?' asked Desborough Topping.

'I am in no mood to talk of crashes, my dear Topping,' said Cosmo Blair. 'This, my dear Topping and my dear Shortlands, is the happiest day of my life.' He advanced to the table, and rested his hands on the cloth. 'My lords, ladies and gentlemen, pray silence. Charge your coffee cups and drink to the health of the young couple.'

'Cosmo and I are engaged, Father,' said Clare, in her direct way.

'My God!' said Lord Shortlands. 'I mean, are you?'

Cosmo Blair placed a reassuring hand on his shoulder.

'I think I know what is in your mind, my dear Shortlands. You fear that you are about to lose a daughter. Have no anxiety. You are merely gaining a son.'

'We're going to live at the castle,' explained Clare.

'So that's all right,' said Cosmo Blair. He was a kindly man at heart, and it gave him pleasure to relieve his future father-in-law's apprehensions. 'We shall both be with you.'

There came upon Lord Shortlands an urgent desire to get away from it all. Cosmo Blair's society often had this effect on him. He yearned for Terry. A moment before, he had been thinking of having a third cup of coffee, but now he decided to lose no time in going to her room, where he presumed her to be breakfasting. Terry was always the best medicine for a bruised soul.

He rose, accordingly, and Desborough Topping cocked a surprised eye at him.

'Finished?'

'Yes.'

'Not going to eat anything?'

'No appetite.'

'Too bad.'

'A liver pill, my dear Shortlands,' said Cosmo Blair. 'That's what you want. Take it in a little water.'

'Oh, by the way, Father,' said Clare. 'Adela would like a word with you later on.'

Lord Shortlands started.

'Adela? What about?'

'She didn't say. I just poked my head in at her door and said Cosmo and I were engaged, and she told me to tell you.'

It was a pensive Lord Shortlands who made his way to Terry's room. The news that he was to have Cosmo Blair with him for apparently the rest of his life had shaken him deeply, but not more so than the announcement that Adela wanted a word with him. It too often happened that, when his eldest daughter had a word with him, that word stretched itself into several thousand words, all unpleasant, and in his present low state of mind he felt unequal to anything but the kindest and gentlest treatment.

But he quickly recovered his poise. On occasions like this what a man needs above all else is a clean conscience, and his, on examination, proved to be as clean as a whistle. Except for wanting to marry her cook, introducing impostors into her home and inciting ex-burglars to break open her safe, of all of which peccadilloes she was of course ignorant, he had done absolutely nothing to invite Adela's censure. If Adela wanted a word with him, he told himself, it was no doubt on some trifling matter of purely domestic interest. As he knocked on Terry's door, he was conscious of that moral strength which comes to fathers on whom their daughters have not got the goods.

Desborough Topping, meanwhile, had finished his ham and had gone up to see his wife, his dutiful habit at this time of day. He found her propped up among the pillows with a bed-table across her knees, and was pleased to note that she seemed in excellent humour.

'Good morning, honey.'

'Good morning, dear. Have you seen Clare?'

'Just left her. You mean this engagement of hers? She was telling me about that. You're pleased, I guess.'

'Delighted. I like Cosmo so much.'

'Got the stuff, too.'

'Yes. And isn't it extraordinary that the two things should have happened almost at the same time?'

'Eh?'

'Don't you know? Terry's engaged to Stanwood Cobbold.'

'You don't say!'

'Yes. It's really wonderful. He seems so nice, and of course Mr Cobbold has millions.'

'Yes, old Ellery's well fixed. When did it happen?'

'I heard about it early this morning.'

'Funny he didn't say anything to me about it. He came in and rushed through his breakfast and dashed off. So they're engaged, are they? He looks as if he'd been having a bar-room scrap instead of getting engaged. Got a peach of a black eye. I'd like to know who gave him that.'

An austere look came into Lady Adela's face.

'I can tell you. It was Father.'

'*Father?*'

'He was disgracefully intoxicated last night. I went to his room this morning, and it was littered with bottles.'

Desborough Topping was visibly impressed. He had never supposed his father-in-law capable of such spirited behaviour. He also learned with surprise that he packed so spectacular a punch.

'Gee!' he said feelingly. 'I'm glad he didn't take it into his head to haul off and sock *me*. I thought he looked a little peaked this morning. Well, say, he must have been pretty bad. I was discussing Cobbold's eye with him, just now, and he'd forgotten all about it.'

'I will refresh his memory,' said Lady Adela coldly. 'But that wasn't Stanwood Cobbold that Father hit. It was a friend of his, a Mr Cardinal. Mr Rossiter is really Stanwood Cobbold.'

Desborough Topping sat down on the bed. His air was that of one who is being tried too high.

'I don't get this.'

'Well, I must admit that I am not very clear about it all myself. According to Terry, Stanwood found himself unable to come here, and this Mr Cardinal made a bet that he could come instead of him and not be found out.'

'Sounds crazy.'

'Very. I intend to have a word with Mr Cardinal.'

'He's gone to London.'

'When he gets back, then.'

'But you say Cobbold couldn't come, and he did come.'

'Oh, that part of it is easy enough to understand. After a day or two he found he was able to, and he couldn't keep away from Terry. So he came to the inn, and I suppose Spink told him he could get into the castle by pretending to be Mr Rossiter.'

Desborough Topping whistled.

'Then Spink –'

'Exactly. It was a deliberate plot on Spink's part to get possession of that stamp. I shall give him notice immediately.'

'I would. The guy's a crook. These thriller fellows are right. Butlers want watching. I remember in *Murder at Murslow Grange*. . . . What are you planning to do with the stamp?'

'I've been thinking about that. We shall never know now whom it really belongs to. I think you had better have it.'

'Me?'

'Well, nobody claims it, and it's about time you had some sort of return for all you've done for us. After all, you have been supporting the whole family for years.'

Desborough Topping was moved. He bent over and kissed his wife.

'I call that mighty good of you, honey. I'll add it to my collection. It isn't every day that one gets the chance of laying one's hands on a Spanish *dos reales* unused, with an error in colour. But tell me more about the old man. Sozzled, was he?'

'Disgustingly.'

'Did you see him?'

169

'No, I did not actually see him. I heard a crash in the early morning –'

'Oh, there was a crash? I thought so.'

'It seemed to come from the library, so I started to go there, and I had nearly reached the door when Mr Cardinal came rushing out with his eye all swollen. He told me that Father was in there in a terrible state. He said he had broken a window and hit him in the eye, but that I wasn't to worry, because he could get him to bed all right.'

'Gee!'

'So I decided to leave everything to him. I am very angry with Mr Cardinal. but I must say he seems a capable young man. He must have managed, for I heard nothing else. Then, some time later, I thought I would go to the library again and see what damage had been done, and there was Terry sitting on the sofa with Stanwood Cobbold. At half past two in the morning!'

'Gosh!'

'He had his arm around her waist.'

'Well, I'll be darned!'

'When he saw me, he jumped up, of course, and it suddenly struck me that he was not wearing spectacles.'

'Eh?'

'What you had told me of your suspicions had made me doubtful about him, and then I remembered that Spink in one of his letters, when the Rossiters had the castle, had mentioned that the son wore spectacles. So I asked him who he was, and he said he was Stanwood Cobbold. And then he told me that he and Terry were engaged.'

'But what were they doing in the library?'

'I suppose they both heard the noise and went to see what had happened, and then they sat down for a talk before going to bed again. Just imagine! At half past two in the morning! Terry really is the most reckless child. Thank heaven she's going to be married.'

'And to a fellow who'll have all the money on earth, if his father loosens up. Which he will, of course. Old Ellery will be tickled stiff about this.'

'You had better send him a cable, telling him what has happened. A nice, cordial cable, coming from an old friend. Go and do it now.'

'Yes, dear.'

'And find Father and tell him I want to see him.'

'You wouldn't let him have his hangover in peace?'

'Certainly not.'

'Just as you say, dear.'

It was some little time before Desborough Topping returned.

'I've sent the cable. I said: "Well comma Ellery comma old socks comma how's every little thing stop Your son Stanwood just got engaged to Lady Teresa Cobbold stop Charming girl stop Congratulations and all the best stop." Was that all right?'

'Splendid. Did you find Father?'

'I hunted everywhere. That's what kept me. But I couldn't locate him. Then I met Clare, and she told me that he and Terry had gone off to London. She met them starting out to make the train. She said they were planning to lunch somewhere.'

'But Father hasn't any money. I gave him five pounds on his birthday, but he must have spent that when he went to London to meet Stanwood. Where could he have got any more?'

'Ah,' said Desborough Topping guardedly. 'There's an interesting piece in the paper this morning about the Modern Girl,' he said, hastily changing a subject that threatened to become embarrassing. 'I'll fetch it for you.'

Chapter 20

Lord Shortlands's decision to visit London that morning had been one of those instantaneous decisions which men take in sudden crises. No sooner had he learned from Terry of the ingenious ruse whereby Mike, some seven hours earlier, had succeeded in checking his daughter Adela's advance on the library than the idea of absenting himself from Beevor Castle for awhile had come to him in a flash.

It was with mixed feelings that he had listened to her story. A fairminded man, he admitted that it had been essential for

Mike, confronted with that menacing figure, to say something that would ease the strain, but he made no secret of his regret that he had not said something else. Within thirty seconds of the conclusion of the recital he was urging Terry to get dressed as quickly as possible and accompany him to the metropolis while the going was good.

This craven flight would, of course, merely postpone the impending doom, but he had a feeling that he would be able to face Adela with more hardihood after a lunch at Barribault's or some similar establishment, and he had not forgotten that he still had in his possession the greater part of the ten pounds which Desborough Topping had given him on his birthday. His frame of mind was somewhat similar to that of the condemned man who on the morning of his execution makes a hearty breakfast.

They took the eleven-three train, stopping only at Sevenoaks, and their arrival at the terminus found the fifth Earl still gloomy and, in addition, extremely bewildered. It may have been because his mind, with so much on it, was not at its brightest, but he had found himself quite unable to follow Terry's tale of her matrimonial commitments. There were moments when he received the impression that she was going to marry young Cardinal, others when it seemed that she was going to marry Stanwood Cobbold, and still others when she appeared to be contemplating marrying both of them.

All very obscure and involved, felt Lord Shortlands, and not at all the sort of thing which a dutiful daughter should have inflicted on a father who had had about an hour and a half's sleep. The one fact that emerged clearly was that if ever there was a time for hastening to his club and calling for the wine list, this was it, and he proceeded to do so, arranging with Terry, as before, to meet him in the lobby of Barribault's Hotel at one-thirty. This done, he sped like an arrow to the Senior Buffers.

Terry, for her part, went off to saunter through the streets, to eye the passers-by, to think opalescent thoughts and to pause from time to time to breathe on the shop windows, particularly those which displayed hats, shoes, toilet soap and jewellery. All these things she did with a high heart, for she was feeling – and,

172

in the opinion of many who saw her, looking – like the Spirit of Springtime. She lacked the money this time to buy a new hat, but found in her crippled finances no cause for dejection. Hers was a mood of effervescent happiness which did not require the artificial stimulus of new hats. She floated through a world of sunshine and roses.

Joy, it has been well said, cometh in the morning. Whatever doubts and misgivings may have disturbed Terry in the darkness, they had vanished in the light of the new day. She was now able to appraise at their true value those babblings of Stanwood Cobbold which had seemed so sinister in the small hours. After what had passed between her and Mike in the library last night, it was ridiculous to suppose for an instant that he did not love her, and her alone. Stanwood Cobbold, in suggesting that his fancy might rove towards motion picture stars, had shown that he simply had no grasp of his subject.

She found herself blaming Stanwood Cobbold. Nobody, of course, who enjoyed the pleasure of intimacy with him, expected him to talk anything but nonsense, but he need not, she felt, have descended to such utter nonsense as that of which he had been guilty last night. She had just decided that she would be rather cold to him on her return, when she saw that there would be no need to wait till then.

An hour's aimless rambling through London's sunlit streets had taken Terry to Berkeley Square, and she had paused to survey it and to think with regret how they had ruined this pleasant oasis with their beastly Air Ministries and blocks of flats, when she was aware of a bowed figure clumping slowly towards her on leaden feet. It was Stanwood in person, and so dejected was his aspect that all thought of being cold left her.

'Stanwood,' she cried, and he looked up like one coming out of a trance.

'Hiya,' he said hollowly.

He made no reference to the circumstances of their last meeting. Presumably he had not forgotten them, but more recent happenings had relegated them to the category of things that do not matter. He gazed at Terry dully, like a hippopotamus that has had bad news.

'Hello,' he said. 'What are you doing here?'

173

'Shorty and I broke out of the Big House and came in to have lunch. What are you?'

Stanwood's attention seemed to wander. A blank expression came into his eyes. It was necessary for Terry, in order to recall him to the present, to kick him on the ankle.

'Ouch!' said Stanwood. He passed a hand across his forehead. 'What did you say?'

'I asked what you were doing in London?'

A look of pain contorted the young man's face.

'I came to see Eileen.'

'How is she?'

'I don't know. I haven't seen her.'

'Oh? What train did you catch?'

'I came by car. Hired it at the inn. Terry, I'm feeling shot to pieces.'

'Poor old Stanwood. Has something gone wrong?' Terry looked at her watch. 'Hullo, I must be getting along. I'm meeting Shorty at Barribault's at half past one. I'd ask you to join us, but I know he wants to be alone with me. He's feeling rather low today.'

'I'll bet he's not feeling as low as I am. A worm would have to pin its ears back, to get under me. I couldn't lunch, anyway, Simply couldn't swallow the stuff.'

'Well, walk along with me, and tell me all about it. What's the trouble?'

'It started with this letter,' said Stanwood, falling into step at her side. 'This letter from Eileen that I found at the inn.'

'Addressed to you?'

'Yay.'

'You mean you registered at the inn under your own name?'

'Sure.'

'God bless you, Stanwood! Not that it matters now, of course.'

'Nothing matters now,' said the stricken man.

It seemed to Terry ironical that on this day of days it should be her fate to associate with none but the crushed in spirit, and she found herself thinking wistfully of Mike. Mike might have his faults – her sister Adela by now had probably discovered dozens – but he was not depressing.

'Cheer up,' she urged.

'Cheer up?' said Stanwood, with a hollow, rasping laugh. 'Swell chance I've got of cheering up. For two pins I'd go and bump myself off.'

They walked on in silence. Stanwood seemed to be enveloped in a murky cloud, and his gloom, for misery is catching, was communicating itself to Terry. In spite of herself, those doubts and misgivings were beginning to vex her once more. There was about Stanwood in his present mood something that chilled the spirit and encouraged morbidity of thought. It was as if she had had for a companion the Terry Cobbold in mittens and spectacles of whom she had spoken to Lord Shortlands, and that this mittened Terry Cobbold were whispering, as she had so often whispered, that no good ever comes of getting entangled with Greek gods.

'All alike,' this Prudent Self seemed to be murmuring. 'They're all alike, these good-looking young men. Remember how you felt about Geoffrey Harvest at the beginning. You thought him perfect. And what a flibbertygibbet *he* turned out to be!'

She wrenched her mind free from these odious reflections. She refused to think of Geoffrey Harvest of abominable memory. Mike was not Geoffrey Harvest. She could trust Mike.

'Well, tell me about the letter,' she said. 'Why was it so shattering?'

'It was in answer to one I had written her, begging her for Pete's sake to tie a can to that crazy notion of hers about not marrying me because I've no money. I told you about that?'

'Yes, I remember.'

'She said she still stuck to it.'

'But didn't you expect her to? She wouldn't change her mind right away. I don't see why that letter should worry you. Why did it?'

'Because I read between the lines. There's more to it than meets the eye. Have a look at it,' said Stanwood, and thrust a hand into his breast pocket. 'You'll see what I mean.'

There was nothing of Augustus Robb about Terry. She had no desire to read other people's letters even when invited to, and she was just about to say so when the hand emerged, brandishing before her face a large white envelope, and there floated to her nostrils a wave of scent.

There are certain scents which live up to the advertiser's slogan 'Distinctively individual.' That affected by Miss Eileen Stoker was one of these. It was a heavy, languorous, overpowering scent, probably answering to one of those boldly improper names which manufacturers of perfume think up with such deplorable readiness, a scent calculated to impress itself on the least retentive memory. It had impressed itself on Terry's memory the day before, when she had first made its acquaintance on Mike's sleeve. They had turned into Duke Street now, and Barribault's Hotel loomed up before them, a solid mass of stone and steel, but not so solid that it did not seem to sway drunkenly before Terry's eyes.

As if in a dream she heard Stanwood speaking.

'Remember what I was saying last night about the old Army game? How I thought all that boloney about the money was just Eileen's way of easing me out because she was stuck on someone else? And remember what I told you about Mike and her at that party of mine? Remember me saying I thought he was making a play for her? Well, look. When I got to London, I called her, and she hung up before I'd had time to say a couple of words. And when I rushed around to her hotel, she wouldn't see me. And that's not the half of it. Listen. You've not heard anything yet. I was in the small bar at Barribault's just now, and Aloysius McGuffy told me that she and Mike were lunching there yesterday. What do you know about that?'

Terry forced herself to speak. Her voice sounded strange to her.

'There's no harm in people lunching together.'

Stanwood was not prepared to accept this easy philosophy.

'Yes, there is.'

'I used to lunch with you.'

'That's not the same thing. There are lunches and lunches.'

'It doesn't mean anything.'

'Yes, it does. It means that they're that way.'

'Why?' said Terry, fighting hard.

They had reached the sidewalk outside Barribault's Hotel,

and Stanwood halted. His face was earnest, and he emphasized his words with wide gestures.

'I look on that lunch as a what-d'you-call-it; a straw showing which way the wind is blowing. If it wasn't, why was Mike so cagey about it? Did he mention it to you? Of course he didn't. Nor to me. Not a yip out of him. Kept it right under his hat. And why? Because it was a –'

Stanwood paused. A light wind had sprung up, and a straw which showed which way it was blowing had lodged itself in his throat, momentarily preventing speech. And before he could remove this obstacle to eloquence and resume his remarks, there occurred an interruption so dramatic that he could only stand and stare, horror growing in his eyes.

On the sidewalk outside the main entrance of Barribault's Hotel there is posted a zealous functionary about eight feet in height, dressed in what appears to be the uniform of an Admiral in the Ruritanian navy, whose duty it is to meet cars and taxis, open the door for their occupants and assist them to alight. This ornamental person had just swooped down upon a taxi which was drawing up at the kerb.

In addition to being eight feet high, the Admiral was also some four feet in width, and his substantial body for a moment hid from view the couple whom he was scooping from the cab's interior. Then, moving past him, they came in sight.

No member of the many Boost for Eileen Stoker clubs which flourished both in America and Great Britain would have failed to recognize the female of the pair, and neither Terry nor Stanwood had any difficulty in identifying her escort. Mike Cardinal passed them without a glance, his whole attention riveted on his fair companion. He was talking earnestly to her in a low, pleading voice, one hand on her arm, and as they paused for an instant at the swing door his eyes met hers and he gave her a Look. Lord Shortlands, had he been present instead of at the moment turning the corner of the street, would have been able to classify that look. It was of the kind known as melting.

Duke Street swam about Terry, wrapped in a flickering mist. From somewhere in the heart of this mist she was vaguely aware of the hoarse cry of a strong man in his agony, and when some little while later the visibility improved she found that she was alone.

She stood where she was, pale and rigid. The life of London went on around her, but she gave it no attention. 'Fool!' she was saying to herself. 'Fool!' And the Terry Cobbold in spectacles and mittens sighed and said: 'I told you so.'

She was aware of a voice speaking her name.

'Ah, there you are, Terry. Not late, am I?'

It was a new and improved edition of Lord Shortlands that pawed the sidewalk outside Barribault's Hotel with his spatted feet. His childlike faith in his club's champagne had not been betrayed. He had trusted it to buck him up, and it had done so. His manner now was cheerful, almost exuberant. He had no reason to suppose that the meeting with his daughter Adela, when at length he returned to the castle, would be in any sense an agreeable one, but he faced it with intrepidity. This was due not merely to the champagne, which had been excellent, but to the fact that he had just had an inspiration, and that had been excellent, too.

If Terry was going to marry this young Cardinal, he told himself – and a careful review of their conversation in the train had left him with the conclusion that this was what she had said she was going to do – why should not young Cardinal, admittedly a man of substance, lend him that two hundred pounds?

Lord Shortlands, as a panhandler, was a man who had his code. It was a code which forbade the putting of the bite on those linked to him by no close ties. Acquaintances were safe from the fifth Earl. They could flaunt their bank rolls in his face, and he would not so much as hint at a desire to count himself in. But let those acquaintances become prospective sons-in-law, and only by climbing trees and pulling them up after them could they hope to escape him. Unless, of course, like Desborough Topping, they had taken the mad step of having joint accounts with Adela. He regarded the financial transaction which he had sketched out as virtually concluded, and this gave to his deportment a rare *bonhomie*.

'Come along,' he said jovially. Abstention from breakfast had sharpened his appetite, and he was looking forward with

keen pleasure to testing the always generous catering of Barribault's Hotel.

Terry did not move.

'Let's go somwhere else, Shorty.'

'Eh? Why?'

'I'd rather.'

'Just as you say. The Ritz?'

'All right.'

'Hey, taxi,' said Lord Shortlands, and the Admiral sprang
to do his bidding. 'Ritz,' said Lord Shortlands to the Admiral.

'Ritz,' said the Admiral to the chauffeur.

'Ritz,' said the chauffeur, soliloquizing.

Lord Shortlands produced largesse. The Admiral touched his
hat. The chauffeur did grating things with his gears. The cab
rolled off.

'Terry,' said Lord Shortlands.

'Shorty,' said Terry, simultaneously.

Lord Shortlands, who had been about to say 'Do you think
that young man of yours would lend me two hundred pounds?'
gave way courteously.

'Yes?'

'Oh, sorry, Shorty, you were saying something?'

'After you, my dear.'

Thus generously given precedence, Terry hesitated. She had
an idea that what she was about to say might cast a cloud on
her companion's mood of well-being. Shorty, she knew, thought
highly of Mike.

'I've made a mistake, Shorty.'

Lord Shortlands looked sympathetic. He often made mistakes himself.

'A mistake?'

Terry forced herself to her distasteful task.

'I'm not going to marry Mike.'

'What!'

'No,' said Terry.

Lord Shortlands sank back in his seat, a broken man. The
day was still as fair as ever, but it seemed to him that the sun
had suddenly gone out with a pop.

Chapter 21

Butlers, like clams, hide their emotions well. In the demeanour of Mervyn Spink, as he drooped gracefully over the telephone in Lord Shortlands's study at four o'clock that afternoon, there was nothing to indicate that vultures were gnawing at his bosom. Sherlock Holmes himself could not have deduced from his deportment that he had recently been deprived of his portfolio after a scene which – on the part, at least, of Lady Adela Topping, his employer – had been stormy and full of wounding personalities. Outwardly, he remained his old calm elegant self, and his voice, as he spoke into the instrument, was quiet and controlled.

'Hullo?' he said. 'Are you there? The office of the *Kentish Times*? Could you inform me what won the three-thirty at Kempton . . .? Thank you.'

He hung up, his face an impassive mask. It was impossible to tell from it whether the news he had received had been good news or bad news. He left the study, and made his stately way to the hall. There was always some little task to be done in the hall – ash-trays to be emptied, papers to be put tidy and the like – and though under sentence of dismissal he was not the man to shirk his duties. 'You leave tomorrow!' Lady Adela had said, putting a good deal of stomp into the words, and he was leaving tomorrow. But while he remained on the premises, his motto was Service.

As a rule, at four in the afternoon he could count on having the hall to himself and being able to scrounge his customary half-dozen cigarettes from the silver box on the centre table, but today it had two occupants. Lord Shortlands, looking as if the rescue party had dumped him there after a train accident, was reclining bonelessly in one of the arm-chairs, Terry sitting in another. She looked up as the butler entered. Her face was pale and set.

'Is Mr Cobbold back, Spink?'

'Yes, m'lady. I fancy he is in his room.'

'Will you give him this note, please.'

'Very good, m'lady.'

Lord Shortlands came to life.

'Spink.'

'M'lord?'

'Has – ah – has Mrs Punter arrived?'

'Yes, m'lord.'

'Ha!'

Mervyn Spink waited respectfully for further observations but, finding that the other had gone off the air, withdrew, and Lord Shortlands turned to Terry. His voice was low and hoarse, like that of a bandit in an old-fashioned comic opera.

'Terry!'

'Yes?'

'Did you notice anything?'

'How do you mean?'

'About that viper. The man Spink. Did you see a sort of gleam in his eye?'

'No.'

'I did. A distinct gleam. As if he had got something up his sleeve. You heard what he said? Mrs Punter's back.'

'Yes.'

'Horrible gloating way he said it. I suppose he's been smarming round her ever since she arrived. That's where he scores, being a butler. No barriers between him and the cook. There he is, right on the spot, able to fuss over her to his heart's content. Probably told her she must be feeling tired after her journey, and insisted on her having a drop of sherry. Just the sort of little attention that wins a woman's heart. Not that it matters much now,' said Lord Shortlands heavily. 'If you aren't going to marry this young Cardinal, I'm dished, anyway.'

Terry sighed. At lunch and during the return in the train and subsequently while she was writing that note, the fifth Earl had gone into the matter of her broken engagement rather fully, and it seemed that the topic was to come up again.

'I'm sorry,' she said.

'I still can't understand why you're giving the chap the push.'

'I explained.'

'Well, I don't see it. Why shouldn't he lunch with this woman? Old friends, apparently.'

'I told you. It was the way he looked at her.'

'Pooh!'

'And after what I went through with Geoffrey –'

'Pooh, pooh!'

A single 'Pooh!' is trying enough to a girl whose heart is feeling as if it had been split in half, but Terry, by clenching her fists and biting her lip, had contrived to endure it. The double dose was too much for her.

'Oh, for goodness' sake do let's stop talking about it, Shorty.'

Lord Shortlands heaved himself out of his chair. He could make allowances for a daughter's grief, but her tone had hurt him.

'I shall go for a stroll,' he said.

'Yes, do. Much better than sitting here, waiting.'

At the thought of what he was waiting for, Lord Shortlands shivered.

'I shall go for a stroll around the moat. The moat!' he said broodingly. 'Might drown myself in it,' he went on, brightening a little at the thought. But the animation induced by this reflection soon waned. 'I wonder where Adela's got to.'

'She's probably gardening.'

'Well, this suspense is awful. I'm in such a state of mind that I almost hope I'll run into her,' said Lord Shortlands, and went out, and a few moments later Terry was aroused from her thoughts by the entry of Stanwood Cobbold. Stanwood was looking tense and grave, as became a man whose heart was broken. To him, as to Terry, that glimpse of Mike and Eileen Stoker at the door of Barribault's Hotel had come as a shattering blow, withering hopes and destroying dreams.

'Oh, there you are,' he said sepulchrally. 'Spink gave me your note.'

'What! But it was meant for Mike.'

'Sure, I know. But Spink got mixed. You can't blame him. He's just been fired, he tells me, and I guess it's preying on his mind. So you've given Mike the razz?'

'Yes.'

'Quite right,' said Stanwood warmly. 'Show him where he gets off. Later on, when I'm feeling sort of brighter, I'm going to write Eileen a letter, telling her where *she* gets off. Who

182

was that female in the Bible whose work was always so raw?'

'Delilah?'

'Jezebel,' said Stanwood, remembering. 'I've heard Augustus Robb mention her. That's how I shall begin. "Jezebel!" I shall begin. That'll make her sit up. And there's a Scarlet Woman of Babylon that Augustus sometimes wisecracks about. I shall work her in, too. The great question now is, do I or do I not poke Mike in the snoot?'

'No!'

'Maybe you're right,' said Stanwood.

He relapsed into a brooding silence. Terry was wishing that he would go away and leave her to her misery, but as it was evident that he was determined to remain and talk, she sought in her mind for something to talk about which would not make her feel as if jagged knives were being thrust through her heart.

'Have you seen Adela?' she asked.

'Her Nibs? No? Why?' said Stanwood, in sudden alarm. 'Is she looking for me?'

'Not that I know of.'

'Thank God! If I never meet that dame again, it'll be soon enough for me. Why did you ask if I'd seen her?'

'I don't know.'

'Well, I wish you wouldn't. You gave me goose prickles. Some party, that, last night.'

'Yes. I never knew you had such ready resource.'

'Eh?'

' "It's all right, ma'am. We're engaged." '

'Oh, that? Well, I had to say something.'

'I suppose so.'

'And it worked. Gosh!' said Stanwood, starting. It was plain that an idea of some kind had agitated the brain behind that brow of bone. 'Golly! You've given me a thought there. Look! Why shouldn't we?'

'Why shouldn't we what?'

'Be engaged.'

Terry gasped.

'You mean really?'

'Sure.'

'Are you choosing this moment to ask me to marry you?'

'You betcher, and I'll tell you why. You want to show Mike where he gets off. I want to show Eileen where she gets off. You're feeling licked to a splinter. I'm feeling licked to a splinter. Let's merge.'

'Oh, Stanwood!' said Terry, and began to laugh.

Stanwood eyed her askance. He did not like this mirth. Her laughter was musical, but he soon began to entertain the idea that there was something of hysteria in it, and at the thought of being alone with a hysterical girl his stout soul wilted. He was none too sure of the procedure. Did you burn feathers under their noses? Or just slap them on the back?'

'Hey!' he cried. 'Pipe down!'

'I can't. It's too funny.'

Stanwood began to be conscious of a certain pique. He had offered this girl a good man's – well, not love, perhaps, but at any rate affection, and he could see no reason why a good man's affection should be given the horse's laugh. His manner became stiff.

'I can't see what's so darned funny about it.'

And Terry, suddenly sobered, found that she, too, was unable to do so.

'I'm sorry I laughed,' she said. 'But you startled me. You'll admit you were a little sudden. Are you really serious?'

'Sure.'

Terry was looking at Stanwood, thoughtfully, weighing him up. She liked him, she told herself. She had always liked him. He made her feel motherly. And he was a man you could trust. She could think of many worse things that the future could hold than marriage with Stanwood Cobbold. To marry Stanwood would be to put into snug harbour out of the storm. Perhaps this was what Fate had designed for her from the start – a quiet, unromantic union with no nonsense about it, solidly based on friendship.

It would mean, too, that she would be able to leave the castle, to go out into the wide world where there might be a chance of forgetting, and she realized now how vitally this mattered to her. I can't do it, she had been saying to herself in a hopeless, trapped way, I can't go on living all alone in this awful place where everything will always remind me of

184

Mike. She saw that she was being offered release from prison.

'If it's the money end you're worrying about,' said Stanwood, 'that's all right. Father will cough up, when he hears it's you I'm marrying.'

'I'm not worrying about that, my pet,' said Terry. 'I'm worrying about you and what you're letting yourself in for.'

'If it's okay by you, it's okay by me.'

'Sure?'

'Sure.'

'Quite sure?'

'Absolutely sure. You betcher. Why not?'

'I'm afraid I shall always love Mike,' said Terry, with a little choke in her voice.

'And I shall always love Eileen, darn her gizzard. But what does it matter? Don't talk to me about love,' said Stanwood, plainly contemptuous of the divine emotion. 'Love's a mess. Look at all the bimbos you see that start out thinking they're crazy about each other. For the first couple of months they can't quit holding hands and feeding each other with their spoons, and after that they're off to the lawyer to fix up the divorce so quick you can't see them for dust. To hell with love. Feed it to the birds. I want no piece of it.'

'Friendship is the thing, you think?'

'Sure. If a fellow and a girl are just buddies, they stay buddies.'

'There's something in that.'

'And we've always got along together like a couple of gobs on shore leave. We'll have a swell time. It's like that song I remember – "Tumty tumty tumty tumty, I was looking for a pal like you".'

Terry sighed.

'Well, all right, Stanwood.'

'Check?'

'Yes.'

'Swell. I'll kiss you, shall I?'

He did, and there followed a silence not untinged with embarrassment. To each of the plighted pair it seemed a little difficult to know what to say next. It was a relief to both when Lord Shortlands reappeared, back from his stroll round the moat.

The moat, as always, had lowered his spirits dangerously. It was a sheet of water on which he never looked without despondency. His manner was so dejected that Terry lost no time in imparting news which she felt sure would bring the sparkle back to his eyes.

'Adela has given Spink the sack, Shorty.'

For an instant, as she had foreseen, the words acted as a tonic. But, like the one which Stanwood was accustomed to imbibe in his dark hours, its effects, powerful at first, were evanescent. What did it profit, Lord Shortlands was asking himself, that Beevor Castle should be freed from Spinks, if he himself remained unable to acquire that two hundred pounds?

'And Stanwood and I are engaged,' said Terry.

The fifth Earl clutched his forehead. That feeling of bewilderment, of having an insufficient grasp on the trend of things, which had come to him in the train, was troubling him once more.

'You and Stanwood?'

'Yes.'

'Not you and young Cardinal?'

'No.'

'But you and Stanwood?' said Lord Shortlands, feeling his way carefully.

'Yes.'

Lord Shortlands's face cleared. He had got it at last.

'I hope you'll be very happy,' he said. 'Stanwood, my boy, I have only this to say: Be good to my little girl – and can you lend me two hundred pounds?'

If Stanwood was surprised, he did not show it.

'Sure,' he said agreeably.

'My dear fellow!'

'At least, when I say "Sure",' said Stanwood, correcting himself, 'I mean I can't.'

'You can't?' moaned Lord Shortlands, in the depths.

'Not yet, what I mean. I don't have it. Father cabled me a thousand bucks the other day, but most of it's gone, so you'll have to wait till I can pop it across him again.'

Hope stirred feebly in Lord Shortlands's bosom.

'And when do you anticipate that you will be able to – ah – pop it across him?'

Stanwood reflected.

'Well, I usually find it best to give him about a month to sort of simmer.'

'A month?' With Mervyn Spink out of the place and unable to exert his fatal fascination, a month seemed to Lord Shortlands no time at all. 'Why, that will be admirable. In a month from now, you think –?'

'Oh, sure. Maybe less.'

Lord Shortlands closed his eyes. As on a former occasion, he seemed to be praying. When he opened them again, it was to observe that Spink had shimmered silently in.

'New York wishes to speak to you on the telephone, sir,' he said, addressing Stanwood.

'New York?'

'Yes, sir.'

'Gosh, that must be father,' said Stanwood, and hurried out.

Lord Shortlands found himself filled with an ungenerous desire to triumph over a fallen rival.

'I hear you're leaving us, Spink,' he said, with unction.

'Yes, m'lord.'

'Too bad.'

'Thank you, m'lord. I shall be sorry to terminate my association with the castle. I have been extremely happy here.'

'Made some nice friends, eh?'

'Yes, m'lord.'

'You'll miss them'

'Yes, m'lord. But there are consolations.'

'Eh?'

'I have been fortunate in a recent investment on the turf, m'lord. Silver King in the three-thirty race at Kempton Park this afternoon at a hundred to eight. What a beauty!' said Mervyn Spink, momentarily allowing his human side to come uppermost, a thing which butlers seldom do unless they are leaving tomorrow.

Lord Shortlands's jaw had begun to droop slowly, as if pulled by an invisible spring. He spoke in a hushed voice, in keeping with the solemnity of the moment.

'How much did you have on?'

'Fifty pounds, m'lord.'

'Fifty *pounds*! At a hundred to eight?'

'I felt that it was not a moment for exercising caution, m'lord. I invested my entire savings.'

Mervyn Spink withdrew, unnoticed as far as Lord Shortlands was concerned, for the latter had leaped to the writing-table and was doing sums with a pencil and a piece of paper.

Presently he raised an ashen face.

'Six hundred and twenty-five quid! That viper has trousered six hundred and twenty-five quid! I told you that one of these days he would strike a long-priced winner, but you wouldn't listen to me.' He paused, and mopped his furrowed brow. 'I'm going to the library to lie down,' he said. 'Adela won't think of looking for me there. If you meet her, tell her you haven't seen me.'

He tottered out. He had been gone perhaps two minutes, when there was a cheerful sound of whistling without, and Mike came in.

Chapter 22

From the first moment of his entry it was abundantly evident that Mike was feeling pleased with himself. His whistling had suggested this, and his attitude confirmed it. He exuded light-heartedness and *bien être*, and the thought of anyone being pleased with Mycroft Cardinal, the Emperor of the flibberty-gibbets, was so revolting to Terry that she stiffened and drew herself up coldly. Her bearing, as she faced him, was that of a Snow Queen. Icicles seemed to be forming on her upper slopes.

This, however, appeared to have escaped Mike's notice, for, swooping down on her, he kissed her fondly; then, placing a hand on either side of her waist, picked her up and waved her about for awhile, concluding by lowering her into her chair and kissing her again. His manner was entirely free from any suggestion of diffidence or uncertainty as to his welcome.

'My angel! My seraph! My dream kitten!' he said. 'I feel

188

as if I hadn't seen you in years. And yet you don't look a day older.'

Terry did not reply. It is not easy for a girl who has been intending to be distant and aloof to think of anything good to say under such conditions.

'Notice the eye?' said Mike.

Terry directed what she hoped was a chilling and indifferent glance at the eye. She had already observed that its sombre hues had vanished.

'I had it painted out at a painting-out shop. For your sake. Augustus Robb warned me that girls didn't like men with bunged-up eyes, and you can always go by him. And now, my child, I have news. Where's Shorty?'

'In the library, I believe.'

'I have tidings for him that will bring the sparkle back to his eyes and make him skip like the high hills. Augustus is in again!'

Terry did not understand him, and signified this by raising her eyebrows coldly.

'Yes, Augustus has started functioning once more. He is going to carry on from where he left off last night. I sought him out this morning and grovelled. I said that it was merely strained nerves that had caused me to kick him, and begged him to take the big, broad view. His manner was a little stiff at first, but eventually he relented. If I would go to his gentleman friend in Seven Dials and borrow his tools, he said, he would do the rest. "Tell him," he said, "that Gus wants the old persuaders." So I called on the gentleman friend – a charming fellow, whose only fault, if you can call it a fault, was that his eyes were a bit close together, and gave him the password, and I've just seen Augustus and handed over the old persuaders. He promised to get to work immediately. Your sister Adela, I have ascertained, is out in the garden, no doubt making the lives of the local snails a hell on earth, and Desborough Topping is in his room, having an indoor Turkish bath for his lumbago, so the coast is clear. If Shorty's in the library, he's probably caddying for Augustus at this very moment with a song in his heart, realizing, as you will have realized, that he will soon be sitting on top of the world. Augustus guarantees to bust that pete in five minutes.'

He paused. A duller man than he would have noted that Terry was not responsive.

'I had anticipated a certain amount of girlish joy,' he said.

'Oh, I'm delighted.'

'Then why aren't you squeaking? I should have thought such news would have been well worth a squeak or two.' Mike paused again, and sniffed. 'Odd smell in here,' he said. 'Can it be I?'

Terry's lip curled. The smell to which he alluded had not escaped her.

'You've probably not noticed it,' she said coldly, 'but you are reeking of scent.'

'Am I? So I am. Tut, tut.'

His reaction to a discovery which should have bathed him in shame and confusion seemed to Terry entirely inadequate. Would nothing, she was asking herself, stir this man's conscience?

'And I'm not surprised,' she said bitterly. 'Did you enjoy your lunch?'

Mike seemed perplexed.

'How have we got on to the subject of lunch? We were talking of scent.'

Terry bit her lip. It was showing a disposition to tremble, and she would have preferred to die the most horrible death rather than shed tears.

'Why lunch?' asked Mike.

'I happened to see you going to lunch today.'

'I didn't know you were in London.'

'No.'

'Were you at Barribault's?'

'I was on the pavement outside.'

'And you saw me going in?'

'Yes.'

'Then you saw me at my best,' said Mike. 'You saw me in the act of giving a prospect the works, and that is the moment to catch me.'

'What do you mean?'

'I've got La Stoker signed up on the dotted line. From now

on, for a period of five years, the dear old firm will peddle her at ten per cent of her stupendous salary. It's an iron-clad contract, and if she attempts to slide out of it she'll get bitten to death by wild lawyers. And I did it. I, Cardinal. I'm good, I tell you. Good, good, good!'

Terry gasped. Her heart, which she had supposed crushed and dead, gave a sudden leap. There shot through her a suspicion, growing with the moments, that the Lady Teresa Cobbold had made a fool of herself. And at the same time, tentatively at first but rapidly gaining in strengh as the purport of his words came home to her, soft music began to play in the recesses of her soul.

'Oh, Mike!' she said.

'I should have begun by telling you that, in that cable of his recalling me to the office, my boss mentioned that La Stoker had severed relations with her agent before leaving Hollywood and had made no new commitments, and he urged me to get in touch with her and secure her custom. "Give her the old oil," he pleaded, in effect, and I gave it her abundantly. I laid the foundations of my brilliant campaign yesterday with a lunch which set the office back about twenty bucks and had her rocking on her French heels, and today I took her out again and polished her off. But it was in no sense a walkover. The Stoker is one of those dumb females whose impulse, if you ask them to do something, is to say "Well, I dunno" and do the opposite, and there were times, I confess, when I felt like giving the thing up and getting what small consolation I could from beating her over the head with a bottle. Still, I triumphed in the end, and why on earth you're not leaping about and fawning on me is more than I can understand. What's the matter with you?'

Terry choked. Odd things were happening inside her. Carried away, no doubt, by that soft music, her heart appeared now to have parted completely from its moorings and to be going into sort of adagio dance.

'Was that really it?'

'Was what really what?'

'Was it really just a business lunch?'

'Strictly business.'

'Oh, Mike!'

'You may well say "Oh, Mike!" I was superb. I played on that goofy dame as on a stringed instrument. I gave her everything I'd got; the whispered compliment, the gentle pressure of the hand, the smile that wins, the melting look –'

Terry laughed shakily.

'I saw the melting look.'

'You did? Good Lord, I hope you didn't think –'

'That's exactly what I did think. I thought it was Geoffrey Harvest all over again. Well, you never said a word to me about it,' said Terry defensively.

'The Cardinals don't talk. They act.'

'And you sneaked off at dawn –'

'It wasn't at dawn. I took the nine forty-five. And I didn't sneak off. I strode from the house with my chin up and my chest out, twirling my clouded cane. So you thought I was a flibbertygibbet?'

'Yes. Flitting from flower to flower.'

'Is that what flibbertygibbets do?'

'Yes. They're very like butterflies in their habits. And it's no good looking at me in that reproachful way, as if you were King Arthur and I was Guinevere –'

'It isn't exactly reproachful. Sadness was what I was trying to register. You must know that you're the only girl in the world I could possibly love, and that only an absolute nitwit would go flitting elsewhere if he'd got you. Don't you ever look in the glass?'

'Well, I stick to it that it was a perfectly natural mistake to make. There were you, devouring this woman with your eyes –'

'I was thinking of that ten per cent.'

'– and generally behaving like Great Lovers Through the Ages. Anyone would have been misled. Stanwood was.'

'Stanwood.'

'He was among the spectators.'

'Egad! What did he think?'

'The worst. Well, when I tell you that he spoke of writing a letter to Miss Stoker calling her the Scarlet Woman of Babylon –'

'Where on earth did Stanwood ever hear of the Scarlet Woman of Babylon?'

'Apparently Mr Robb chats with him about her sometimes. And then he came to me and asked me to marry him.'

'To – what?'

'To marry him. And I said I would.'

Mike tottered.

'You said you would?'

'Yes. It was his idea. He said it would show you where you got off.'

Mike drew a deep breath.

'If Shorty kicks at paying three guineas to have your head examined,' he said feelingly, 'I'll put up the money myself. Let me tell you something for your files. You're not marrying any blasted Stanwoods. You're marrying me.'

'Yes, I see that now.'

'Got it clear in your little nut, have you?'

'Quite.'

'It's a pity you were ever uncertain on the point, for look what you have done. Playing with hearts, I call it. Now I have the unpleasant task of telling an old friend that if he doesn't lay off, I'll push his face in. And what makes it so extremely awkward is that I don't believe I can push Stanwood's face in, unless I seize a happy moment when he's looking the other way.'

'Will you really tell him?'

'Of course.'

'Oh, Mike, how noble of you. I was wondering how I could do it.'

'Where is this home-wrecker?'

'Telephoning. His father rang him up from New York.'

'Well, here's something that may comfort you. I doubt if we shall have much moaning at the bar when we break it to him that the deal is off. Towards the end of lunch, when the main business details had been settled, I worked like a beaver in his interests, and La Stoker is now prepared to marry him any time he says the word. I might perhaps have mentioned that earlier.'

'You might.'

'My old trouble. Playing for suspense. But let's not talk about Stanwood. His romance is merely a side issue. Ours is what matters.'

'Yes.'

'Have you any objection to getting married like lightning?'

'Not if it's to you.'

''At's the way to talk! It will be. I'll see to that. Well, that's what we'll have to do, because time is running short. I've got to sail next week.'

'How pleased all the girls in Hollywood will be to see you again.'

'Are there girls in Hollywood?'

'Stanwood says so.'

'I don't suppose I shall so much as notice them.'

'How about if they come squealing "Oh, *Mike,* darling"?'

'There is such a thing as police protection, I presume. But I was saying. About getting swiftly off the mark. It must be a simple ceremony at the registry office for us.'

'Beak Street?'

'Or Greek Street. For goodness' sake don't go to the wrong place, like Augustus Robb's girl. And now to tackle Stanwood. Ah,' said Mike, as a thunder of large feet approached along the corridor, 'here if I mistake not, Watson, is our client now.'

Stanwood Cobbold came charging into the room, as if bucking an invisible line.

Chapter 23

That his conversation on the telephone had been one fraught with interest and of the most agreeable nature was manifest at once in Stanwood's whole appearance. His eyes were starting, his hair ruffled where he had clutched it with an excited hand, and his face as nearly like the Soul's Awakening as it was possible for it to look. Picture a hippopotamus that has just learned that its love is returned by the female hippopotamus for which it has long entertained feelings deeper and

warmer than those of ordinary friendship, and you have Stanwood Cobbold at this important moment in his life.

'S-s-s-s –' he began, like a soda water syphon, and Mike
rapped the table, calling for order. One has to be pretty sharp
on this sort of thing at the outset.

'Spit,' he advised.

Stanwood did not spit; but he swallowed once or twice, and
seemed to get a grip on his emotion. His voice, when he started
again, was calmer.

'Say, I've just been talking to Eileen.'

'It's a small point, but you mean your father.'

'No, I don't mean my father. I mean Eileen. I called her up
after I was through with Father. It's all right. She's going to
marry me.'

'Marry you?'

'Sure.'

Mike frowned.

'Just a minute.'

'Can't stop,' said Stanwood, exhibiting restiveness. 'I've got
to rush to the inn and hire that car again and go in and see
her.'

'Nevertheless,' said Mike, 'I repeat. Just a minute. You say
you're going to marry La Stoker?'

'Sure.'

'That wasn't the story I heard. The way I got it was that
you were going to marry Terry.'

'Oh, gosh!' said Stanwood, pausing. He seemed disconcerted.
It was plain that Terry had to some extent slipped his memory.

'Yes, what about me?' said Terry. 'Are you proposing to
throw this eager heart aside like an old tube of tooth paste?'

Stanwood reflected. It was not long before he reached his
decision.

'You betcher. You don't mind, do you?'

'Not a bit,' said Terry.

'Swell,' said Stanwood.

'It's just as well that you've got that settled,' said Mike,
'because Terry is going to marry me, and the last thing we
wanted was you clumping up the aisle, shouting "I forbid the
banns!"'

195

Stanwood gaped.

'She's going to marry you?'

'Yes.'

'What, even after —'

'Mike has explained everything, Stanwood,' said Terry.

A look of awe came into Stanwood's face. He regarded his friend with reverence. If Mike had explained everything, that look seemed to say, then Mike, as the latter had so often had occasion to point out himself, was good. He shook Mike's hand, and said that that was dandy.

'He turns out to be as pure as the driven snow.'

'Rather purer, if anything,' said Mike. 'Your foul suspicions were entirely unfounded, my dear Stanwood. Ask your girl friend, when you see her, and she will tell you that I was merely signing her up in my capacity of junior partner in the firm of Schwartz and Cardinal, ham purveyors of Hollywood. The whole thing was a simple business transaction, entirely free from all taint of sex. There is absolutely nothing between your darned Stoker and me, and there never has been anything. For your information, I wouldn't touch her with a barge pole.'

'Oh, say,' said Stanwood, wounded, and Terry asked if that was not a little severe. Mike considered.

'Yes,' he agreed. 'I'm sorry. I went too far. I *would* touch her with a barge pole, provided it was a good long one.'

'Thanks, o' man.'

'Not at all.'

'So that's all right,' said Terry. 'I'm so glad everything's settled, Stanwood.'

'Yes,' said Mike. 'One likes to see the young folks happy.'

'How sensible of her not to mind about you having no money.'

'Eh?' said Stanwood. 'Oh, but I do have some money. I forgot to tell you. Seems that the little guy with the nose-glasses cabled Father that I was engaged to you, and Father was so tickled that he's deposited a hundred and fifty thousand smackers to my account. That's what he called up about. So I'm nicely fixed,' said Stanwood, and without further words dived through the door en route for the inn and the car that was for hire.

He left behind him a rather stunned silence.

'Well!' said Terry, and Mike agreed that 'Well!' about summed it up.

'I hope he'll be happy,' said Terry doubtfully.

'As a lark,' said Mike. 'Not in the sense that we shall be, of course. Nobody could be. But I see quite a bright and prosperous future for the lad. The Stoker's all right. A little apt to turn the conversation to the subject of her last picture, but he'll enjoy that.'

'I don't like the scent she uses.'

'Stanwood does. He has often told me so.'

'She isn't a flibbertygibbet?'

'Not in the least. A quiet little home body, never happier than among her books. I've read interviews with her that stressed that. And she often puts on a simple gingham apron and cooks a bite of dinner for herself.'

'I'd hate Stanwood to be unhappy.'

'Don't you worry. They're the ideal mates. She's solid ivory from the frontal bone to the occiput, and so is Stanwood. Ah, my dear Shorty,' said Mike, breaking off and addressing Lord Shortlands, who had just entered.

A glance was enough to tell that this was a very different Lord Shortlands from the crushed martyr who had tottered out to go and lie down in the library. It was a near thing, but he looked a little more like the Soul's Awakening than Stanwood Cobbold had done.

Terry glanced questioningly at Mike.

'Shall we tell him at once, or break it gently?'

'At once, I think.'

'All right. Shorty, darling, shake hands –'

'Mitt.'

'Yes, much better. Mitt Mr Cardinal, Shorty. We're going to be married.'

The unmistakable look of the man who feels that the strain is becoming too much for him came into Lord Shortlands's face. He gave the impression of having definitely given up the attempt to cope with things.

'Married?' he said feebly.

'Yes.'

You and Cardinal?'

'Yes.'

'Not you and Stanwood?'

'No.'

'But you and Cardinal?'

'Yes.'

'My God!' murmured Lord Shortlands, passing a hand across his brow.

'The fact is, my dear Shorty,' said Mike, 'things have been getting a little mixed, and it has taken some time to straighten them out. There had been mistakes and misunderstandings, not unlike those which occurred in Vol. II of *Percy's Promise*, a work which you may or may not have read. By Marcia Huddlestone (Popgood and Grooly, 1869). These, however are now at an end, so brush up the old top hat and get ready for the wedding. The bells of the little village church – or, rather, the little Beak Street registry office – are soon to peal out in no uncertain manner. You may take this as official. Have you seen Augustus?'

The Soul's Awakening expression, which had been temporarily erased, came back into Lord Shortlands's face. After what had occurred on the previous night, he had never expected the name of Augustus Robb to be music to his ears, but this was what it was now. Augustus Robb stood very high on the list of men he liked and respected.

'I have, indeed. I've just left him.'

'Why didn't you stay and watch?'

'He wouldn't let me. Said it made him nervous. Very temperamental chap. I told him he would find me here when he was finished.'

'How was he coming along?'

'He appeared entirely confident.'

'Then very shortly . . . Ah!'

Augustus Robb had come into the room, jauntily like an artist conscious of having done a good piece of work. He had an excellent reception.

'Augustus!'

'Mr Robb!' cried Terry.

'Did you get it?' cried Lord Shortlands.

198

''Ullo, cocky. 'Ullo, ducky. Yus, chum, I got it,' said Augustus Robb, replying to them in rotation. 'But –'

An unforseen interruption forced him to leave the sentence uncompleted. 'Ah!' said a voice, and they turned to see Lady Adela in the doorway.

Lady Adela was wearing gardening gloves and carrying the shears which had so intimidated Mike at their first meeting. Her eyes, as they rested upon Lord Shortlands, had in them the stern gleam that is seen in those of a tigress which prepares to leap upon the goat which it has marked down for the evening meal. Her righteous indignation, denied expression by his craven flight to London, had been banking up within her since half past nine that morning, and it was plain that she welcomed the imminent bursting of the dam.

'Ah!' she said. 'I would like to speak to you, Father.' She looked at the assembled company, and added the word: 'Alone.' What she had to say was not for the ears of others.

Augustus Robb was always the gentleman. His social sense was perfect. Besides, he intended to listen at the door.

'Want us to shift, ducky?' he said agreeably. 'Right ho.'

Lady Adela, who had never been called 'ducky' before and did not like the new experience, raised her eyebrows haughtily. It began to seem as if Augustus Robb was going to get his before Lord Shortlands.

'Who are you?' she asked.

'Name of Robb, dearie. Augustus Robb.'

'He's Stanwood's valet,' said Terry.

'Oh?' said Lady Adela, and left unspoken the words that had been trembling on her lips. Vassals and retainers of Stanwood Cobbold were immune from her wrath. Later on, perhaps she would suggest to the dear boy that his personal attendant was a little lacking in the polish which one likes to see in personal attendants, but for the moment his chummy servitor must be spared. All she did, accordingly, was to catch his eye.

It was enough. Blinking, as if he had been struck by lightning, Augustus Robb withdrew, followed by Mike and Terry, and Lady Adela turned to Lord Shortlands.

'Father!' she said.

'Well?' said Lord Shortlands.

In the word 'Well?' as inscribed on the printed page, there is little to cause the startled stare and the quick catch of the breath. It seems a mild and innocuous word. But hear it spoken in a loud, rasping, defiant voice by a man with his chin protruding and his thumbs in the armholes of his waistcoat, and the effect is vastly different. Proceeding like a bullet from Lord Shortlands's lips, it left Lady Adela silent and gasping, her feeling closely resembling those which would have come to the above-mentioned tigress, had the goat on the bill of fare suddenly turned and bitten it in the leg.

Of all moral tonics there is none that so braces a chronically impecunious Earl as the knowledge that he is fifteen hundred pounds on the right side of the ledger. Lord Shortlands had Augustus Robb's assurance that that stamp, for which he had gone through so much, was now as good as in his pocket, and the thought lent him a rare courage. Ancestors of his had been tough nuts on the field of Hastings and devils of fellows among the Paynim, and their spirit had descended upon him. He seemed to be clad in mail and brandishing a battle-axe.

'Well? What is it? It's no good you trying to come bullying me, Adela,' he said, though perhaps Flaubert would have preferred the word "thundered". 'I've put up with that sort of thing long enough.'

Lady Adela was a woman of mettle. She tried hard to shake off the illusion that somebody had hit her between the eyes with a wet fish.

'Father!'

Lord Shortlands snorted. One of the main planks in the platform of those ancestors, whose spirit had descended upon him, had always been a rugged disinclination to take any lip from their womenfolk.

'Don't stand there saying "Father!" No sense in it. I tell you I'm not going to put up with it any longer. I may mention that I had very much disliked your manner on several occasions. In my young days daughters were respectful to their fathers.'

This would, of course, have been a good opportunity for Lady Adela to say that they had probably had a different kind

200

of father, but that strange, sandbagged sensation held her dumb, and Lord Shortlands proceeded with his remarks.

'I've decided to leave this bally castle,' he said. 'Leave it immediately. I have been able to lay my hands on a large sum of money, and there's nothing to keep me. I'm sick and tired of seeing that damned moat, and that blasted wing built in 1259, and all the rest of the frightful place. If it interests you to hear my plans, I'm going to buy a public house.'

'Father!'

'Will you *stop* saying "Father!" Are you a parrot?'

Lady Adela's mind was now so disordered that she could scarcely have said what she was. Whatever it might be, it was something with a swimming head. The only point on which she was actually clear was that she had been swept into the vortex of an upheaval of the same nature as, but on rather bigger lines than, the French Revolution.

'Oh, and by the way,' added Lord Shortlands, 'I'm going to marry Mrs Punter.'

It is proof of the chaotic condition to which Lady Adela's faculties had been reduced that, for an instant, the name suggested nothing to her. Mrs Punter, she was asking herself dazedly. Did she know a Mrs Punter? A member of the Dorsetshire Punters, would it be? Or perhaps one of the Essex lot?

'Punter?' she whispered.

'Yes, Punter, Punter, Punter. You know perfectly well who Mrs Punter is. The cook.'

'The cook?' screamed Lady Adela.

'Yes, the cook,' said Lord Shortlands. 'And don't shout like that.'

When she spoke again, Lade Adela did not shout. Horror made her words come out in a dry whisper, preceded by an odd, crackling sound which it would have taken a very sharp-eared medical man to distinguish from a death rattle.

'You can't marry the cook, Father!'

'Can't I?' said Lord Shortlands, thrusting his thumbs deeper into the armholes of his waistcoat and waggling his fingers. 'Watch me!'

It seemed to Lady Adela, for it was evident that nothing was to be gained by arguing with this unbridled man, that the only course open to her was to fly to Mrs Punter, whom she had always found a reasonable woman, and appeal to her sense of what was fitting. She proceeded to put this plan into action with such promptness that she was gone before Lord Shortlands realized that she had started. One quick leap, a whizzing sound, and she had vanished. And a moment later Augustus Robb re-entered, wearing the unmistakable air of a man who has had his ear to the keyhole.

'Coo, m'lord,' said Augustus Robb admiringly. 'That was telling her!'

'Ha!' said Lord Shortlands, still very much above himself. He strode masterfully about the room, waggling his fingers.

'And I've got something to tell *you*, chum,' said Augustus Robb. 'It's like this.'

He broke off, for Mike and Terry had come in. Terry seemed a little agitated, and Mike was patting her hand.

'Your daughter Teresa,' he said, 'has been suffering a good deal of filial agony on your behalf, my dear Shorty. She was offering me eight to one that we should find you chewed into fragments, and I must say I was anticipating that I should have to dig down for the price of a wreath and a bunch of lilies. But at a hasty glance you appear to be still in one piece.'

Lord Shortlands said that he was quite all right, never better, and Augustus Robb endorsed the statement.

'He put it all over her. Ticked her off, he did. Proper.'

Terry was amazed.

'Shorty! Did you?'

'Certainly,' said Lord Shortlands, and if there was in his manner a touch of pomposity, this was only to be expected after so notable a victory. Wellington was probably a little pompous after Waterloo. 'I have been too lenient with Adela in the past, far too lenient, and she has taken advantage of my good nature. It was high time that I asserted myself. As Mr Robb so rightly says, I – ah – ticked her off proper. She's gone away with a flea in her ear, I can assure you. Ha! You should have seen her face when I said I was going to marry Alice Punter.'

The man was lost to all shame.

'You said that?'

'Certainly.'

'To *Adela*?'

'You betcher. "Oh, and by the way," I said, "I'm going to marry Mrs Punter".'

'But you ain't, chum,' said Augustus Robb mildly. 'That's what I was starting to tell you.'

'Eh?' Lord Shortlands glared formidably. He was under an obligation to this buster of petes, but gratitude was not going to make him put up with this sort of thing. 'Who says so?'

Augustus Robb removed his hornrimmed spectacles, gave them a polish and replaced them.

'Well, I do, cocky, for one, and she does, for another. Because the 'ole thing is, you see, she's going to marry me.'

'What!'

'Yes. It's a long story,' said Augustus Robb. 'I was telling Mr Cardinal and his little bit about it last night. We ought to have got married years ago, only she inadvertently went and waited for me at the Meek Street registry office when I was waiting for 'er at the Beak Street registry office. Shouldn't wonder if that sort of thing didn't often occur.'

Terry gasped.

'Then – ?'

'Yus, ducky. She's the woman I loved and lorst. You could have knocked me down with a feather,' said Augustus Robb. 'I come out of that library after getting that there stamp, and I was doing a quiet shift-ho to my room to hide the blinking thing, when I see someone coming along the passage, and it was 'Er!'

'Good heavens!'

'You may well say "Good heavens!" ducky. It was a fair staggerer. "Alice!" I says, knocked all of a heap. "Gus!" she says, pressing of a 'and to 'er 'eart. "Is it you?" I says. "Yus, it is," she says, "and you're a nice cup of tea, you are," she says. "What 'ave you got to say for yourself?" she says. Whereupon explanations ensued as the expression is, and the upshot of it all is that we're off to Beak Street registry office next week – together, this time.'

'You'll probably find us in the waiting-room,' said Mike. 'My heartiest congratulations, Augustus.'

'Thanks, cocky.'

'If there's one thing I like, it is to see two loving hearts come together after long separation, particularly in Springtime. But have you considered one rather important point? Mrs Punter's ideals are pretty high. The man who wins her must have two hundred pounds to buy a pub.'

'I've got it, and more.'

'Been robbing a bank?'

'No, I 'ave not been robbing a bank. But there's a little bit of money coming to me from a source I'm not at liberty to mention. I could buy 'er 'arf a dozen pubs.'

A faint groan greeted this statement. It proceeded from Lord Shortlands, who at the beginning of the recital had sunk into a chair and was lying in it in that curious boneless manner which he affected in moments of keen emotion. Terry looked at him remorsefully. Augustus Robb's human interest story had caused her to forget that what was jam for him was gall and wormwood to a loved father.

'Oh, Shorty, darling!' she cried. 'I wasn't thinking of you.'

'It's all right,' said Mike. 'He still has us.'

'Yes, Shorty, you still have us.'

'And the stamp,' said Mike.

Lord Shortlands stirred. He half rose in his chair like a corpse preparing to step out of the coffin. He had forgotten the stamp. Reminded of it, he showed signs of perking up a little.

'Gimme,' he said feebly.

'Give him the stamp, Augustus,' said Mike.

Something in the trend events had taken seemed to be embarrassing Augustus Robb. He shifted from one foot to the other, looking coy.

'Now, there's something I was intending to touch on,' he said. 'Yus, I was going to mention that. I'm sorry to tell you, chums, that there's been a somewhat regrettable occurrence. You see, when I come out of that liberry, I put that there stamp in me mouth, to keep it safe like, and what with the excitement and what I might call agitation of meeting 'Er, I –'

'What?' cried Lord Shortlands, for the speaker had paused.

204

He had risen completely from his chair now, and was pawing the air feverishly. 'What?'

'I swallered it, cocky,' said Augustus Robb, and Lord Shortlands's blood pressure leaped to a new high as if somebody had cried 'Hoop-la!' to it. 'Last thing I'd 'ave wanted to 'ave 'appen, but there you are. That's Life, that's what that is. Well, good-bye, all,' said Augustus Robb, and was gone. Lady Adela herself had not moved quicker.

The first of a stunned trio to comment on the situation was Lord Shortlands.

'It's a ramp!' he shouted passionately. 'It's a swindle! I don't believe a word of it. He's gone off with the thing in his pocket.'

Mike nodded sympathetically. The same thought had occurred to him.

'I fear so, Shorty. One should have reflected, before enlisting Augustus's services, that he is a man of infinite guile. One begins to see now why he spoke so loftily about having enough money to buy half a dozen pubs.'

'I'll sue him! I'll fight the case to the House of Lords!'

'H'm,' said Mike. And Lord Shortlands, on reflection, said 'H'm,' too.

A moment later he was uttering a cry so loud and agonized that Terry leaped like a jumping bean, and even Mike was disconcerted. The fifth Earl was staring before him with bulging eyes. He reminded Mike of a butler discovering beetles in his glass of port.

'What the devil am I to do?' he wailed, writhing visibly. 'I've gone and told Adela about Mrs Punter!'

'So you have!' said Mike. 'If I may borrow Augustus's favourite expression, Coo! But have no alarm –'

'She'll make my life a hell! I'll never have another peaceful moment. My every movement will be watched for the rest of my life. Why, dash it, it'll be like being a prisoner in a bally chain gang.'

Terry's eyes grew round.

'Oh, Shorty!' she cried, but Mike patted him on the back.

'It's quite all right,' he said. 'You heard me say "Have no alarm." Will the public never learn that if they have

Mycroft Cardinal in their corner, Fate cannot touch them?'

'You have a plan?' said Terry.

'I have a plan. Shorty will accompany us to Dottyville-on-the-Pacific.'

'Of course!'

'I must try to break you of that habit of yours of saying "Of course!" when I put forward one of my brilliant solutions, as if you had been on the point of thinking of it yourself.'

'Sorry, my king.'

'Okey-doke, my queen.'

'Where is Dottyville-on-the-Pacific?' asked Lord Shortlands.

'A little west of Los Angeles,' said Mike. 'It is sometimes known as Hollywood. We shall be starting thither almost any day now. Just got to get married and fix up your passport and so on. Pack a few necessaries and sneak off to your club and wait there for further instructions. I will attend to all the financial arrangements.'

'My dear boy!'

'What an organizer! He thinks of everything, doesn't he?' said Terry.

'He does, indeed,' said Lord Shortlands.

'And when we get to Hollywood,' said Mike, 'if you feel like making a little spending money, I think I can put you in the way of it. I don't know if you have ever noticed it, my dear Shorty, but you are a particularly good butler type.'

'A butler type?'

Terry squeaked.

'All these years,' she said, 'I've been trying to think what Shorty reminded me of, and now I know. Of course, darling, you look exactly like a butler.'

'Do I?' said Lord Shortlands.

'Exactly,' said Terry.

'And for such,' proceeded Mike, 'there is a constant demand. I cannot hold out hope of stardom, of course; just a nice, steady living. Say "Very good, m'lord".'

'Very good, m'lord.'

'Perfect. What artistry! You will be a great asset to the silver screen. And now we must leave you. My future wife wishes to show me the rose garden.'

'Haven't you seen it?'

'Not with her,' said Mike.

For some moments after he found himself alone, Lord Shortlands stood motionless, gazing into the golden future. Then,
walking jerkily, for he was still enfeebled, he moved to the
mirror and peered into it.

'Very good, m'lord,' he said, extending his elbows at right
angles. 'Very good, m'lord.'

A look of satisfaction came into his face. Butler parts would
be pie.

Mervyn Spink came silently in, and Lord Shortlands, seeing
him in the mirror, turned. As these two strong men, linked by
the bond of thwarted love, faced each other, there was a
silence. Mervyn Spink was feeling that Lord Shortlands was
not such a bad old buster, after all, and Lord Shortlands was
feeling strangely softened towards Mervyn Spink.

'You have heard, m'lord?'

Lord Shortlands nodded.

'A nasty knock, m'lord.'

'Very nasty.'

'We must face it like men, m'lord.'

'You betcher. Be British.'

Mervyn Spink coughed.

'If your lordship would care for a drop of something to take
your lordship's mind off it, I have the materials in my pantry.'

Lord Shortlands moistened his lips with the tip of his tongue.
The suggestion was a very welcome one. It astounded him to
think that he could ever have disliked this St Bernard dog
among butlers.

'Lead me to it, Spink.'

'This way, m'lord.'

'Don't call me "m'lord".'

'This way, Shortlands.'

'Don't call me "Shortlands",' said the fifth Earl. 'Call me
Shorty.'

He put his hand in his new friend's arm, and they went out.